THE VOLUNTEERS

He had less than twelve seconds to live.

He stood up and almost fell again. He yelled, *'Get out, Tim! For God's sake!'*

Through the window, cutting one hand on the jagged glass, his lungs bursting, his heart pounding like a club.

There was a gap in the wall. With a desperate sob Allenby hurled himself the last few feet. He dug his elbows into the ground and pressed his hands to his ears.

But when the mine exploded he heard nothing. It was a new sensation, more like being drowned than buried.

Someone was yelling and sobbing, but he was past recognizing his own voice.

Oblivion when it came was merciful.

Also in Arrow by Douglas Reeman

The Volunteers

Douglas Reeman

ARROW BOOKS

Arrow Books Limited
62-65 Chandos Place, London WC2N 4NW

An imprint of Century Hutchinson Limited

London Melbourne Sydney Auckland
Johannesburg and agencies throughout
the world

First published by Hutchinson 1985
Arrow edition 1986

Printed and bound in Great Britain by
Anchor Brendon Limited, Tiptree, Essex

ISBN 0 09 945950 7

For Audrey,
with love

I

Three of a Kind

The clouds above the port of Liverpool were bunched together for another onslaught although the wharves and docks were still glistening from an overnight downpour.

A typical Liverpool morning, some might complain; it would be April in a few days but looked and felt more like winter. Gladstone Dock was as usual packed with warships of every size and class. Minesweepers to keep the coastline clear, battered little corvettes, frigates, and here and there the longer, more stylish hull of a destroyer.

For this was Liverpool in 1943, the headquarters of the navy's Western Approaches Command from whence each week the convoys left for the corners of the world where the war was being waged with unrelenting ferocity. And yesterday a homebound convoy had passed the Bar Light Vessel after running the gauntlet of the Atlantic, the 'killing ground' as most of the sailors knew it.

The warships, ranked together because of lack of space, appeared to be supporting one another after their ordeal. Convoy escorts, whose efforts kept the routes open for the rusty lines of merchantmen without which Britain could not survive for more than a couple of weeks. Food, oil, guns, ammunition and the most precious cargo of all, men.

Alongside two elderly destroyers, veterans of the Great War, lay another, larger one which seemed to stand out from all the rest. HMS *Levant* had been the senior escort of that last homebound convoy and was only eighteen months old.

She was big and well armed and, apart from a few scrapes around her raked bows, showed little sign of the many convoys she had watched, protected and chased since her keel had first touched water just two miles away at Birkenhead.

The forenoon watch were working unhurriedly about her decks and bridge, thinking probably of the next run ashore into this bombed, defiant and somehow wonderful city. Liverpool had from the very first convoy in 1939 opened its arms and its heart to the thousands of sailors, naval and merchant service who nightly thronged the bars and clubs, their refuge from the Atlantic and its bitter memories.

In his day cabin *Levant*'s commanding officer took a framed photograph of his wife from a desk drawer and stood it in place. He was thirty, but looked older, his face lined and reddened by hours and days on his bridge. The photograph's reinstatement had become symbolic. A return, no matter how brief, to normal. The captain spent his convoys on the bridge or snatching a catnap in his cupboard-sized sea cabin behind it.

He looked around the cabin. Two days ago it had been the overflow from the sickbay, as had the wardroom.

They had lost twenty-two ships on the long haul from Newfoundland, and it was a miracle they had managed to rescue so many of their gasping, oil-soaked survivors.

He glanced at an unopened newspaper which the ship's postman had brought aboard. The news would be all about the Allies' change of fortunes. No more retreats, they were on the offensive. It was proclaimed that even the invincible Afrika Korps would be beaten into submission and driven out of North Africa once and for all. Then where? Sicily and Italy, it sounded an impossible dream after all the losses and setbacks. Norway and France, Greece and the Low Countries, Dunkirk and Singapore. They read like defeats and yet somehow they had given new strength to fighting men and civilians alike.

There was a tap at the door, and he sighed. Defaulters or

promotions, a sailor requesting to see him privately perhaps about a letter which had awaited his return from that awful convoy. It was hard to think of such ordinary matters after the great roaring greybeards in mid-Atlantic, the dull thud of a torpedo and yet another tired merchantman toppling out of line, avoided if not ignored by her consorts. *Close the gap. Do not stop.* The merchantmen were the targets, helpless, obedient only to the flags and urgent signals from their escorts.

But it was none of those things. It was the first lieutenant.

The captain yawned, 'Yes, Number One?'

'Pilot to see you, sir.'

'Yes. I see.' It was coming back to him. A flaw in the pattern of things.

The first lieutenant added unhelpfully, 'There's a signal to say his successor will be arriving tomorrow forenoon, sir.'

'Send him in.'

The door closed and as if from another world the tannoy piped, 'Able Seaman Robbins report to the Cox'n.' *His world.*

He pulled out a clip of signals from his desk and stared at it. Lieutenant Keith Frazer, Royal Canadian Naval Volunteer Reserve, had been in *Levant* for about a year, first as assistant navigating officer and then as navigator. Most big destroyers carried either a regular officer or a very experienced RNR officer for the job, but Frazer had served in two corvettes, one of which had been sunk in collision with a blazing freighter when they had been trying to take off her crew.

There were many Canadians in Western Approaches, ships as well as men, and the mixture seemed to work.

He leafed back to the original signal, that Frazer was to be interviewed about a possible transfer to Special Forces (Navy). He had tried to talk him out of it. Cloak-and-dagger brigade, he called them. The Atlantic could still lose them all the war. No commando exploit could win one. But it had been to no avail. Now Frazer was leaving the ship. It would weaken their close-knit team. He gave a bitter smile. If I was killed on the next convoy I too could be replaced, so why the difference?

The door opened and Lieutenant Keith Frazer stepped into the cabin.

Tall, with the shoulders and stance of an athlete, he already looked a stranger in his best uniform. A change from seagoing gear or a filthy duffel-coat.

The captain studied him gravely. He had got to know his navigator pretty well in the last year. Frazer was twenty-six years old, but the crow's-feet around his eyes and the lines at the corners of his mouth showed experience rather than youth.

'Well, Pilot? No change of heart?'

Frazer smiled and the strain dropped from his tanned face like a mask.

'I guess not, sir.' He turned and glanced around the day cabin. He too was remembering the last convoy. People who did not understand babbled continuously about invasions, the Second Front, an end to the war. In the Atlantic some convoys were better than others, but the toll was always too high.

The captain said, 'I could still make a signal and get you out of it. Special Forces, you never know where you might end up. I've come to rely on you, Pilot.'

Frazer shrugged. It had sounded like an accusation. But he knew his captain and what mattered to him.

He replied, 'I've been on the Atlantic since the beginning, sir. I want to do something else. Where I can see the enemy for a change, instead of being a target or the victim.'

The captain wanted to yawn but held it back. He said, 'I wish you luck.'

Frazer turned slightly, the deckhead light glancing across the gold CANADA on his shoulder. He would miss *Levant*. She was a thoroughbred. No wonder the Old Man was in love with her. He thought suddenly of his father, Bill Frazer to everyone, never William, who lived now in Vancouver, an ocean and a continent away. He too was probably wondering why his eldest son had decided to join the navy, and then to transfer to the Royal Navy for the worst war of all.

Bill Fraser and his father had originally settled in Powell River, and from humble beginnings had carved out one of the biggest timber businesses on the West Coast. Now the company had expanded to Vancouver and north to Prince Rupert, but to Keith Frazer, who had been born in Powell River, his boyhood seemed like a dream. His father was doubtless a millionaire, and although he spent a great deal of his time sailing now, he still kept an eagle eye on the timber empire he had helped to build.

There was no need for Keith to go to sea, he had insisted a hundred times. He was needed in Vancouver, especially now that the company was directly involved with building small vessels for the navy anyway.

Frazer realized that the captain was staring at him and said, 'I'll take my leave then, sir.'

The captain thrust out his hand. It was over.

Outside the drizzle had started and the steel decks shone like glass. Several members of the wardroom stood by the brow which crossed to the deck of a neighbouring destroyer.

They shook hands, unusually silent and solemn. A few seamen gave him the thumbs-up and grinned. He would soon be forgotten. It was the way of the navy. Another ship, new faces. Never go back.

The first lieutenant, whose mind was already working on his daily routine, said, 'Transport's waiting, Keith. Remember, keep your head down.'

On the dockside Frazer paused, the rain bouncing off his cap and raincoat. When he looked back the *Levant* was almost hidden by the two elderly ships alongside. But he knew he would never forget her.

He heard a car start up, the driver revving the engine unnecessarily as he waited for his passenger.

Passenger? To what and to where, he wondered. He must be crazy to leave the world he knew, had learned and worked at since he had volunteered.

Perhaps he had had his mind made up for him. He quickened his pace, suddenly eager to go. To leave the Atlantic and its bloody cruelty behind.

He settled himself in the car and touched his pocket to make certain his orders were still there.

Special Forces. The officer who had originally interviewed him when he had applied for the transfer had been offhand, even rude. He must have been testing him. The fact he was here in this camouflaged car proved that he must have satisfied even him.

The Royal Marine driver saw the lieutenant give a small smile and sighed as the car bounced over some tracks beside a towering gantry. He had picked up plenty of officers like this Canadian. Quite a few had never been seen again.

Some two hundred miles southeast of Liverpool on the outskirts of Canterbury, a very different city, the rain passed over and there was even some determined sunshine.

The Royal Navy Detention Quarters, called Fort Mason, stood quite alone like a grey cliff, the walls too high for any passers-by to see what was going on.

In the centre of the prison, for that was what it had been during the Napoleonic War, was a cobbled square over which the cells of the inmates and the offices of those who controlled them stared like lines of small, mean eyes.

In one such office the senior Master-at-Arms rolled himself a cigarette from a large tin of duty-free tobacco and ran his tongue along the edge of the paper.

'Now then, son, let me just put it to you again – '

The only other occupant of the neat, cream-painted office

was a strongly built man in a sailor's square rig. He had short fair hair, a pleasant, homely face, but one which looked as if it was well able to take care of itself. On his left sleeve he wore the single anchor of a leading hand, on the other the red crown of the regulating branch. Ships' police, sometimes less politely known as 'crushers'.

Mark Ives was twenty-four and looked like a policeman, which was exactly what he had been before joining up. He had been serving in the East End of London when he had made his decision. A lot of friends had left to enlist, several had been killed or taken prisoner overseas. In spite of the bombing of London, Ives felt out of it. Other, older coppers could do his job. He wanted to fight.

In the beginning everything had gone well. His subdivisional inspector had tried to talk him out of joining the navy, much as the Master-at-Arms was about to do regarding his transfer to Special Forces, but he had stood firm. After serving in an old sloop, he had volunteered for Light Coastal Forces and had even completed a course to become a killick coxswain with his leading rate's anchor, aboard an MTB or a motor gunboat.

It was just as if the old police system had picked him out at that moment. He had been transferred to Chatham Barracks, and then to this detention barracks where he had been for nearly five months.

'Look,' the MAA was warming to his theme, 'once you've been in the job you know how it is. You're a copper at heart, and you stay one. You belong here, my son. In a few more months you may rate RPO, just think – a *petty officer*.' He glanced down at the matching gold crowns and leaves on his lapels. 'Why you might even reach Master like me. This bloody war will go on for years an' years yet, you see.' He sounded pleased.

Ives stared through a window and gritted his teeth. Near one end of the square was a high wall. It had been painted white, and then a mountain of coal had been piled against it.

The opposite side of the wall was black where this same pile of coal had been leaning. That wall would now be washed and painted, and then the coal would be moved back in small hand barrows to repeat the whole process over and over again. He watched the bent figures of the prisoners digging with their shovels, their faces and arms shining black in the sunshine. Through the tough glass he could hear the bark of commands, the occasional shrill of a whistle as the prisoners were driven to greater efforts.

As every RPO said to an incoming prisoner, 'You may break yer mother's heart, but you won't break mine.'

What a place. Everything at the double. Poor food, little sleep. Ives often thought the guards would have felt quite at home in a German prison camp.

The Master-at-Arms stood up and joined him by the window.

'You sorry for them? Don't be. Skates, the lot of 'em. Deserters, lower-deck lawyers, hard cases. *Scum*. They're a disgrace to the Andrew.'

'I might as well have stayed in the Job, Master.' He felt like hitting his superior, although his features remained calm. Not because of his words, but because of his attitude. He looked down at some other toiling figures, doing squad drill with full packs and equipment. Except that their packs were loaded with stones and they would march until they dropped. The Master-at-Arms was probably right about them being a disgrace. This treatment might break many of them, but others would become even harder.

Ives had seen the Admiralty Fleet order by accident when he had been working in the regulating office. Special Services. He had heard of them, of course. Raids on enemy coasts, small, quick actions which were highly dangerous.

He saw one of the drilling figures stagger and fall. The rest marched around him, frightened to look or help.

God, anything was better than this hell.

He said evenly, 'I want to go, Master.'

'I see.' He sighed as if unable to believe what he had heard. 'Well you can always apply to come back, my son.'

Ives reached for his cap. The Jaunty was unconvinced. The man in question added, 'You know what they say about a volunteer in this mob? He's a bloke who's misunderstood the bloody question in the first place!' He rocked with silent laughter. 'Never fear, you'll be back, you see if I'm not right.'

He was still chuckling as Ives left to collect his gear and his travel warrant.

The duty Regulating Petty Officer peered in and said, 'You didn't talk 'im round then, Master?'

'No.' He glared at him. 'Get those idle buggers to shift themselves with the coal. They're like a bunch of old women!'

Outside the high studded gates Ives took a deep breath. Even the air tasted different out here. He slung his bag over his shoulder and made his way towards a blue van with the letters RNDQ on its side. He had made his decision. There was nothing to lose. Ives's father had been a copper too and had died in a punch-up at some stupid dog race. His mother had been buried in her little house in Bethnal Green during a hit-and-run raid. Now she lived, broken and completely mindless, in a home. No, there was nothing to lose any more.

The driver said, 'I'm to take you to the station, Hookey. After that, you're on your own.'

Ives nodded then turned to stare at the high, dismal wall. He seemed to hear the Master-at-Arms's last words and shook his head.

Aloud he said, 'Not this time, *my son*. I'll never come back.'

The naval jeep with scratched red-painted wings splashed through a succession of puddles and swung into yet another deserted street.

In the front seat beside the driver Lieutenant Richard Allenby, RNVR, tried to balance a map on his knees and prevent himself from being hurled bodily onto the road.

I must be mad. Raving bloody mad. What is this trying to prove?

Behind him he heard Hazel, his young rating, shifting amongst the tools and other gear which cluttered the jeep. He saw a policeman on a bicycle, wearing a steel helmet, pedalling slowly past, going the opposite way.

The driver muttered, 'Got the right idea, that one.'

Nobody answered him.

Allenby was twenty-five years old and hailed from the county of Surrey. His even features were unusually pale, and his mouth tightly shut.

He could not find the answers to any of his questions. After the officers' training college at *King Alfred* he had been appointed to a minesweeper. He had a knack of understanding mechanical and electrical gadgets that had left some of his instructors openly nonplussed.

Even now on quiet nights he thought about his months in the little minesweeper. Up and down, back and forth, monotony, strain, and every so often sudden death, with a sweeper being blasted to fragments by a mine someone had missed. He had had one chance of transferring to general service but something, a sort of wild impulse, had made him stay on with minesweeping.

His mother, with whom he shared very little of his work and his doubts, often asked him why he didn't get promoted like some of the neighbours' sons, or be in a ship with one of the household names.

'Like the *Hood*?' he had once suggested. Even that cruel joke was lost on his mother.

Two minesweepers had exploded in a single pyre within sight of their base. Nobody was saved, and when the burned and twisted corpses had been laid out for burial Allenby had felt fear for the first time. Before, it had been merely a sensation, elation, madness perhaps, but seeing those pitiful and familiar faces had made him afraid, and had also filled him with hate.

He had applied to join what was laughingly described as the Land Incident Section, Admiralty, which in plainer words meant the mines disposal section. It had meant yet another course at the mines and torpedo school, HMS *Vernon*, in Portsmouth, where he had learned to recognize and deal with the latest German magnetic mines.

Allenby worked on the models and on the real thing with utter dedication, and when he picked up his second stripe he was sent almost immediately to deal with his first challenge. He still did not know how he had managed it, let alone survived until this damp, sunny morning.

Many of his associates, trainee officers like himself, had only gone to their first mines. At least it was quick, and there was never anything to clear up.

The Germans were good at it. Booby traps, other traps to explode the big mines if the first deception failed; it was like fighting a person and not just a machine.

Allenby had dealt with sixteen mines of various kinds, one of which had been in a hospital where seven elderly patients had been too ill to be moved.

Even his mother had been impressed by his George Cross. Pinned on by the King himself.

But Allenby knew that without a change the chance of survival was a bad risk. Sooner or later you overlooked some small difference, or your nerves destroyed your caution.

He had seen the request for applications for Special Service and had put his name down with the same detachment as when he had volunteered for mines disposal.

He had had an interview with two men, a naval officer and another in civilian clothes. Very businesslike, with every detail of his work and successes at their fingertips. They did not try to make him change his mind as he had half expected. Too many young officers had been killed in the long winter nights as they had pitted their skills against the best that the enemy could invent.

Quite the reverse, they had smiled and said he would hear from them soon.

In three days he was ordered to Portsmouth to take up his new appointment.

And then this morning, long before dawn, he had been roused from his bed by the duty officer.

There had been several massive raids on London and the docks, the Army Bomb Disposal units were working full out to deal with bombs that had failed to explode and would most likely be fitted with delayed-action devices so as to cause the most havoc.

Allenby would normally have reacted calmly, gathered his wits like his equipment and gone to work. But his defences were down. He had stepped back from the work the instant he had received his orders to move.

The officer had said flatly, 'There's just nobody else available.' So here he was. One more time. Perhaps the one that would cheat him at the moment of release.

It was on the outskirts of Southampton. Lines of familiar working-class houses, side by side, back to back. He felt his stomach muscles tighten. The worst streets. No side gates, no breaks in the terraced houses where you could run and hide. In another hour he would have been on his way to Portsmouth. Something different. A shift of odds.

He would have to be extra careful.

Hazel, the young rating who had been his assistant for the past few months, was unusually quiet. He was a pleasant youth of nineteen, with fine, almost delicate features. He was well educated, considerably better than his lieutenant, and it was a crying shame he had not been given a commission, Allenby thought. Allenby had mentioned it to the commanding officer.

'Lacks officerlike qualities. Nice enough chap, but – ' That word 'but' made all the difference in the navy.

But Allenby had spoken to others, and his George Cross had been useful for the first time. Hazel had been interviewed again and was getting a chance after all.

When Allenby had told him, the young seaman had hung his head.

'I – I know you're doing it for the best, sir.'

'You don't want it?' Allenby had pretended to be angry. It was hard to do, Hazel was one of those gentle souls who managed to short-circuit even the angriest petty officer.

'I'd rather stay with you, sir.'

If it had come from anyone else Allenby would have been embarrassed. But it was just Hazel's way.

The call to Portsmouth had at least settled things. Hazel would go to *King Alfred* after all. He would probably get chucked out but at least he would have had a fair crack of the whip. He was the sort of quiet one who might win a VC, Allenby decided.

Hazel said sharply, 'There it is!'

The usual, the 'Unexploded bomb' notice, the air of utter desertion and emptiness. As if every living soul had been spirited away. Another policeman waited by the barrier, his features softening with relief as the battered jeep rolled to a halt.

He said, 'Number twenty-eight, sir. Left side. Old Ma Kenilworthy's place, it is.'

When Allenby did not speak he added, 'We've been busy movin' people out all night.'

'We've been a bit busy too.' Allenby patted his crumpled blue battledress to make sure he had everything he might need. He saw the hurt in the policeman's eyes, and was surprised by his own lie. He had not been busy, but had spent the previous evening in the mess, farewell drinks all round. And his head felt like it. That worried him too. There was no room for blurred thoughts.

'You wait here, Tim. I'll take a look-see.'

He saw the driver start with surprise at the casual use of

a rating's name. The driver was new. He'd soon learn. He'd better.

Allenby walked through the barrier and down the centre of the street. Every house alike, and no parked cars, naturally. A cat washing with one paw stopped to watch him as he walked unhurriedly past.

Allenby always pictured it as a scene in a film about cowboys and Indians, the marshal walking up to match pistols with the bad guys. He mentally ticked off the house numbers. It was funny how you could tell they were all empty, he thought. Strips of paper across the windows in case of blast. A faded Union Jack painted above one of the front doors. A welcome home perhaps for some son or husband?

Chalk marks on the walls. So there were still children here, not evacuated like the lucky ones.

There had been one previous bombing in the street. It must have been early in the war, he thought. A solitary bomb had knocked down a house, and the disposal crews had shored up the two adjoining ones to leave a neat, clean gap. It was like a missing tooth. He wondered briefly what had happened to the people. He quickened his pace, his eye taking in two important details. In the gap between the houses the fire service had constructed a large, metal static watertank. In some air raids there were not enough hydrants to supply the hoses. But the tank would also afford cover if the worst happened.

The other sign that caught his eye was a hole in one of the sloping roofs, the remains of a parachute wrapped around the chimney. Number twenty-eight. He turned and looked along the empty street. The jeep and the policeman were hidden from view, and only Hazel, his heavy satchel across one shoulder, stood watching him.

Allenby felt his lips twist in a smile. Poor chap, he was more scared of being selected for a commission than he was of any mine. He had always had absolute faith in Allenby, and never suggested even once that they had been lucky with this job or that job.

He walked to the front door and pushed it open. The hallway was narrow, and full of dust from the roof. Normally, he guessed, it would be spotless. An old lady living alone. Maybe that was her cat?

He stood motionless, getting his bearings, his ears pitched to the slightest sounds, except that there was nothing to hear. Allenby gripped a door handle which obviously led into the front room. He opened the door very slowly, holding his breath. It grated against something solid and would not budge. It was the mine. It had to be. Suspended by its parachute. One false move or knock and you'd had it.

He swore under his breath and went out the front door. He waved to Hazel and when he came panting down the street Allenby explained what had to be done.

That was another thing about Hazel, you never had to repeat a single word.

'I'll have to go out the back and break in through the other door, the kitchen, I think. You stay in the hall outside the front room.'

He glanced up the street. Some pieces of newspaper had come to life and were rolling about on their own.

Allenby added shortly, 'This needs to be fast. There's a bloody breeze getting up. We don't know how long that thing has been hanging there.'

Hazel nodded, his features concerned. 'I'll rig the telephone, sir.'

'No time, Tim. If I yell out, you run like hell for that watertank. If the mine goes off you should be safe there until rescue arrives.'

He realized that Hazel was staring at him, eyes wide with sudden shock.

'You mean – ' He struggled for words.

Allenby patted his arms, 'I mean, we've got to be careful on this one.'

He went through the house and into the kitchen. There was a small yard outside which backed on to another exactly like it. There were photographs on the mantelpiece, one of a soldier in a beret with a tank behind him. A ration book lay forgotten on the kitchen table.

He wondered momentarily what some of his brother officers would think if they knew he had been brought up in a house not much bigger than this one.

He went into the yard and peered into the next room through the only other window.

As he shaded his eyes and pressed his face to the glass he felt the familiar twist in his stomach.

There it was, hanging through the smashed ceiling, long and evil, grimy with the filth of exhaust gas from the aircraft which had released it. About eight feet long, maybe a bit more. At a guess, like one he had dealt with just a week back. His mind grappled with the details, the margin of success and otherwise. This kind was packed with fifteen hundred pounds of explosive, hexanite. Deadly and devastating. He thought he saw the mine quiver and guessed that the parachute lines had slackened slightly.

With a hammer he smashed the window until there was ample room to climb through. Even after all this time he hated destroying other people's property. That was his mother, he thought with a grin. *We're not made of money. Some of us have had to work hard for every penny.* And so on.

He saw a shadow through the crack in the hallway door and knew Hazel was there. Ready to push through an extra tool if needed. His just being there made all the difference.

Allenby ran his fingers over the side of the mine. It was like ice. He held his breath again as his fingers found the fuse cap. The parachute lines were taut, and the bulbous nose of the mine's cylinder shape rested in the remains of an old sofa. He withdrew the safety callipers from his pocket and fitted them to the fuse. They would keep the fuse from moving and coming alive while he was working.

'*Bloody hell!*'

Hazel called in a fierce whisper, 'What's happened, sir?'

'The fuse is bent. Won't budge. I shall have to unscrew the damned keeping ring by hand. Give me the spanner.' For a moment their fingers touched through the small gap in the door and Allenby heard himself say, 'It's a Charlie. If the fuse goes you've got twelve seconds, right?'

'Right, sir.' The fingers vanished. Then he said in a small voice, 'What about you?'

'I shall be through the back window faster than a priest out of a knocking shop, believe me, Tim.' He pictured his possible escape route. Out through the back yard. A place where they delivered coal. Not much but it would support the weight of a house if need be.

He wiped his forehead with his sleeve, what the hell was the matter with him? It was not the first fuse that had jammed. Dust filtered down onto his wrists as he worked steadily and with regular pauses to watch his progress.

The breeze was getting up, and he almost cried out as a loose slate clattered down the roof and shattered on the pavement outside.

He thought suddenly of his last leave, perhaps the first time he had realized his nerves were getting raw.

His mother had been going on about shortages and queues and had suddenly remarked, 'But, of course, you aren't troubled with things like that in the services!'

He had seen the warning light in his father's eye, that quiet docile man who never complained about anything. He had only one leg; the other he had lost as a young sapper on the Somme.

Allenby had heard his own voice, high and almost unrecognizable. 'For Christ's sake, you don't know what it's like. How can you? Every day men are getting killed and maimed and all you can bleat about are your bloody rations!'

The keeping ring moved very slightly, perhaps an eighth of an inch. The worst was over. Soon the repair teams would arrive and put a tarpaulin over the old lady's roof, and the houses would fill with ordinary, decent people again.

A brick fell beside him; it had missed his head by inches. Even as he stared at it he heard a slithering sound and to his horror saw the great steel cylinder drop just a few inches before the parachute lines checked it again.

Allenby stared at it, frozen, unable to accept it. There was a sudden whirr of mechanism, the sound was almost gentle.

He had less than twelve seconds to live.

He stood up and almost fell again. He yelled, '*Get out, Tim! For God's sake!*'

Through the window, cutting one hand on the jagged glass, his lungs bursting, his heart pounding like a club.

There was a gap in the wall. With a desperate sob Allenby hurled himself the last few feet. He dug his elbows into the ground and pressed his hands to his ears.

But when the mine exploded he heard nothing. It was a new sensation, more like being drowned than buried.

Someone was yelling and sobbing, but he was past recognizing his own voice.

Oblivion when it came was merciful.

2

Prothero's Navy

Lieutenant Keith Frazer tapped on a door marked 'Special Operations, No Admittance' but no voice called out for him to enter. It was hardly surprising, he thought, the door was solid steel.

He pushed it open and stared round a long, low room with a curved ceiling. It was incredible to think that this maze of rooms and passages was deep beneath part of Portsmouth Dockyard. It must have been a wine or spirit store at one time. Two Wrens were hammering at typewriters but both looked up as he entered. They were young and seemed tired, and their shirts did not look crisp as was expected in the Wrens.

No wonder, he thought. The air was damp, stale and confined. A place under siege.

'Sir?' The nearest girl glanced at his gold shoulder flash. 'You must be Lieutenant Frazer.'

Frazer grinned. 'That's right.' He had been making so many explanations in so many offices since he had left Liverpool it was refreshing to discover someone who apparently knew exactly what was happening.

Liverpool, the *Levant*, even the Atlantic, all seemed lost in time, and yet it had been only two weeks since he had reported to another office here in Portsmouth near the barracks.

He said, 'I think I'm expected, Miss er – '

She had a friendly smile and looked as if she was about to tell him her name. If so, she decided against it.

She said, 'The Boss is with the Commodore. You are to wait in the next office. Second Officer Balfour will take care of you.' She dropped her eyes to her typewriter and then asked, 'Do you know a Lieutenant Allenby, sir?'

He turned his cap round his fingers. Allenby, he was one of the team. They had met only briefly at the pistol range where they had been put through their paces at hand-shooting by two tough Royal Marine sergeants. They had been shown how to use a commando knife too. It looked as if he was going to get closer to the enemy than he had expected.

'Allenby,' he said. It formed slowly in his mind. A pale, unsmiling face dominated by dark brown eyes. Withdrawn, or maybe he just didn't like Canadians. 'Yes, I did meet him for a few seconds.'

She nodded and slammed the typewriter carriage into position.

He asked, 'Bit of a lad, is he?'

She looked up and Frazer was shocked to see that her eyes were brimming with tears.

'I – I'm sorry, hell, I had no idea what – '

The other Wren darted round her desk and guided him to the next door. Her head did not reach his shoulder but she seemed to have the strength of an able seaman.

'It's all right, Lieutenant. Just forget it.'

He found himself in the next room, slightly longer and brightly lit to reveal all the cracks and stains which even the wall maps and charts could not completely disguise.

Second Officer Balfour, like the Wrens in the outer office, had slung her jacket with its two blue stripes across the back of her chair. She too was young, with short auburn hair, blue eyes and a nice mouth.

She said, 'Sit down. The Boss will be here soon.' She was smoking a cigarette and leaned back to watch him through the smoke as he settled in a chair. Every other chair and table seemed to be filled with files and clips of signals.

Frazer said, 'I'm afraid I upset one of your girls just now.'

The blue eyes were motionless. Not even a blink.

'She'll be fine. Bad news.' She threw the cigarette into a metal bin. 'There's a war on.'

Frazer changed tack. In *Levant* he had created his own system. He had been respected for it, even by the captain. Here he just seemed to get more and more confused.

He said, 'I'm supposed to see the Operations Officer as well.'

She gave a brief smile. 'You're seeing her right now.' She leaned over the desk and held out her hand. 'Lynn Balfour.'

Frazer could not help noticing the way her shirt curved around her breast when she reached over the desk. She had a firm, warm handshake.

He said uncertainly, 'I guess you know about me anyway.'

She opened her packet of cigarettes but did not offer him one.

'Yes. I study all the details. Part of the job.' She rested her elbow on the arm of her chair and studied him thoughtfully.

'You come from a rich family, you could have stayed at home. Instead you went to sea.' She glanced away, her body restless beneath her shirt as if she had remembered something bad.

'Lost one ship, became navigating officer of a fleet destroyer.' She looked at him and gave a small grimace. 'No easy thing that. It's 1943 and there are still some idiots in high places who would rather have an elderly relic brought in from retirement than allow reservists, hostilities-only officers, into vital posts.' She smiled. 'Especially chaps from the colonies!'

He laughed. 'What about the Boss?'

Her smile went. 'You must decide for yourself.'

'Anyone else coming?'

She answered severely, 'Too many questions.' She relented

very slightly. 'Lieutenant Allenby. He joined us late. He's
been ill.' She shrugged as if it was of no importance. 'But
he's an explosives expert, so it didn't matter too much.'

'I see.'

'You don't, best keep it that way.' She picked up a telephone. 'Now, if you'll excuse me, I've things to do.'

Frazer relaxed. What would Caryl, or some of the other
girls he had known in Vancouver and elsewhere, make of
Second Officer Lynn Balfour, he wondered. In some ways
it was harder for the people in Canada to understand the
war. There were no obvious shortages, no air raids, not too
many uniforms once you got away from the ports and larger
towns. And yet it was worse when the troopships, the
convoys and the aircraft left for far-flung theatres of war
which ranged from Iceland to Burma. How could they share
it? Here in England it was different, and he had long decided
it was better to share the good and the bad with the people
you were trying to defend. Only the casualty lists were the
same on both sides of the Atlantic.

The Wren officer glanced at her watch and said, 'He's here
now. That red light will flash, and in you go.' She bit her
lip and added, 'What the hell has happened to Allenby? The
Boss won't thank him for keeping him waiting.'

The red light did indeed flash and Frazer stood up,
wondering as he did so what sort of giant he was about to
meet.

The outer door opened and shut with a bang and he saw
the girl staring at the newcomer with sudden surprise.

It was Allenby. Without his raincoat he looked somehow
too young for his rank and the decoration on his left breast.

Second Officer Balfour asked quickly, 'Is something
wrong?'

But Allenby looked directly at Frazer. Seeing someone
familiar, even if he had only known him for a matter of
minutes, seemed to give him strength.

'That girl out there. The Leading Wren. I just met her.'

His faced looked damp, as if he might be sick. The little lamp flashed again, and this time was accompanied by an impatient buzzer.

As the Wren officer hurried to open the other door Frazer took Allenby by the arm and said, 'Easy, Dick.' It was strange how the fact he had remembered the pale lieutenant's name helped to steady him. 'We'll talk about it later, eh?'

But Allenby did not hear him.

'That Wren. Her name's Hazel. I think I killed her brother.'

The office into which the two lieutenants were pushed without ceremony was probably the same size as the other one. But it seemed almost filled and overcrowded by the huge figure who stood, beefy hands on hips, in a raincoat which looked lik a tent.

He stabbed a finger at two canvas-backed chairs. 'Frazer? Allenby?' He nodded curtly. 'Punctuality rates very high with me.' He raised his resonant voice. 'Lynn! Ring Gieves and tell them my new reefer is still too tight.'

Frazer heard the girl call through the door, and wondered what it would be like to work for this man. The Boss.

The latter stripped off his raincoat and Frazer realized that his size was no illusion.

He wore a blue battledress with the shoulder straps of a commander RNVR. Very rare in high places, as Second Officer Balfour had commented. He had a giant girth, heavy shoulders which were surmounted by a large head. He was nearly bald, but his scalp was like tanned leather, and he had a short piratical beard; like a figure from *Boys' Own Paper*.

'I'm Prothero,' he announced in his deep voice. 'I command the Special Boat Operations Section. Here and on the ground, so to speak.' It seemed to amuse him and his weathered face creased into a grin.

Frazer noticed his eyes were very small, like chips of

washed-out blue glass. In his big features they looked almost incidental.

'Rear Admiral Oldenshaw is in overall command but he's away.' He did not elaborate.

'I'll get right down to it.' He leaned back on his heels as if to proportion the weight. 'We've had a lot of success in the Med. There'll be a lot more once the Germans are completely out of North Africa. Our work is tough, it makes big demands and all our people are handpicked for their various talents.' The small eyes rested momentarily on Allenby, but only for an instant. 'You can forget most of what you've learned. This is the thinking man's navy, no place for your feather-bedded regular. We are here to *fight*, not to carve out a career. No passengers.'

Frazer guessed he made this speech quite often.

'Fact is, we use any type of vessel that suits the operation in hand. We cooperate with the other Special Services when we have to. The Levant Schooner Force, the SAS, even the Long-Range Desert Group and Commando. The work involves stealth, the ability to mingle with local vessels, but to use initiative and guts if Jerry gets too nosy, which he has, and will a lot more when he is forced back to Sicily and the mainland.'

He lowered his voice. 'You've both got excellent records. You, Allenby, have more than proved your courage and resourcefulness. You're going to need both. Frazer, you're a small-ship man and by all accounts are a dab hand as a navigator, much of which you picked up before the war, sailing with your father. According to him anyway.' He saw the surprise on the lieutenant's face. 'Raced with him at Cowes, as a matter of fact.'

Allenby tried to relax, but felt ice-cold even in the damp, humid air and had to clench his knuckles against his thighs to stop himself from shaking.

He tried to listen to what Commander Prothero was

saying, but instead he kept seeing the girl's face. It was so obvious, she even looked a bit like his dead assistant.

Dead, that was the word. He went over it again, as he had since he had been dragged out of the debris, barely able to breathe, temporarily deafened by the blast he had not even heard, but without a mark on him. That same mine had knocked down six streets. His commanding officer had visited him in hospital. It was just one of those things. Allenby had done more than almost any other render-mines-safe officer. He could not be blamed. Allenby had tried to ask about Hazel.

It was the usual story. Hazel had simply disintegrated. Not a button or even a strip of uniform. Nothing.

His superior had asked, 'Did you not think of rigging the telephone, Dick?' It was unnerving the way Frazer had recalled his first name.

'There was no time, sir. There was a breeze.' After that he had recalled very little.

'You told him to run for it when the fuse started?' He had smiled sadly. A silly question for one as experienced as Allenby, he probably thought.

And that was the terrible doubt. Allenby could not remember. Had he hurled himself to safety and left Hazel standing there within a foot of that long smoke-stained cylinder?

Someone at the hospital had tried to console him. 'He wouldn't have felt a thing.'

Not for long anyway. But surely even in the split second before the mine had exploded Hazel must have wondered about the lieutenant he had trusted and worshipped since their first meeting. And then the Leading Wren. When she had told him who she was in a flat, unemotional tone he had felt the walls begin to cave in. He had started to explain, to describe it, until his memory had tricked him yet again.

He had been aware of voices in the other room, and the fact he was late for his appointment with the commander,

and he had been unable to move as she had said quietly,
'Well, sir, at least you've come out of it all right.' Her eyes
had been on his George Cross ribbon. If she had hit him her
words could have had no greater impact.

Prothero's voice thrust through his thoughts like a ram.

'No questions, Allenby? All quite clear is it?'

Allenby stared at him like a trapped animal. 'I – I'm sorry,
sir.'

Prothero smiled but there was no warmth in it. 'You
are a brave man, Allenby. Courage is not always enough,
however. Too many hopes, too many lives may rely on
you in the future, perhaps even before you have become
accustomed to our ways in the group.'

Frazer said abruptly, 'He's had a bad time, sir.'

Prothero did not move his small eyes from Allenby. 'I
know. I know all about both of you. Despite that, you are
here, and in this section you do not have the exclusive right
to be miserable. *Do you understand?*'

Allenby nodded. 'Yes, sir.'

'Good.' He rested his buttocks on his table so that his
considerable belly stood out like a bay window.

'You will take forty-eight hours' leave to deal with your
personal affairs. Second Officer Balfour will attend to travel
warrants and the like. When you report back you must expect
to move at short notice.'

Frazer asked, 'May we know where, sir?' At this stage he
did not really care but wanted to draw Prothero's fire from
Allenby. He saw Allenby glance at him. Curious, grateful?
It was hard to tell.

'No.' Surprisingly, Prothero gave a great grin. 'But as it
is too far for you to return to Canada in the time, I would
suggest you take a girl and a bottle up to London, right?'

The door opened slightly. 'Gieves on the phone, sir.'

'Very well, Lynn.' The meeting was apparently over.

Frazer and Allenby left the room and glanced at each other.
Allenby asked, 'Will you?'

Frazer laughed. 'What, the girl-and-bottle bit? I shouldn't
think so.' He looked at the Wren officer who was staring at
some new signals, one hand thrust into her hair like a claw.
Unless. He dismissed the idea and asked, 'What about you,
Dick?'

Allenby already knew what he would do. There never
seemed an alternative.

'Home, I suppose.' He looked quickly at Frazer's profile.
A strong face, someone you could trust. He was a Canadian
and probably expected him to ask him to his home for their
short break from duty. Forty-eight hours. He thought of the
dull, suburban house, his mother's incisive voice, everything.
It made him feel cold. How could he?

'Good. I envy you.'

Allenby said, 'Perhaps next time we could – '

Frazer smiled. 'Sure. Why not?'

The Wren officer said, 'If you drop in after lunch I'll brief
you and give you your new passes.' She looked from one to
the other. 'Welcome to the Club.'

Frazer watched her. It was an act. She had been hurt,
badly.

She turned to Allenby. 'One thing. How do you do it?'
She saw the immediate guard drop behind his eyes, and added
more gently, 'I saw the pictures in the papers of you in that
hospital, just sitting on that bloody great mine and chatting
with the old lady in bed, and making the nurse laugh. I
couldn't have done it. I don't know anyone else who could.'

Allenby looked at the floor, confused. 'I never thought
much about it.' In spite of his guard he shot a glance at the
outer door. 'Not until the last one.'

Frazer watched the girl, saw the compassion in her eyes
before she too returned to her role in the drama.

She said softly, 'Well, don't you worry about Leading
Wren Hazel. She'll get over it given time.'

Allenby clenched his fists. 'You see, I can't remember.
Maybe I did forget – '

Frazer said, 'Come on. I'll take you for a drink.' He glanced at the Wren. 'Maybe we could – '

She opened a file of papers. 'Could what?'

Frazer shrugged. 'I've been too long at sea, that's my trouble.'

She grimaced. 'Perhaps you should take up the Boss's suggestion.'

Frazer felt himself flushing. 'Were you listening, for God's sake?'

She laughed. 'It is what the Boss *always* says!'

In the outer office there were two different girls at the desks. Frazer could almost feel Allenby sigh with relief.

He glanced at the lieutenant's pale face. So that was what a hero looked like.

Almost to himself Allenby said, 'As a matter of fact – ' He hesitated. 'Keith, isn't it? Well, as a matter of fact, I was scared, every single time.'

Frazer laughed. 'We're going to get on just fine.'

Allenby stared at him, unable to stop himself.

'Look, I wonder if you'd like to come home with me?'

It was against everything he had planned and guarded since he had entered the navy, and Frazer guessed as much.

He answered softly, 'Sure, I'd like that.' It was settled.

A seaman pushed his head around the door and shouted, 'Air-raid warnin', gents!'

Mark Ives stood up and studied himself in a mirror at the tailor's shop attached to naval stores. On his sleeve the new badge of leading coxswain was still like part of the dream, the unreality of it all.

The elderly petty officer who had been his guard and instructor since his arrival chuckled, 'Bit better than a crusher, eh?'

Ives shook his head. 'I didn't believe they could fix things so easily. Before it's always been draft chits, duty rotas and

requests to see the Old Man about the slightest thing.' He
grinned. 'This'll do me.'

The petty officer filled his pipe and said, 'You're entitled
to forty-eight hours, y'know.'

Ives checked over his pile of brand-new gear. It would be
good to get back to something like Coastal Forces, if that
was what the job entailed. Small ships, and a feeling of self-
dependence which was lacking in carriers and cruisers. He
controlled the urge to laugh. Or in detention quarters
especially.

Ives said, 'I'll stay put. Talk to some of the others.'

The PO watched him and liked what he saw.

He said, 'You're to be a replacement. I'm not supposed to
say, but I think you should know.'

Ives shrugged. 'What happened to the other chap?'

'Dunno for sure. It's pretty hush-hush in the mob you're
joining. But it was a raid of sorts, a raid what went wrong.'

Ives looked at the commando knife and the holster in
which he would be carrying his newly issued revolver when
he went on active service. He had used it on the pistol
range, but was already an excellent shot and had been in the
Metropolitan Police display team in those far-off days.

A good all-rounder they had said. Rugger, boxing and a
fair hand with revolver and rifle. It was coming in useful at
last.

The face reappeared in the doorway. 'All clear, gents. False
alarm, it's another raid on London.'

The PO said, 'Poor sods.'

Ives saw it clearly in his mind. The piles of rubble. Gaping
holes, upended double-decker buses. His London. The catch
in your throat when you rounded a corner and a tearful
voice screamed, 'Thank Gawd, 'ere's a copper!' And then the
clearing up. The removal of the dead. Putting a face on it no
matter what you felt inside.

He picked up the knife and drew it slowly from its scab-
bard. Now he had a chance to hit back.

The stores petty officer joined them at the counter.

'Sign here then.' It didn't matter to him if it was a would-be hero or a prisoner awaiting a court martial. Everything had to be signed for.

Alone in her brightly lit operations office Second Officer Balfour watched the door close as a Wren carried the travel warrants out to await collection by the two lieutenants. She thought about them briefly. Allenby was nice, but seemed withdrawn to the point of self-destruction. She found she could accept such complications since she had transferred to Prothero's Special Section. Secret or not, it was known by almost everyone as Prothero's Navy. It fitted him.

She thought too of Frazer, the tall Canadian. She had seen him watching her body and guessed he would be an easy one to fall for.

The thought stabbed at her like a dart.

She had hung a 'Do not disturb' sign on her door. Prothero was on his way to Plymouth for a meeting and to watch a commando exercise. He might ring her in the dogwatches but not before. She shifted in her chair and then pulled open the bottom drawer of her desk. It lay there glinting at her, a half-empty bottle of gin. It had been full, when?

She groped for a tin of peppermints and suddenly thought of the small, dedicated section of girls she controlled. Did any of them know or guess? Prothero obviously did not, otherwise he would have sacked her and sent her back to general duties, like being a quarters officer at some dismal Wrennery.

She shook a teacup into the litter bin and filled it deliberately with neat gin.

Aloud she whispered, 'Oh God, help me.' Then she drank it down, gasping at the rawness of it in her throat, at the gesture which did not seem to help.

She reached behind her and drew a wallet from her reefer jacket and laid it on the desk.

It was always the same. Sometimes it took longer than others. Then she slipped out his photograph and stared at it. It was as if she might have missed something although she had studied it a million times.

Just another naval lieutenant, squinting at the camera on that last morning. That so very special morning when – a tear splashed on her wrist and she hurriedly replaced the picture in the wallet.

Oh Paul, I miss you so.

The telephone jangled by her elbow and the empty cup.

'Second Officer Balfour, Operations.'

The voice asked something and she replied, 'I'll ring back.'

She could barely see through the mist in her eyes, but nothing in her voice betrayed her. Yet.

She put down the telephone very carefully and straightened her tie.

She said, 'It won't do. It simply will not do.'

But the words bounced back at her, like they always did.

Commander Aubrey Prothero listened to his own heavy breathing while he stared at the coloured map that lay weighted down on a table. A solitary shaded light glared down, suspended on a long flex, so that everything beyond the map was excluded in shadow.

A strip of coastline. It could have been almost anywhere from North Africa to the Adriatic. Large scale, with groups of coloured pins and paper arrows to indicate the various zones and possible objectives.

It was very quiet, he thought, rather like his HQ in Portsmouth. Here in Plymouth they had also suffered badly from air raids, and this section's offices were protected by concrete and steel from everything but a direct hit.

As if from miles away he heard the muffled bellow of a

gunnery instructor as another company of raw recruits was initiated into the mysteries of parade training, rifle and bayonet drill, although what use it would be to seagoing personnel was beyond Prothero.

He was feeling his age after his madcap drive to Plymouth. His crazy Royal Marine driver had excelled himself. Even so he had been late and that troubled him.

He felt the other two occupants of the still room watching him. They had said nothing about his lateness, but were probably glad to have found a flaw in his rules on the matter.

Why? Perhaps one of the girls in the SDO had mixed up the signals, or had retyped the times wrongly. It was surprising that Lynn Balfour had not noticed it. Not like her at all.

He glanced up quickly. Both of the other officers were soldiers, a brigadier and a major. Their medal ribbons from forgotten campaigns gleamed in the harsh light, but above them their faces were in total shadow. It was like being with two decapitated corpses.

'Sorry to rush you, Aubrey, but we've been caught napping.'

Prothero almost added 'again', but refrained; he was still thinking about Second Officer Balfour.

He said, 'It's a bit dicey, even for our chaps.'

The brigadier said, 'Our forces in North Africa are going like fury. We heard today that Rommel has been flown out on the direct orders of Hitler himself. He's had to hand over the whole of the Afrika Korps, or what's left of it, to von Arnim. It will be all over soon, a couple of weeks at the most. It looks as if Hitler is prepared to sacrifice the lot of them. No Dunkirk for *him*.'

Prothero leaned on the map, his big hands like lumps of coral. It was hard to accept that Rommel, the Desert Fox, who had won the respect of his own men and the Eighth Army alike, had given in. It would do more harm to the Germans' morale than anything.

He heard the table creak under his weight. The map was a small section of the northern coast of Sicily. Not a healthy place at any time. When the Germans retreated there from North Africa it would be doubly dangerous to land or retrieve agents even with the aid of the so-called underground there. They were mostly bandits.

He said, 'I've been unhappy about the situation in Sicily for months, although I found it difficult to get much sympathy for my views.' He did not conceal his bitterness. 'Now we might be too late. When the Germans are finally out of North Africa the Allies will want to invade Sicily and Italy with as little delay as possible. Before Jerry has time to regroup, to set up extra coastal defences. For once the enemy will be on the defensive. We shall see how he likes it.'

The major said gently, 'You mentioned a new team?'

'Yes. Good men.' In his mind he saw Allenby's defensiveness, Frazer's attempt to defend him. Together they should more than replace the ones who had been killed or gone missing.

He said, 'We have to make contact with the Sicilians. Terrorists, partisans, whichever fits your point of view. It will be too late once the invasion starts. Those buggers will play one side against the other like the Yugoslavs have done. It's now or never. Work with us, or be treated like the enemy.'

The brigadier did not conceal his relief. 'My section will give you all the help it can.'

The major's face dipped into the light as he opened some papers.

'The Canadian, Frazer, what's he like?'

Prothero considered it. 'Good. Headstrong but not reckless. The kind of man who can act quickly and encourage those who depend on him. He should have had a command by now. Bloody waste.' He almost added 'as usual'.

The buck had been passed.

Prothero said, 'I'll get back right away.' His driver would

love that. 'Leave it to me. I'll let you have the time and
method in a few days.'

The brigadier stood up. 'Anything we can do right now?'

Prothero shrugged his massive shoulders.

'Pray,' he replied.

A messenger guided him out into the evening air. It was
not much like spring, he thought.

He allowed the plan to take shape in his mind as he walked
unseeingly past some saluting sailors. Soon a new pointer or
flag would appear on the map, the idea would become a fact.

He despised men like the two he had just left. They cared
nothing for those who carried out their harebrained schemes.
They were merely pawns, faceless units. Only the mission,
and the next after that, counted. It was up to Special Operations to make sure that men did not die for nothing.

Prothero saw his driver waiting beside the car and quickened his pace.

It was just that it got harder each time.

3

A Piece of Cake

As Prothero had hinted, things moved fast when he had got approval from higher up.

With some soldiers and a few Royal Marines, Frazer and Allenby found themselves packed into a Dakota troop carrier and winging their way south to Gibraltar. There they had barely time to take a bath before they were taken, or rather escorted, by a severe looking provost marshal to a motor torpedo boat and were dashing through the night into the Mediterranean.

Crouched in one corner of the MTB's tiny wardroom Allenby had tried to drag his mind from that last mine, to recover the one missing fragment of memory. He thought too of the Leading Wren's words, the way that the second officer had attempted to soften them by asking him about the mine at the hospital.

He had thought also of his brief return home, the extraordinary change in his mother's attitude when he had introduced her to Frazer. Allenby had cursed himself more than once on the way there; Frazer was said to be a millionaire's son, a well-known yachtsman, all the things that Allenby could only imagine. He would be shocked by the shabby, semidetached house, the small back garden where his father did his best to grow vegetables, to 'Dig for Victory'. All the houses in the respectable road were shabby, tired out by war. No repairs, too many air raids, not enough men around to paint and patch up.

But Frazer had settled down as if he was really enjoying himself. He had obviously won his mother's heart, and gone further to make Allenby's father talk about the Somme, something which was almost impossible to do.

He had said in his soft drawl, 'My Dad was there, Mr Allenby. Passchendaele as well.'

The old man's eyes had misted over but he had given the small smile that Allenby had always known and loved.

'It's not something you forget, er, Keith.'

On their way back to the station Frazer had remarked, 'Good people. I hope they liked me.'

Frazer had spent most of his time on the MTB's bridge, chatting with her youthful CO and peering at the chart while the boat scudded and bounded through the night.

The places on the North African coastline read like milestones of the war. Now the tide was turning and at least this phase of it was all but ended.

Oran, bombarded by the Royal Navy to destroy the warships of their ally after the French government had surrendered to Hitler. It had been necessary, for if the ships had fallen into enemy hands the balance of naval power would have swung against Britain. Nevertheless, the French who had remained in Tunis and Algeria had never forgotten or forgiven.

There were other names which had reappeared again and again in the early bulletins. Benghazi, Tobruk, and finally El Alamein where the Eighth Army had made a last desperate stand and had won.

If the MTB's skipper had known anything about their mission or final destination he kept it to himself.

Frazer had recalled what Second Officer Balfour had said about secrecy. It was a pity he had not been able to speak to her again before they had been driven to the naval air station. He had called at the Ops Room, but each time she had been unable to see him. In a conference, or involved with her many duties. Or so they had said. He still wondered about it.

Four days after leaving Gibraltar they groped their way into the Tunisian port of Sousse.

Frazer and Allenby stood side by side on the bridge as the MTB picked her way nervously amongst partly submerged wrecks and floating debris until signalled alongside a make-shift jetty which looked as if it had been built by children.

The MTB's skipper grinned. 'There's a jeep waiting for you. I'll have your gear shipped over.' He glanced across at the town, blasted buildings, eyeless windows and drifting layers of smoke. 'I've been based here,' he said. There was something like pride in his voice. 'It's only a hundred and fifty miles to Sicily, and I think my flotilla has hunted every inch of it. The Germans have been trying to supply the Afrika Korps by sea at night. Now they're attempting to evacuate their tanks and troops the same way. The seabed must be strewn with them.'

They shook hands, and Frazer was reminded of the moment he had left the *Levant*. It must be a month ago, he thought. It seemed like a century.

The jeep was waiting as promised. Seated at the wheel was a very bronzed young man in khaki shirt and shorts. He wore no markings or badges, but as he got down from his seat he slapped a naval cap on his head and saluted.

'Able Seaman Weeks, sir. Naval Party Seventy-Five.'

Frazer nodded. He wanted to grin, but the young sailor looked deadly serious. Not even the name of a ship for their new enterprise. A number, like a crate of stores.

They clambered in and the sailor said, ' 'Bout eight miles, that's all, sir.' They roared away, the wheels spewing out sand and dust like something solid.

Fraser felt the heat on his face. Searing, not like anything he had ever experienced. Heat and a strange heavy smell. The vastness of the desert, he thought. A place littered with

burned-out and gutted tanks and half-tracks, smashed
weapons and the too familiar wooden crosses.

They headed north towards Tunis, the piece of coastline
which they had passed during their last night in the MTB.

'Is there much going on, Weeks?'

The rating glanced at Frazer; his eyes were very innocent.
'Can't really say, sir.' You could take that either way. *Careless talk costs lives*, the posters proclaimed, or the wittier
ones like, *Be like dad, keep mum*.

The HQ of Naval Party Seventy-Five looked for all the
world like a junk yard. There was a ragged line of salvaged
vehicles, mostly German and Italian, piles of crates, jerrycans
interspersed with sandbagged and camouflaged gun emplace-
ments. There were several blackened craters around the place
if anyone needed reminding how close the enemy air bases
were.

And here was the sea, like a friend. Deep blue and
untroubled once you looked beyond the wrecks and half-
submerged hulks that lay nearer to the beach.

'You're here then.'

Frazer and Allenby found themselves face to face with a
tall, hatless naval officer in khaki. His tarnished shoulder
straps showed him to be a lieutenant commander, but from
his appearance and the heavy pistol at his belt he looked
more like a soldier. They both saluted and the other man
gave a great grin. It made him look about ten years younger,
Frazer thought.

The other man said, 'I command here. John Goudie's the
name.'

He did not need to elaborate. Goudie had distinguished
himself in motor gunboats from one end of the Med to the
other, and before that in the narrow seas when little else had
stood between the victorious Germans and the white cliffs
of Dover.

Three Spitfires roared low overhead and Goudie said, 'The
RAF have been pretty good. They've kept the Krauts from

bothering us too much. We don't need aerial pictures right now, thank you very much.' He sounded light-hearted, not a care in the world.

Frazer glanced at Allenby and wondered what he thought. It was usually hard to know what he was thinking. Chalk and cheese, but they got on.

He thought of his visit to Allenby's home, the way Allenby seemed to watch his mother, dreading what she might say. But Frazer had felt only admiration for the woman and her one-legged veteran husband. The house had looked rundown, but it seemed to represent what he had come to love about England. A tattered defiance that nothing could break. Even the way Allenby's mother had laid out her high tea for them. It must have been more than a week's ration.

That had been when he had made his one mistake. He had offered to write and ask his own folks to send some food parcels. Allenby's mother had regarded him coolly. 'We can manage, thank you. You get used to it. It's never been easy in this house.'

A defence, an accusation because her husband had been unable to obtain proper work since his war – it was difficult to say. Afterwards Allenby had tried to apologize but Frazer had said, 'She was right, eh? That sort of remark makes me no better than some cocky Yank!'

Lieutenant Commander Goudie led the way to a small hump of rock and loose stones and pointed down into an oval natural harbour. Apart from the scattered debris of war, it looked as if it had been there since time began. There were the sounds of saws and hammers, and jazz from a loud-speaker by some low camouflaged tents.

As they approached the base Frazer watched the comings and goings of the inhabitants. Most of them wore nothing but shorts, they might have been anybody. But all were young and looked very fit and tough. It was another navy, and most of them were obviously amused by the two new arrivals in their uncomfortable uniforms.

Frazer thought suddenly of the *Levant* and wondered if they had already forgotten him. Where was she now? Steaming back into Halifax, Nova Scotia, or charging up and down the lines of merchant ships as they prepared to leave St John's in Newfoundland?

Goudie said, 'In here. Welcome to the mess.'

It was a slightly larger tent than the others and filled with crude trestle tables, ration boxes and cases of small-arms ammunition.

Goudie said, 'Sit here, gentlemen. With your backs to all that squalor you won't feel so bad.' He waited as a sailor entered with a tray under his arm.

Goudie raised an eyebrow. 'Large gins, I think.'

Frazer watched him as he opened a canvas satchel and dragged out some papers. Very cool and self-possessed, he thought. But wound up like a wire. If half the things he had heard about Goudie's exploits were true it was a marvel he was still joined together.

Goudie looked up and said abruptly, 'I expect the Boss has put you in the picture?'

They nodded and took their gins from the messman. Frazer thought it was strange to hear Prothero's name mentioned out here. He seemed to belong back in the UK. He almost choked as he realized the glass was full of neat gin. It was like fire. He saw Allenby's eyes watering as he tried to stop himself from coughing.

Goudie grimaced. 'The water's not good. Jerry poisoned some of it before he left, bless him. And our ice-making equipment is still in Alex, I understand!' It seemed to amuse him.

'Now.' He laid a well-worn map on the table. 'North coast of Sicily, and *here* – ' he jabbed the map with a teaspoon, 'is the objective.'

Objective. Despite the heat and the gin it was like a douche of ice water. They were going into action without any time for further preparation.

Goudie saw their expressions and said mildly, 'Well, we were expecting you earlier, and we were *not* anticipating that your unfortunate predecessors were going to get the chop, right?'

Frazer opened his mouth to ask the question but shut it as Goudie added, 'Anyway, the enemy has left us no choice. Jerry is pulling out of North Africa so fast it will be a race. But the raid, *our* raid, is to be on a brand-new power plant which the Germans have been building in Sicily. As you may know, the island gets all its power from the mainland by overhead cable across the Messina Strait. If we invade,' he smiled, 'when we invade, we shall have to make sure that the cable stays intact. But that is a headache for the brown jobs when they finally stumble ashore. This new installation is important for another reason. If we wait until all the German forces have pulled back to Sicily and the Italian mainland, the enemy will be ruthless with anyone who attempts to use sabotage against them. The Resistance, or whatever you choose to call them, are our only hope. They have no love for the Italian Government and hate the Germans for suppressing their activities far more efficiently than the Carabinieri ever could.'

Allenby spoke for the first time. 'It's to give the Resistance confidence, is it? To show them we are prepared to back them up to and after the eventual invasion?'

Goudie nodded. 'You have a quick mind. That's good.'

Frazer looked at the map. 'How do we get there, sir?'

'The seas to the north and west of Sicily are alive with craft. Vessels taking part in the North African evacuation, the movement of stores and ammunition, and of course the fishing fleet without which there would be more trouble for the Germans. Before, it was comparatively easy for the enemy. All our ships were needed to fight the convoys through to Malta and beyond, and our submarines were worked to death tracking down Rommel's convoys back and forth to Italy. Now we and the Americans have a round-the-

clock air umbrella, and our Light Coastal Forces hunt from
Sousse and Bône even in broad daylight.' He looked at each
of them in turn. 'So we ought to be able to slip through
the patrols, rendezvous with the Sicilian patriots, blow the
objective and then pull out. We should have the advantage
of surprise. Nothing like this has ever been attempted against
the northern coastline. Farther to go, but less well defended.'
He frowned. 'Or so the brains of Intelligence assure me.'

A bugle shattered the silence beyond the tent and Goudie
shrugged apologetically. 'We have the Royal Marines here.
They do most of the fighting in the SBS but they do like to
cling to a bit of ceremonial, bloody desert or not.

'Go with Able Seaman Weeks and get settled in. You'll
not be here long, I think.'

Frazer grinned. 'Sounds ominous.'

Goudie eyed him thoughtfully. 'It is.'

Outside, the sun seemed hotter than ever.

Allenby said, 'It's not quite what I expected.'

Frazer clapped him on the arm and laughed. 'A fine under-
statement, Dick, I'm proud of you!'

Goudie dropped the tent flap and signalled to the messman
for another drink.

A young lieutenant entered from the opposite end and
flopped down in a canvas chair.

'What are they like, sir?'

'Fine.' Goudie felt his eyes mist as the gin burned his
tongue. 'It's a straightforward job. In and out, no messing.
Piece of cake.'

The lieutenant picked up a much handled copy of *Lilliput*
and thumbed over the pages, looking for the one and only
nude.

'I expect that's what Bill Weston thought, sir.'

Goudie swung on him, his eyes blazing. 'Well he's dead,
isn't he? It was probably his own big-headed fault too. Lucky
it happened when it did. We would have lost the boat and
the whole bloody crew otherwise!' He tried to put down the

glass but it was shaking too badly and he signalled for another drink instead.

The lieutenant stood up and stammered, 'I'm sorry, sir. I didn't mean to imply – '

Goudie waved him down again. 'Forget it. It's the war and what it's doing to us. You saw Frazer, the Canadian lieutenant? Well, every bullet we use, each can of petrol we burn up was probably fought through the Atlantic by Frazer and men like him. Allenby's different. He's spent his time sweeping mines, then not content with that he went ashore to nobble the bloody things when they dropped in towns and harbours. *Both brave men.*'

He looked at his refilled glass as if he hated it. 'Now they've come to *our* war. Where they'll have to learn to dirty their hands with the rest of us.'

Lieutenant Commander John Goudie, Distinguished Service Cross and Bar and twice mentioned in dispatches, stood hands on hips and stared down at the little harbour.

'Well, there she is, gentlemen.'

Frazer glanced at his tanned profile and sun-bleached hair. Whatever tension he had sensed in Goudie before their rough and ready lunch seemed to have vanished, if it was ever there. He followed the direction of Goudie's gaze and mentally picked his way amongst the assorted litter of craft. Some were using the partly submerged wrecks for moorings, others lay together as if dozing in the blazing glare.

There was a sleek, grey-painted launch which could have begun life as a private yacht and Frazer said, 'She must have cost a bit.'

Goudie laughed. 'Next to her.'

Next to her. Frazer saw a strange, low-hulled vessel that looked very like a barge, except that it was bristling with twin-barrelled cannon for anti-aircraft defence.

Goudie explained, 'It's a Siebel ferry. We captured her

from Jerry just a couple of weeks ago. Fast, shallow draft, rather like a superior landing craft, they've been using hundreds of them for supplying and later evacuating the Afrika Korps. Very heavy armament for their size, and magnificent engines, naturally.' The last word sounded bitter.

Frazer recalled what he had heard about Light Coastal Forces. How their MTBs and MGBs were powered by high-octane petrol engines, while their opponents mounted powerful diesels which did not 'brew up' at the first salvo of tracer.

Goudie said, 'The base plumber has done a great job on her, she's running as sweet as a nut.' He looked at Frazer. 'She's yours.'

Frazer stared back at him. 'Mine?'

Goudie turned to Allenby. Even though he had changed into khaki shirt and slacks he still seemed apart from all the others.

'You both have watchkeeping certificates. You will take over if the job goes rotten on us.'

Frazer said, 'D'you think the Germans will swallow it, sir?'

'Hope so. It's all we've got at the moment.' Goudie smiled cheerfully. 'Twenty marines, some well-placed explosives, should be home for breakfast. Piece of cake.' It seemed to be his favourite expression.

He became serious. 'You've a new killick coxswain, good chap by all accounts, called Ives. The rest are Lieutenant Weston's old crew. Most have been in action several times.'

'Weston? He was the one who – '

Goudie eyed him impassively. 'Yes. The one.'

Goudie walked down the slope, his eyes everywhere as he glanced around his command. Special Services, and the SBS in particular, had learned to use anything and everything that lay to hand, and to use it to deadly effect.

Goudie waved casually to the moored Siebel ferry and a small dinghy cast off immediately.

He said, 'There's a subbie aboard, named Archer. Good chap in a scrap. But watch him. He's getting a bit bomb-happy.'

Frazer asked, 'How many in the company?' It was all moving too fast. Suddenly he had a command, a German ferry which he was obviously expected to take into an enemy harbour. Just like that. Goudie did not appear to have any doubts about it.

Goudie said, 'Twenty, excluding Archer, the coxswain and a petty officer called Gregson, the only "regular" in the boat.'

They were ferried out to the craft by a solitary oarsman, a sailor who was so covered in oil and grease he looked as if he had just crawled through the bilges.

Frazer climbed up the low side and heard Goudie say, 'No side party, I'm afraid, or band.'

Goudie's manner and casual comments were beginning to grate on Frazer's nerves. What the hell was the matter with him?

Allenby said, 'Look at that.' He was pointing at the German flotilla insignia that was painted on the low, boxlike bridge.

A big, fair-haired man stepped from the shadows and saluted. In the midst of the new paintwork and patched-up bullet holes he looked very clean and somehow reassuring.

'Ives, sir.' He looked at Frazer. 'Acting Cox'n.'

Frazer smiled. He liked that. Ives had done his homework, otherwise why did he not select Allenby?

'I'll take you round the boat, sir.'

Frazer said, 'I saw you at Eastney Barracks.'

'Right, sir.' He touched the holster on his hip. 'This is more like it.'

He led the way up the first ladder to a long empty space where troops and stores could be carried.

Allenby was reminded of the unexploded mines he had dealt with and all the false alarms. The deserted streets and the familiar man in blue who always waited to hand over to him.

He whispered, 'He looks like a policeman, Keith.'

Goudie grinned. 'He was.'

Then Frazer and Allenby seemed to find themselves completely in Ives's hands; Goudie had disappeared.

They clambered through the long hull, spoke to the artificer and the two stokers who ran the engines, and the assorted bunch of hands who did everything else. Gregson, the petty officer, was a gunnery man and, despite his crumpled khakis, had a ramroad aloofness which marked him as a Whale Island refugee. The subbie, Archer, was a suave, eager-looking young man with ginger eyebrows to match the two wings of hair which poked around his stained cap. He looked slightly crazy, Frazer thought. Too ready to smile, which made him appear all the madder.

'Satisfied?' Goudie was back as suddenly as he had vanished.

'Well, naturally I'd like more time to – '

Goudie cut him short. 'There isn't any. I shall see that you've finished loading by sundown. Then you can get under way. I'll fill you in on the other items later.'

'You're coming with us, sir?' Why should he be surprised? Goudie was not likely to trust a green newcomer. The Atlantic counted for nothing out here, Goudie had made that very clear.

'Of course.' He eyed him for several seconds, his bleached hair moving slightly in a furnace breeze. 'Look, if you can't handle it, say so and I'll have you replaced.' He was not smiling now.

Frazer said calmly, 'Forget it.' He looked away to hide his anger. 'Sir.'

Goudie nodded. Satisfied.

'Well, let's go out and make a bit of history, eh?'

Allenby saluted as Goudie jumped lightly into the dinghy.

He said, 'And we only just got here.' He sounded crestfallen.

Frazer turned his back on the dinghy.

'Sorry you volunteered, Dick?'

Allenby looked at his new friend and shook his head.

'Not any more.'

He was astonished to find that he meant it.

4

To Hell with Caution

Frazer awoke with a start, his mind instantly recording the pitch and roll of the unfamiliar hull, the regular thud of the engines.

An anonymous shadow hovered beside the bunk. 'Char, sir. Oh-three-'undred, an' a bit choppy.' He vanished.

Frazer threw his legs over the side of the bunk and pushed his fingers through his unruly hair. He had not felt clean since they had left England. He sipped the hot tea and grimaced in the darkness. Even that tasted of diesel.

He switched on a small light and pulled on his old sea boots. They had become part of himself during all those convoys, flat calms when the U-Boats came in surfaced for the kill, or raging gales when all you thought of was staying afloat and to bloody hell with the enemy.

He peered at his watch and remembered that last time he had seen Caryl. That had been on a week's leave in Toronto. He could see it all, the big room at the Royal York Hotel, the inability to get a drink when he needed it most. It was the same watch. Like the boots. The luminous face glowing in the dark as she started to cry. 'I can't go through with it.' Frazer sighed and got to his feet, the deck dropping beneath him like a springboard. In his mind's eye he could see the Sicilian coast, just as he had memorized the other details of the raid. If Goudie caught him out it would not be for a loss of memory.

They had been at sea for two days, or would have been

by the time they reached the tiny fishing village where the enemy were completing their generating plant. Small it might be, but it made good sense. At the briefing before they had got under way Goudie had pointed out a useful pier on the plan, and a narrow-gauge railway that ran from a nearby quarry, something which would certainly appeal to the Germans.

Frazer clipped on his pistol belt and thought of the man who was coming with them. He was called Major Thomas, but what regiment he belonged to or his actual role in the Special Services was impossible to fathom. As Allenby had remarked wryly, 'Thomas? Never in your life. With an accent like his he should be on the other side!'

A last look round. That at least was the same as the Atlantic. Once you were on the bridge, you never knew when you would leave it.

Outside the cabin it felt cool, even blustery. Frazer climbed into the squat bridge and waited for his eyes to become accustomed to the shadows. Just after three in the morning, and they were heading south now towards Sicily having spent the whole of the two days circling and weaving up and around the coast, well clear of patrols and the enemy's RDF.

Some of it had been unnerving, although Frazer had had nothing but admiration for the Boss's arrangements. Once, during their first night at sea, a submarine had surfaced nearby. They had heard the roar of compressed air as water was forced from her ballast tanks, the sound of a hatch banging open, the snick of a breech block as her deck gun was loaded.

Goudie had already said that the submarine would be there. The link between them and HQ and eventually he supposed the Admiralty and that dank cellar beneath Portsmouth Dockyard.

No signals were exchanged, but Frazer had sensed her there, had felt the hairs rising on his neck. You could call them U-Boats or submarines according to your loyalty, but he hated all of them.

Allenby came out of the darkness. 'Morning, sir.'

Frazer grinned. 'For God's sake, Dick. Wait till I'm in command of something other than this barge!'

Together they climbed onto a metal grating in the forepart of the bridge. Goudie's mechanics must have got a move on. There was still a smell of fresh paint in the damp air, and Frazer saw the pale outline of a boxlike chartroom which had been hastily thrown together, made mostly of old packing cases and then painted grey to match the rest of the superstructure. It was not thick enough to stop a child's bow and arrow but, once sealed, was completely dark from the outside, so that if required charts and local maps could be studied under the most powerful lights.

The open hold was littered with big crates which were clearly marked with Wehrmacht stencils. But their contents were not part of the North African retreat; each crate concealed two heavily armed Royal Marine commandos. God help anyone who tried to shift one of them by mistake.

Goudie came from the chartroom. 'All quiet?' He nodded to Fraser. 'Did you snatch an hour?'

Frazer replied, 'Better than I thought.'

Goudie was not listening. 'Better get the people to action stations.' He melted into the darkness and Frazer guessed he had gone to confer with the mysterious Major Thomas.

Frazer looked around his strange command. Either his eyes were getting used to the gloom or the sky was already lighter. He saw the lookouts on either side of the bridge, the upended barrels of the flak guns framed against the creaming bow wave alongside. But still no division between sea and sky, and no stars either. A blustery morning perhaps. It might be an unexpected ally.

Sub-Lieutenant Archer's tall figure appeared at the steel bridge gate.

Allenby said, 'Send the hands to action stations, Sub. They can take their time that way. No noise.'

Archer answered calmly, 'They know what to do. There's no need to tell them.'

Frazer turned, one elbow propped on the glass screen.

'Tell them anyway, Sub. And from now on I don't repeat orders, right?'

Allenby said quietly as the sub-lieutenant clattered down the bridge ladder, 'You didn't have to speak up for me, Keith.'

Frazer was surprised that Archer had made him so angry. He said, 'I felt like it. Trouble with you, Dick, is that you've spent so much time swapping yarns with magnetic mines you probably find the Archers of this world a bit dull.'

Allenby smiled. He had been out of his depth with Archer, and Frazer knew it. Archer was all the things which he had wanted to be. Well educated, good family, the right accent, the casual authority that even now, and in spite of his George Cross, made him feel like a nobody.

He crossed to the helm and compass where Ives stood like a rock.

'All right, 'Swain?'

Ives smiled. 'Fine, sir. Never thought I'd end up steering a thing like this.' He jerked his head astern. 'Be better if we had no tow. Easier to manoeuvre.'

Allenby agreed. That was one of Goudie's ideas. An ancient, twin-masted schooner with Italian markings was zigzagging back and forth across their wake on a long towline as if trying to break free.

Goudie had said, 'Jerry needs time before he acts. Like most people in combat, he sees what he expects to see. That schooner might give us a few minutes when we most need 'em. While the Krauts are investigating our *find*, we'll blow their arses off. Piece of cake.'

Allenby found himself pondering for the first time on their chances of success, even survival.

The intelligence reports had been adamant that there was no German garrison at the fishing village. Every trained soldier was needed on the southern coast in case the Allies launched an invasion as the last of the Afrika Korps were captured or driven out. They would be required to guard the airfields too, for if they hoped to hold Sicily they needed constant fighter protection.

He rejoined Frazer on the grating. 'Right on time, er, Keith.'

Frazer looked at his shadow. Nervous, he wondered. Unlikely after what he had been through.

He said, 'We've got enough explosives down below to wipe out half the island. Rather you than me.'

Allenby shrugged. 'One charge will have to be set off immediately. I've been ordered to lay a second delayed-action one before we pull out.'

Frazer listened to his change of tone. Allenby felt about trick charges and booby traps much as he did about submarines.

Ives whispered, 'Here comes the major, sir.'

Major Thomas had a pair of powerful night glasses slung around his neck and a German machine pistol tucked under one arm. Like most of the detachment, Frazer thought, who seemed to prefer captured enemy weapons to their own. Was it because ammunition was easier to find, or because they did not want anything that might identify them later on?

He asked, 'Where are we?'

Frazer gestured across the screen. 'Thirty miles northeast of Palermo. The last of the Lipari Islands is about eight miles off the port beam.'

Thomas hunched his shoulders and stared into the darkness.

'It is the best approach. Little chance of being picked up on their RDF.'

Frazer listened carefully. Thomas spoke perfect English,

but it was without tone. Like a man who is stone deaf. There was something alien about him. Inhuman.

'Flare, sir! Bearing Green four-five!'

It was a long way off, emerald green as it drifted beneath some fat-bellied clouds.

Frazer lowered his glasses. A local signal probably. A patrol boat investigating some returning fishermen. The Germans left most of the inshore patrols to the Italians. But you could never be certain. He heard one of the gunlayers shifting his sea boots on the damp steel as he swung his double-barrelled cannon towards the lonely flare.

Thomas snapped, 'The sea's getting more choppy. The bastards will sleep soundly in their beds tonight.'

He moved away and Allenby said softly, 'Wouldn't like to get on the wrong side of that one!'

Goudie appeared next. 'Reduce speed now.'

'Slow ahead together.' Frazer felt the hull sidle into a deep trough. 'Send Archer aft to watch over the tow. We don't want that bloody schooner coming aboard.'

They were almost up to the rendezvous now. So far it had gone like clockwork. Frazer wondered what the Sicilians would be like. He had heard Archer speaking of them disdainfully as 'a bunch of ignorant bandits'.

'Signal, sir! Fine on the port bow.'

Frazer nodded. 'Stop engines.' The hull began to rock and dip uncomfortably as the sea took over. The signal reappeared, a small torch, very low down and reflected on the waves.

And waves they were, Frazer thought. The poor marines would be wondering how much longer before they could be released from their hiding places. He hoped they would not be too sick to move.

Thomas said, 'Fishing boat. Have it covered.' The nearest guns dipped and then settled on the small vessel as it loomed out of the darkness.

Thomas added, 'It's the right one.' He sounded very tense.

Then he said, 'You come with me, Allenby. I've detailed some men to assist you.'

'Another flare, sir. Same bearing.'

They watched the bright green flare. Like a droplet of molten glass.

Goudie said, 'Somebody's awake, it seems.'

Thomas did not rise to it, and Frazer had the feeling they disliked each other. Or maybe it was just the usual division between navy and military.

The fishing boat came alongside with a violent thud, and Frazer heard Petty Officer Gregson snarling at someone to drag more fenders between the two hulls. It was a dangerous moment. There were not enough hands to man the guns and work the lines and fenders at the same time. Too many chiefs and not enough Indians, Frazer thought.

Was that how Lieutenant Bill Weston had been killed. Transferring commandos or agents while in enemy-patrolled waters?

Allenby paused to glance at the bridge then lowered himself onto the fishing boat's deck. Even in the dark he knew it was filthy; it stank of fish and bilge water.

A squat figure in a sheepskin jerkin stepped from the tiny wheelhouse and waited for Thomas to join him.

Allenby glanced round as two muffled figures followed him with satchels of explosives. He thought suddenly of Hazel, of the dead sailor's sister in Portsmouth. The despair and anguish in her voice when she had spoken to him.

Thomas said shortly, 'This is Maroca. He is the leader.'

Maroca watched Allenby in the gloom. He made no attempt to offer his hand or showed any emotion. Perhaps anyone in uniform was automatically suspect to him.

Thomas added, 'Everything's clear. There is a patrol boat at the pier. It always ties up there. We'll go in without any more delay. You all know what to do.'

He spoke crisply and with confidence but Allenby had the strange feeling it was for Maroca's benefit. As if in their brief exchange beside the wheelhouse Thomas had discovered some unexpected flaw in his plan of attack.

'Don't forget. The patrol boat is to be taken intact.' He spoke quickly to Maroca in fluid Italian and the latter nodded and then showed his teeth in the darkness.

'Cast off then.' Thomas waved to the big Siebel ferry and the two hulls began to move apart even as Frazer restarted his diesels.

The fishing boat's engine coughed into life. Another smell to add to the rest.

But filthy or not, the fishing boat showed a good turn of speed. Thomas sensed Allenby's surprise and said, 'They use it for running contraband and guns. They're used to this kind of thing.'

Again the slight inflection. Polish? It seemed likely.

Thomas said suddenly, 'One thing. Maroca says that his people have cut the telephone wires to the plant.' He was containing his anger with an effort. 'Too damned early. If the Germans or the local police check on the place, they're bound to investigate. Bloody fools, can't trust any of them.'

Allenby considered what it could mean. The enemy might have attacked and overpowered Maroca's men, and would be waiting for the raiders to appear. Allenby had heard something of what the Germans did to the Resistance or terrorists; even a naval uniform would not protect him.

He thought of that morning in the hospital, the old lady in her bed which had been propped within a few feet of the hole made by the parachute mine, the nurse who sat with her holding her hand while he had worked on the mechanism to render it safe. If men like Prothero and Major Thomas could shorten the war by direct action, surely this was worth all the risks?

He thought too of his father, the way he and Frazer had got on so well. He had shown the tall Canadian his *Daily Mail* war map on which he had moved the flags of friend and foe alike so many times it was filled with holes.

With some pride his father had said, 'When we were all alone in the war after Dunkirk I tried to join the Home Guard. But they wouldn't have me because of the leg. I could have done something if they'd tried to invade. I've not forgotten how to use a Lee-Enfield. You don't after being at the Somme.'

What would his mother say now if she could see him with Thomas and the villainous-looking Maroca? Not her idea of the war at all.

It seemed an age before lookouts sighted the coast. It was just a darker shadow without substance but, like the desert, you could smell it, sense its strange air of menace.

Allenby turned to his new assistants. He did not know their names. Thomas had said it was better not to. Just in case.

He said, 'Stay close. We'll do the hardest one first. Have it ready. Once the Siebel ferry is alongside we can arrange the bigger one. It'll wake the dead.' He wanted to return to the ferry and tell Frazer about the cut telephone lines. He ought to know.

One of the men rolled up his balaclava helmet and Allenby saw that it was Able Seaman Weeks who had been the first one to greet them from Naval Party Seventy-Five.

Even in the darkness Weeks saw his surprise and said simply, 'The Skipper told me to come along, sir. He thought you'd prefer to have someone you know with you.' He slapped the soldier on the back and added, 'No offence, mate.'

Allenby smiled in spite of his tight nerves. Frazer would think of something like that even though he was in greater danger than anyone, standing on top of a floating bomb.

Weeks added, 'Anyway, I'm a torpedoman.' That settled it.

Thomas snapped, 'Dead ahead.' He unslung his machine pistol and cocked it. Around the littered deck others were doing the same, and Allenby saw one man with his body hung about with grenades. Like obscene fruit.

Far inland a searchlight darted its beam at the clouds, licked across them and then went out again.

Allenby knew that the whole operation depended on perfect timing. If Maroca's men had made one mistake they could easily make another.

Another half-hour dragged by, and sounds of the engine, the spray battering over the boat's blunt bows seemed tremendous, impossible not to hear.

Allenby asked quietly, 'What about prisoners, sir?' It was just something to say. To ease the awful tension.

Maroca leaned towards him and replied thickly, 'No prisoners.' He was grinning, enjoying Allenby's sudden anxiety.

Thomas remarked, 'Stay out of it. They're different.'

The outline of a pier made black lines on the choppy water and still there was no challenge, no rattle of machine guns. He thought of Maroca's words and guessed that any such guards were already dead.

And there was the moored patrol boat. Even in the darkness Allenby could see her clean rakish lines. An Italian motor anti-submarine boat. Their means of escape when they had completed what they had come to do. But first they had to take her.

He imagined he heard the distant thud of Frazer's diesels, but guessed that this little place was used to the comings and goings of German and commandeered vessels.

Thomas pulled his beret down over his forehead and said, '*Now*. Before some bloody sentry gets edgy.'

Allenby swallowed hard. It was like those deserted streets all over again. With only the unknown at the end of them.

Obedient to the rudder, the Siebel ferry swung in a slow arc, the tethered schooner dragging astern.

Frazer said, 'Keep a good look out.' He glanced up at the

stumpy tripod mast. 'Put a good man up there, Sub. These diesels drown out everything, but he might hear something.'

Archer touched a man's arm and watched him climb the ladder.

Frazer half smiled. Archer was still sulking after his 'bottle'. He thought of Allenby. He was a strange one. Never gave much away or volunteered an opinion. But the way he threw explosives about showed he was an expert in his new trade.

Goudie said, 'What's taking so long, for Christ's sake?'

Frazer glanced at him. He could see most of his face now, just as he could recognize some of the others around him. It was getting brighter by the minute.

Archer suggested, 'Maybe the fishing boat's broken down, sir.'

Frazer looked away as Goudie swore horribly. It was not Archer's day.

He peered at his watch. Again it reminded him of that unsatisfactory night at the Royal York Hotel. What had he really expected? That she would fall into his arms and make passionate love even though they were soon to be parted again. Every time you did an Atlantic convoy the odds against you mounted. Frazer had survived one sinking, but had known men who had been bombed or torpedoed several times. Eventually their extra time had run out.

Caryl was vivacious and desirable and came from a respected Vancouver family, and then –

Goudie asked irritably, 'Is it time?'

'Yes.' Frazer wondered how long he had been staring at his watch.

'Full ahead both engines!'

The man on the mast yelled, 'Ship dead astern! Closing fast!'

'Stand by all guns!'

Frazer ran to the rear of the bridge and trained his glasses over the screen. That bloody schooner had hidden the other vessel's swift approach but as he settled on the shadow he saw a rising moustache of white foam from the newcomer's bow wave as she tore in pursuit.

Goudie said, 'Thomas has taken the interpreter with him. Of all the bloody luck.'

Frazer asked, 'E-Boat, d'you think?'

Goudie shook his head. He of all people would know what an E-Boat looked and sounded like.

He came to a decision. 'Switch on the searchlight. Two can play silly buggers.' He groped down in the darkness and when he stood up again Frazer saw he was wearing a German officer's white-topped cap.

The big searchlight hissed into life and cut a blue path directly astern. Everything stood out with glacier brightness, the schooner with her flaking Italian flag painted on her side, the bubbling wake which surged past her, and about half a cable farther on was the other boat.

She was small and low-lying, with just a single cannon like an Oerlikon mounted on her foredeck. There were several sailors too, gripping handholds for support as their craft bounced through and over the choppy waves. They were Italians, but Frazer concentrated on her wheelhouse. Two different uniforms, he thought, one with a cap like Goudie's.

Goudie said, 'They often carry Germans. To make certain their allies don't make a foul-up.' He glanced up at the big scarlet ensign that rippled from the tripod mast. 'That would have been good enough to fool the Eyeties.' In the blue glare the cross and swastika stood out on the flag stark and clear. 'If we open fire now, it'll rouse half the coast. It might even catch Thomas and his party in the open before they can land.' He rubbed his chin, watching the other vessel through narrowed eyes. 'Dead slow, if you please. Drop some fenders outboard as if we're open for visitors.' He sought out Gregson. 'Warn the Royals. It'll have to be quick. Tell Sparks to keep listening watch. If those bastards start to transmit we'll open fire. Then we can try to pick up Thomas and your chum and get the hell out of it.'

He did not sound too hopeful, Frazer thought. When daylight came they would not get very far before the planes found them. The more he thought about it, the flimsier the plan of attack became. Suppose the patrol boat was not there? How would they get away?

Goudie was saying, 'Here they come.' He spoke so gently he could have been watching a shoal of fish. 'They're bound to take a look at the schooner, what did I tell you?'

'D'you think they're checking on us, our number maybe?'

'Doubt it. What with the shambles in North Africa and troops coming back in anything that will float, even the Germans will be in a twist. But they will want to know why we're up here to the north of the island.' He released a sigh as a metallic voice echoed across the narrowing gap. Goudie unclipped the loudhailer and shook it above his head to show it was out of order.

Frazer heard a thud as one of the crates in the hold spare was levered open. The atmosphere was so tense it was barely possible to breathe.

At the nearest gun mounting the seaman who was strapped behind it eased himself very slightly to one side so that the twin muzzles were pointing directly at the approaching launch. One of the Germans was waving his arm and gesturing at the glare.

'He wants us to switch it off.' Goudie unbuttoned his holster. 'Can't have that, can we?'

How many times had Goudie done this sort of thing, Frazer wondered. It was unbelievable, chilling, the way the enemy were standing with heaving lines, their single cannon unmanned. One of them was waving and trying to make himself heard above the growl of engines and the slosh of trapped water between the two hulls. Yards, then feet; Frazer could feel his heart thumping louder even than the engines.

Two lines snaked across the glare and were deftly made fast by the British seamen.

Then he heard a sharp cry of alarm. Something or someone had accidentally betrayed their true identity. Two pistol shots cracked against the bridge and shattered the screen on the other side. The Italian sailors, so relaxed a moment ago, were frantically tearing at the lines that held the enemies together, and it was then that Frazer saw the most terrifying sight of all. The commandos scrambled up from their hiding place in a silent, deadly arrowhead. Their teeth and eyes shone in the searchlight, and their blackened faces only added to the sense of nightmare.

The Italians seemed to crumple before them as they swarmed across their deck. Here and there a commando dagger glinted just briefly in the searchlight and then it was done. The two Germans came out of the wheelhouse, their hands in the air; it had taken only three minutes.

'Cut the searchlight!' It was like being blinded as the beam died.

Goudie shouted, 'Open her seacocks, and make sure the corpses go with her. If a patrol comes looking for her they'll only find the schooner. With luck they'll think it was a skirmish between the patrol boat and some terrorists.' He did not turn as one terrible scream broke the stillness.

Frazer had been about to ask about the two Germans. He knew it was pointless now. He felt sick.

Goudie said, 'Better us than the Sicilians, you know. Those bastards would make it last longer if they got their hands on them.'

He watched the commandos leaping aboard, the lines being cast off. 'Good show. No casualties.' He looked at the Italian launch; it was already settling down, beginning to founder. 'Now we must make up for lost time. To hell with caution, full speed ahead and cast off that ruddy schooner. Without her, I think the Krauts would have put out a radio alarm.'

Frazer passed his orders and wondered how his voice

stayed so calm when his whole body was shaking in protest and disgust. When he next looked at Goudie he saw that he was smiling, as if at some private joke.

He checked the compass and groped his way into the wooden chartroom. Around him the hull quivered and rattled as the engines worked up to maximum revolutions. He thought of the abandoned vessels as they fell farther and farther astern, one with its dead crew still aboard. Frazer recalled *Levant*'s captain, when one of the convoy escorts had been caught napping by a German bomber. The ship had broken in half while manoeuvring at full speed. There had been very few survivors.

He had commented, 'Vigilance. You must never take anything for granted. You'll go under if you do.'

The crew of the patrol boat had just paid for their lack of vigilance.

Archer climbed onto the bridge, and as Frazer left the chartroom he saw the tall sub-lieutenant hold a wristwatch to his ear, his features set in a frown of concentration. When he lowered his arm Frazer saw there was a smear of blood on his cheek. In two strides he crossed the bridge and tore the watch from his hand. 'We're not down to stripping corpses yet!' Then he flung the watch over the side.

He saw Archer's eyes light up like twin lamps and then heard the dull thunder of an explosion. It even seemed to touch the hull, like a bodyblow.

Goudie, who had been watching the little drama with the watch, said calmly, 'Save it for the enemy. I think the balloon is about to go up.'

5

The Raid

Allenby crouched on his knees and peered up at the gaunt steel pylon. It was still bare of cables and he guessed it would be the first of a line across the island once the German engineers had finished their work.

Able Seaman Weeks watched as the lieutenant ripped open his pouch and deftly laid out his tools on the rough ground. The soldier waited nearby, his eyes on the pale, blocklike shape of the new generating plant, seemingly oblivious to the terse commands, the scampering partisans as they ran for cover and fanned out towards the village.

Allenby felt the ground beneath his knees. It was like rock and, despite the nearness of the sea, gave no hint of moisture.

He said, 'Just one leg of the pylon should do.' He found it easy to concentrate on the job in hand, to ignore the fact he was actually in hostile territory. Later perhaps – he felt his lips tighten as he fastened the grip on the wire which Weeks was unreeling for him. There might not be any 'later'. He wondered how Frazer was getting on and tried to picture the map and the chart as he had last studied them. Thirty miles east of Palermo where there was a big German garrison. It was a bloody wonder they had not got wind of the raid already. Allenby checked his racing thoughts. He must concentrate. This was his job. The others would manage on their own.

Major Thomas ran, half-crouching, across the narrow track and stared down at him.

'Ready?'

Allenby nodded without glancing up. It was getting lighter all the time. The pier and the sleeping patrol boat were invisible from here, and the village merely a huddle of pale shapes. But it would not last.

He replied sharply, 'Nearly. I'm going to drop this pylon across the railway tracks. It will take about a minute more.'

Thomas grunted and raised his night glasses. 'The partisans say the whole village is in hiding or gone to the hills.'

Allenby looked at the soldier. 'Carry on.'

Thomas added, 'I was here a few weeks ago.' He seemed to need to talk. 'The patrol boat's captain is coming over to our side. He's not waiting for an invasion. He'll take our party to the rendezvous.'

The soldier came bouncing down the ridge, his blackened face split by a grin.

'All done, sir.' As he threw himself down, his leather jerkin worked up over his battledress and Allenby saw the flash of the Royal Engineers on his shoulder.

He heard himself say, 'My father was a sapper too.'

The man eyed him curiously but said nothing.

Thomas waved his arm at several running figures, and one in the familiar sheepskin coat skidded to a halt. Maroca could move fast when he wanted to.

Thomas's runner said, 'Thought I heard a shot.'

Thomas ignored him and spoke in a fierce whisper to the squat partisan.

Then he said, 'The Carabinieri are in the new building. When the wires were cut –' he shot Maroca an angry stare, 'they took cover with the engineers.'

Maroca muttered, 'Then they all die together.'

Allenby said, 'It will be loud. I suggest you take cover. With the ground this hard the blast will be like a daisy-cutter.'

Thomas regarded him bleakly. 'I know your work, Lieutenant!'

Weeks tore off his balaclava and pressed his hands to his ears as Allenby said, 'Here goes then.'

The explosion was like a thunderclap and for what seemed like an age it was barely possible to breathe as dust and sharp fragments of stone and sand rained down over them. Allenby felt the earth jerk beneath his body and knew the pylon was down. As he lurched to his feet he saw its vague outline sprawled across the narrow-gauge railway in a tangle of buckled girders.

Weeks said softly, 'No trains today!'

Thomas waved his machine pistol and, with Maroca loping beside him, ran along the track towards the new concrete building.

Allenby gasped as a thin line of bright green tracer slashed down from the top of the pale building; he heard the bullets cracking and ricocheting amongst the stones like enraged hornets.

Weeks exclaimed, 'That's bloody torn it!' He cocked his sub-machine gun and banged the magazine with his palm to make sure it was firm.

Allenby waited until the sapper had gathered up one of the satchels and then ducked as more sporadic firing ripped above his head. They, whoever *they* were, could see nothing in the gloom and swirling dust. But once daylight came they could pin the raiders down and wait for help to arrive.

Allenby wiped his lips with his hand. The building should have been empty, the guards accounted for by Maroca's men, instead – He dragged Weeks by the sleeve. 'Round here. We must get closer.'

Weeks bobbed his head. 'Right bloody potmess this has turned out to be!' Surprisingly he grinned. 'Trust the army, eh sir?'

Shots were coming from the village now, and Allenby saw chips of concrete flying from the high wall as the partisans' bullets wasted themselves.

Thomas was back again, his breath loud and painful.

'I'll give you covering fire, Lieutenant. Get up there and lay a charge at the corner.' He peered at his watch. 'The marines should be in position now. About bloody time!'

Allenby crawled farther along the litter of rocks and discarded building equipment.

He heard a man scream out in agony and the sound was like a blow. He tried not to think of the nearness of danger and death. He told himself again and again, he was used to that. Nothing new.

Weeks said, 'No windows, sir.'

Allenby groped for his pouch again. If Goudie were here he would have said, 'Piece of cake.'

He gestured to the soldier. 'Second charge. Lively.'

The man crawled up beside him. 'There, sir. Gap in the wall.' It was probably intended to allow access for power cables.

Allenby pressed himself against the wall and watched as the soldier moulded the explosive charge into place. Once he looked up and saw the top of the wall framed against the sky. Paler still, but with ranks of low scudding clouds to hold back the dawn a little longer.

It only needs one brave soul to look over the edge. A grenade would do for the lot of us.

'All done, sir.'

Allenby heard shouts from above, Italian not German. Why did that matter so much?

Weeks said, 'The partisans have pulled back.' He sounded stunned. 'We *must* have their cover!'

Allenby looked round. Being against the wall was like being in a trap. He clenched his teeth and felt the grit between them, like that day when they had dug him out after the mine had exploded.

'No time for anything fancy. They'll be onto us at any second.' He lit a fuse with his lighter, the flame like a beacon in the grey light.

'Run!' They stumbled down the slope like drunks and

Allenby thought he saw Thomas and some of the others scattering towards the nearest cottages.

The explosion was more like a muffled thud after the first one which had brought down the pylon, and Allenby heard the debris cascading down and upending scaffolding and a concrete mixer in a miniature avalanche.

Thomas yelled, 'Now! *Attack!*'

Voices and shots echoed around the hillside and Allenby saw some of Maroca's men pushing forward again, firing as they ran. Somewhere a whistle shrilled and Weeks said heavily, 'Here come the Royals, bless 'em!'

The big Siebel ferry was hidden by a jutting elbow of land, beyond which Allenby knew there was the newly constructed jetty. Thomas rushed past and shouted, 'Wasted fifteen minutes!'

Allenby sighed. Was that all? It seemed like hours.

More crouching shapes ran towards him, and he recognized them as part of the Royal Marine detachment. They were carrying more explosives, their bodies bent double under the weight.

Allenby nodded. 'Follow me.' It was strange to think that, had the fishing boat been sunk before they could get ashore, these marines would be trying to do it all on their own.

The firing was less and more erratic and Allenby heard the sharp crack of grenades as Maroca's men flung them into the building. One marine, a corporal, said, 'Ready when you are, sir.' He sounded tense, wild. Like a horse scenting blood.

Allenby clambered up the fallen concrete, his eyes streaming from smoke and the sting of small-arms fire. He saw the outline of the big generators, the catwalk which ran around the inside of the place; two corpses lay upon it.

Thomas touched his arm and asked sharply, 'Can you do it?'

Allenby saw a figure being pursued along the catwalk, pushed and harried by some of the partisans. He looked away as the man's scream cut down to a gurgle.

He said huskily, 'It's not like the machinery which Intelligence described. It will take a much larger charge.' He looked at the corporal. 'The two red packs. Get them now.' He glanced at Thomas. 'I'll need half an hour, you see – '

Thomas peered at him, his face so close Allenby could feel his fury.

'*Half an hour?* The Krauts will be here in ten minutes at the most!'

A man ran through the smoke and babbled something in Thomas's ear.

The major said evenly, 'We have trouble with the patrol boat. I shall deal with it.' He spoke slowly, carefully, as if he were afraid Allenby would not grasp the significance of his words. 'The boat's captain must have thought the raid had gone wrong.'

Allenby stared at him. 'That's what *I* think, as it happens!' He peered round as another terrible scream cut across his nerves like a knife. 'Can't you control those savages?'

Thomas stepped back, and by accident or design allowed the muzzle of his machine pistol to hover towards Allenby's stomach. Weeks and the soldier stared at the gun with sudden anxiety, as if it could not be happening.

'You attend to your task. I shall deal with the boat.' His eyes shone like stones in his blackened face. Then he swung on his heel and left.

Allenby waited until he could trust his own voice. 'Go and help the others with the charges, Weeks.' He felt sickened by what he had seen, by Thomas's inhuman anger.

The sapper humped two satchels onto his shoulders and followed Allenby deeper into the unfinished site.

The dust and trapped smoke mercifully hid some of the carnage, but great patterns of blood lined the walls like unmoving spectres where the grenades had blasted the defenders to fragments. In the poor light the blood looked like tar.

Allenby went about his work, his mind grappling with his revulsion, hanging on to the job he knew so well.

He heard someone groping towards him and without looking knew it was Maroca.

Allenby said, 'Tell your men to clear the village. Everyone out.' The man said nothing and Allenby swivelled round on his knees and added harshly, 'Right now!'

Some marines bounded past to lay the extra charges against the dust-covered machinery. Allenby watched them lash and tape it into place as he added slowly, 'Otherwise I'll blow up the lot of us.'

The marines melted away to rejoin the others and Allenby heard the stammer of machine guns and rifle fire. But it did not seem important, or that it concerned him in any way.

Maroca grinned and tried to laugh. 'You joke, huh?'

'No joke.' Allenby stood up and saw Weeks raise his tommy gun threateningly. Even now the Germans might be coming along the coast road, unless they were stone deaf.

Maroca stared from the piled explosives to the coils of fuse wire which lay by Allenby's feet.

Maroca shook his head. 'You're mad!' His eyes shifted as Allenby bent down over the detonators. 'I do what I can.'

Allenby strode across the floor and seized him by his filthy coat.

'They're *your* people, for Christ's sake! Don't you care any more?'

Maroca shook him away and ran through the building as if he expected Allenby to shoot him down.

Allenby looked at his hands. They were steady enough. Detached. Perhaps he had gone past it, round the bend as they termed it. Bomb-happy. The thought made him smile but he controlled it instantly. *If I begin to laugh, I shall not be able to stop.*

A sailor peered through the breach in the wall and saw him standing beside the explosives.

He shouted, 'Time to pull out.' His eyes stayed on the

explosives. 'They're ready to set the time fuses in the ferry
when you says the word, sir.'

More shots, and a great gout of flame from the hillside
where some tracer had touched off a fuel store.

Allenby looked up at the clouds. Suddenly it was daylight.
Grey, cool, but daylight.

Bullets whimpered through the building, and he saw the
soldier fall on his face, without even a cry.

Weeks ran to help him but Allenby said, 'No use. Keep
down.' He had seen enough dead men in his young life to
recognize this one.

Suddenly they had the place to themselves, apart from the
corpses. Even the sailor had vanished. Allenby shook
himself. He had forgotten to ask about Frazer. He looked
at the dead soldier, his blackened face screwed up at the
moment of impact. Who was he?

Weeks said awkwardly, 'I can hear a vehicle, sir, a tank or
Jerry half-track most like.'

Allenby nodded. He too heard the distant clink and clatter
of tracks. Delayed-action, they had told him. The Germans
would defuse the charges in minutes, thanks to Major
Thomas and his bloody allies.

'Fall back to the pier, Weeks. Tell them I am going to fire
the charge myself. When it blows, set the ones on the ferry,
right?'

Weeks stood firm, and did not even duck as a heavy bullet
slammed into the machinery behind him.

'I'll stay with you, sir. Just in case.'

Allenby swung on him angrily and instantly relented. The
same quiet faith as Hazel would have shown. As he always
had, even at the end.

'Why not?' He began to pay out the wire, with Weeks
keeping beside him all the way.

There was more firing now, machine guns of a different
pattern, probably from the patrol boat. Suppose the boat
went without them, or the Italian change of heart and loyalty

prevented their escape, what then? Thomas would go to earth with Maroca and the partisans, while the raiders – he shuddered. The Germans would show no mercy after what had happened.

'Far enough, sir.'

Allenby got down on his knees again. From a corner of his eye he saw a gleam of pewter, the sea. It should be blue as it always was in travel pictures and stories, Allenby thought vaguely.

'You OK, sir?'

Allenby tugged down the peak of his cap. The marshal again.

'Here we go.' He pressed the switch and ducked his head as the hillside erupted in a deluge of rock and concrete. When the smoke finally drifted clear the building was reduced to half its height, and the inside had caved in amongst the new machinery like a violated tomb.

Allenby raised his head. 'Bloody hell!'

Weeks hurried after him, his ears still numb from the explosion. But through and above it all he saw only Allenby. The pale and strangely determined lieutenant who rarely smiled, who found time to save a few stinking Sicilians when his own life was in the balance.

Weeks saw the end of the pier, and two dead marines being dragged towards the moored boat. They all had a very good chance of being killed. But the sea was here, and to Weeks that meant just about everything.

Lieutenant Keith Frazer strained his eyes above the bridge screen and watched the land as it appeared to pivot across the bows.

'Midships! Steady!' He heard Ives murmur a reply and thanked God for his coolness so far.

They had stopped the engines only once and that was to drop a boat with half a dozen marine commandos who would rendezvous with Thomas and take command of the Italian patrol boat. Even through his concentration the realization kept hitting him like a fist. It had all been too casual, with no apparent thought for the Italians' change of heart. He had seen the flash of tracer from the pier, the ripping sounds of bullets spraying the wooden pier where the squad of marines should be in position.

A lookout in the blunt bows yelled, 'Anchored barge dead ahead!'

'Full astern together!' The bridge shook as the big diesels responded instantly.

Lieutenant Commander Goudie's lean figure ran to one side as he snapped, 'Get past it!'

'Stop starboard.' Frazer gripped the screen to steady his nerves. 'Half ahead port, starboard fifteen.'

As they swung crabwise towards where the new jetty and loading bay were supposed to be, Frazer felt the ferry's flank crash against the moored craft and then drag it alongside, its cable wrapped around the Siebel ferry's rudder.

Frazer said, 'Half ahead together.'

Ives said, 'Helm's jammed, sir.'

Goudie joined Frazer and said softly, 'Doesn't matter now.' He raised his voice. 'Stand by in the bows! Archer, get those men ashore as soon as you can!'

Frazer tried not to lick his lips. He knew that one of the machine gunners was staring at him, probably measuring his own chance of survival in what he saw.

He thought of Allenby. Was he still alive, or lying out there badly injured by the explosion?

The first one had been bad enough, but the second had seemed more menacing. As if a volcano had erupted.

The lookout shouted, 'That schooner's heading seaward, sir! Port quarter!'

Frazer did not need his binoculars. The partisans were getting out, or some of them were.

Goudie glanced at him. 'Stop engines.' He moved nearer

so that the others could not hear and waited as Frazer passed
his orders and brought the ferry and its tethered companion
towards the promontory.

He said in a tightly controlled whisper, 'The schooner is
valuable to them. It doesn't mean they're saving their own
skins!'

Frazer watched as the bows loomed over the snub-nosed
jetty where the enemy had been preparing a bay for loading
and unloading fast supply boats. The road and the railway
would have done the rest.

He said, 'I'd have thought the RAF could have done it
better with one blockbuster.'

Goudie watched him. 'These people have got to manage
on their own when we pull out. We don't want the Sicilians
to remember that our bombers wiped out their village, do
we?'

Frazer tensed as the ferry sidled against the pale concrete.
When the charges in the hold were exploded it would probably destroy the whole place anyway. He examined his feelings and was surprised to discover he did not care. It was
war at first hand. Not through a gun or bomb sight. He had
seen plenty of innocent people in the air raids on Liverpool
and Southampton laid out in rows to await their mass graves.
Well, now it was their turn.

He shouted, 'Stop engines, get the Chief and his men on
deck!'

Men were leaping ashore with Sub-Lieutenant Archer,
pistol in hand, in the lead.

Frazer saw the rest of the marines trotting forward to
disembark. With all the explosions it seemed likely the enemy
must soon react.

The marines could deal with this lot, but they could hardly
be expected to take on a Panzer division from Palermo.

As the engines rumbled into silence he heard the sound of
shots, hoarse shouts of command as the other raiders ran
towards the pier and the coastal track. Ives stood down from

the wheel and automatically wiped the compass with his sleeve to clear away the drifting dust.

Frazer smiled, 'Time to go.' He saw the ERA and his two stokers hurry along the narrow side deck. Did it mean they would all end up as prisoners, or worse? He had often considered being killed, blown up or drowned. It was common enough in the Atlantic. But a prisoner? Shut up like a criminal was different.

Goudie said, 'Be ready to hit the deck. They may have a few sentries around in spite of all the shit.'

The gunner's mate peered up from the hold, his cap still at exactly the correct angle.

'All set to blow, sir.' He sounded very calm.

Frazer took off his cap and ran his fingers through his hair. Perhaps *Levant*'s skipper had been right after all about the cloak-and-dagger brigade.

A seaman ran towards them and peered from Petty Officer Gregson to Goudie. 'I just seen Mr Allenby, sir.' He was gasping for air. 'He's goin' to blow the whole place hisself. Able Seaman Weeks is stayin' with 'im.'

Goudie snapped, 'What about Major Thomas, how far – ' He checked his sudden anxiety and said, 'We'll have to set our delayed charges right away. When that lot goes up, we'll have company for certain.'

Frazer seized the seaman's arm. 'How was he, man? Doesn't he know the risk he's taking?'

The seaman shrugged, glad to be away from it. 'Cool as a cucumber 'e was, sir. Bloody marvel.'

Frazer said, 'I'll wait here in case – '

Goudie jerked his head at the seaman and pulled Frazer to one side.

'No time for heroics. You go to the pier and take command of the boat. If it's still in one piece,' he added bitterly. 'It *is* why you are here. I will decide the rest, right?'

Frazer eyed him angrily. 'If you say so, sir.'

Goudie said almost to himself, 'Always trying to prove

something.' To Petty Officer Gregson's upturned face he added, 'When, or should I say *if*, we ever manage to invade the Italian mainland we'll not get farther than the bloody beaches unless we learn to hate the bastards!'

Gregson controlled a grin. He had known Goudie long enough to recognize all the signs. A good officer, but a bastard if you crossed him. He never forgot anything.

A seaman who had been sitting on the explosives called, 'What d'you make of it, PO?'

'I don't never think about it, son. I leave thinkin' to 'orses, they've got bigger 'eads, y'see.'

The eighteen-year-old seaman sighed. Silly old sod. A real barrack-stanchion. No place out here with us.

Frazer walked along the jetty. Two corpses lay on their backs near a striped guard hut. Their weapons and boots were gone, and one of them seemed to stare at Frazer as he passed, as if to make a last plea for life. Both had had their throats cut. Frazer thought of the glinting daggers aboard the Italian patrol boat. Near enough to feel their strength and their terror.

He saw Archer and two armed sailors with one of the marines. The latter had been slightly wounded and had his arm in a sling, a cigarette dangling from his mouth despite the obvious risk.

Archer watched Frazer warily. 'We're going for the boat, sir.'

'Yes. There's nothing else big enough.'

One of the seamen cocked his head to listen. 'Tanks on the road, sir.'

Archer glared at him. 'One anyway.' He fiddled with his pistol. 'That's all we bloody need!'

A handful of Royal Marines ran past, one giving the thumbs-up to their wounded comrade. He shouted, 'Two of the lads bought it! We're going under the pier.'

Frazer strode on, his ears and eyes grappling with the menacing crackle of gunfire and the fact that landmarks stood out much more clearly in the grey light. In an hour it will be full daylight no matter how dense the clouds are. If we get the patrol boat under way the most she can do is eighteen knots provided they've not sabotaged anything. His mind hurried on as he mentally pictured the chart. They'd not get far before the Jerries found them.

When he rounded the side of the headland where the construction engineers had carved it away for the jetty, he saw the pier, and towards the end of it the patrol boat which they had expected to greet them with open arms.

Everyone knew that once the Allies invaded Sicily and then Italy only the Italians caught on the wrong side of the line would remain loyal to Germany. Major Thomas must have convinced the patrol boat's skipper that he would be well rewarded for his sudden change of allegiance.

Archer strode beside him and exclaimed, 'It's over. They've taken the boat.'

Frazer quickened his pace. It was strange about Archer. He sounded disappointed he had been unable to join in.

A black-faced marine, his sub-machine gun tucked under one arm, greeted the two naval officers with a chuckle. 'All yours, gents. The Eyeties are under guard.'

Frazer climbed swiftly onto the vessel's deck. She was sleek and graceful but armed only with two twin-barrelled cannon. Some of the seamen were already checking them and fitting fresh magazines. One, whom Frazer recognized as their only signalman, was hauling down the ensign, his feet astride one of the dead Italians.

'Take charge, Sub.' He found he was listening. Waiting for that one last explosion. Wondering about his new friend Allenby.

Archer gestured with his pistol. 'Single up all lines. Stand by to cast off.' The ERA and his two stokers stumbled below and with barely minutes to accustom themselves to the strange engineroom brought a confident vibration to the hull.

Frazer looked into a cabin; it was littered with papers and

official documents. The boat's skipper, he was about his own age, lay back in his chair a pistol hanging from one hand. He still grasped a framed photograph of a young woman in the other hand despite the fact a bullet had blown away half his head. A sense of shame, or was it honour that had stopped him at the last moment?

Feet pounded along the pier and he heard Goudie's incisive voice call, 'The Jerries are in the village! All guns train on the end of pier!'

He found Goudie in the small wheelhouse where Ives and the young signalman seemed to fill the place.

Frazer looked at him. 'You're not leaving Allenby?'

Goudie darted a glance at his watch. 'Our own delayed charges will blow in fifteen minutes. Do you want to go up with them?'

Archer's voice intruded. 'Singled up to head and stern ropes, sir.'

Frazer looked round for some sort of engine control, but there was only a telephone. The ERA replied instantly, as if he had been pressed against it.

'Fine motors, sir. I can give you full power when you say the word.'

Frazer stared fixedly through the wheelhouse windows. He could sense Ives at the wheel, and could hear Goudie's uneven breathing.

It was bad enough leaving a torpedoed ship in a convoy. But even then you tried to do something.

Goudie said calmly, 'I'm waiting.'

'What about Major Thomas?'

'Oh, he's staying with the partisans, didn't I tell you?'

'No, you did not.'

He turned sharply as two of the wheelhouse windows cracked from top to bottom and scattered broken glass across the line-handling party below.

The hull lifted and surged against the pier, and for a brief instant Frazer thought they had been straddled by artillery fire. Voices shouted through the din, and Frazer saw the land up by the village suddenly blacked out by smoke and flying fragments.

Nothing and nobody could survive that.

Goudie seemed to tear his eyes from the swirling clouds of smoke. 'That gives us just under ten minutes, so cast off and steer north. Otherwise a coastal battery might catch us before we can change course to the rendezvous.' He was in control again. Relaxed.

Frazer crossed the deck, his eyes stinging with despair. He recalled Allenby's pale face in the bunker after he had spoken to the Wren, and again when he had taken him to his home to meet his folks.

He said, 'Let go head rope, bear off forrard!'

He picked up the handset and waited for the ERA to acknowledge.

The signalman shouted, 'Here they come, sir!'

Frazer stared. 'Belay that order! Get those men aboard!'

As the last line was flicked from its bollard and the engines churned the choppy water into froth, Allenby, with Weeks on his heels, pushed his way into the wheelhouse.

Goudie regarded him impassively. 'You're late.'

Weeks chimed in, 'He went to the ferry too, sir. Just to make sure the fuses were set right.'

Ives called, 'Steady on nor'west by north, sir.'

Frazer wrapped his arm around Allenby's shoulders. He was covered in filth and thick dust. 'You crazy bastard, you might have been killed that second time!'

Allenby looked across at Goudie's expressionless face.

'No chance. The fuse was incorrectly set.'

Later, as the patrol boat, with her dead commander lolling unheeded in his chair, worked up to her full speed and the sea parted across her stem in two creaming banks, they heard the final charges explode. Offshore it was too misty to see anything, but the explosion seemed to linger on, like sullen thunder over hills.

Allenby walked to the rear of the wheelhouse and stared up at the White Ensign which the signalman had found in the Italians' own flag locker. Perhaps for a deception of their own?

He said, 'I hope they got away safely.'

He knew that the others did not understand although Weeks would probably tell the tale later with relish. How he threatened to blow up the partisan leader if he refused to warn the villagers. Would they have done it for us? He smiled, the weariness dropping instantly from his face. Unlikely. But it was worth it.

He watched the land fading away in spray and mist, and a shaft of sunlight as it managed to break through the low clouds. It was like defusing a mine and rendering it safe. When it was done, after all the sweating anxiety and chilling fear, you just wanted to be alone.

Hemmed in by others as the boat tore across the lively water Allenby was still alone.

He saw two gulls wheeling above the masthead. *I made it.* Just once more, I made it.

6

Quite a Night

The sun blazed relentlessly across the tents and salvaged vehicles of Naval Party Seventy-Five. In the small bay the varied collection of small craft including the captured Italian patrol boat lay quite motionless. Only their masts and upper-works appeared to move as they weaved in the heat.

Allenby tugged down the peak of his cap and stared across the anchorage wondering how it was possible for so many people to keep out of sight in this barren place.

He looked at the Italian patrol boat and recalled how he and Weeks had been dragged aboard at the last minute even as she made to get under way. The feeling of wild exultation as they had thumped his shoulders and shouted above the din. Now it seemed more like a dream, some parts vivid and terrifying, others overlapping and vague. Their escape from the village had been without incident. That was almost harder to understand than their getting into the place undetected. Right at the prescribed time and place two powerful destroyers and relays of long-range fighter-bombers had closed around them for their return to base. At the time Allenby had seen their escort as evidence of their importance, a gesture to mark what they had achieved.

Goudie had waited until they had moored the patrol boat and had then put paid to any such ideas.

They had done well, but the true purpose had been to draw the enemy's attention from another part of the Sicilian coastline, he did not say where, so that arms and ammunition could be landed for the main partisan group.

'They need weapons desperately. Men like Maroca – ' he had spat out his name, 'cannot be expected to fight with shotguns and shovels!'

Once in sight of the North African coast Frazer had stopped the engines and had buried the dead Italians at sea. Allenby wondered if any of the others knew Frazer had buttoned the dead officer's picture of his wife or girlfriend inside his uniform before he was tipped over the side.

Allenby lifted the flap of their tent and ducked into it. The trapped air made it like a kiln.

Frazer was bending over a mirror and shaving himself with great concentration. He was naked but for his sandals and Allenby saw the way he snatched up a towel to wrap around his well-made body. It was automatic and nothing to do with modesty. Allenby had seen it once before, the great burn on his side, like rough parchment.

Frazer saw his expression and shrugged. 'Just a habit. Sorry.'

Allenby sat on his camp bed and watched him.

'How did it happen?'

Allenby was usually withdrawn, even shy in spite of the daily danger he took for granted. But there was something about Frazer. He made even sharing a confidence seem easy.

'Our skipper tried to get alongside a burning ship in a westbound convoy. He was a good man to serve under. Just a two-ringer, like we are now. He was usually so damned careful, and an ace at ship-handling. It must have been the freighter. She was Canadian too. Maybe he knew some of them.' He shook his razor on the sand. 'Anyway, the next thing, we hit her, and the sea carried us into her again and then we too were ablaze.' His eyes were distant and did not focus on Allenby. He was back there in the cold Atlantic with burning fuel demolishing life rafts and men with savage efficiency.

'I was picked up eventually. Not many of us left though.'
He lowered the towel and examined the brutalized flesh with
something like hatred. 'They say I was lucky. I guess I was.'

He saw the letter in Allenby's hand. 'News from home,
you lucky sod!'

Allenby tried to hide it. It did not seem right that he
should have one when it was unlikely Frazer would get a
letter for months, even if it eventually caught up with him.

'From my mother.'

Frazer mopped his cheeks. 'All right?'

'My dad's not too well.' It was strange for his mother
to mention that. She usually wrote about how they were
'managing', as she called it. 'He insists on doing his
firewatching. Doing his bit.' His mouth twisted in a sad
smile. 'Not easy with just one leg.'

Frazer sat down beside him and watched him thoughtfully.
'Can't be much fun, sitting on top of a factory or somewhere
looking for incendiary bombs every night, eh?'

Allenby nodded. He must be really ill. His mother would
have kept quiet about it otherwise. To stop him worrying.

Frazer said, 'I wonder how much longer they'll keep us
here? I feel like a run ashore somewhere. Even Sousse would
have charm after this dump.'

Allenby looked at him. 'I'd like that.'

Frazer asked quietly, 'Have you got a girl back in England,
Dick?'

Allenby stood up as if to adjust the tent flap. 'Nobody
definite, I – I mean not regular.' He looked at Frazer despair-
ingly. 'I'm doing it again, Keith. No, I've no girl.' A note
of defiance crept into his voice. 'I've had a few chances, but
not the right one.'

Frazer nodded. 'Like me. I feel I'm missing out somehow.'

Allenby looked away. Frazer, with his looks and his background, should have no difficulty at all. Whether he had
much feeling for them was something else. But Allenby had
never even touched a girl other than an unsatisfactory cuddle

in a cinema, and a dangerously near thing with his commanding officer's wife. Even now he sweated about that.

Nobody else seemed to have any trouble, he thought. He had listened to the seamen, and especially the watchkeepers on those long days sweeping for mines. Every time libertymen returned on board they were crowing over their conquests. The married ones seemed to be the worst. Perhaps he was inwardly afraid of getting some awful disease. The sailors even joked about that. 'Getting a dose' or 'catching the boat up' – they were not put off by the risks. It was even accepted in the wardrooms. If an officer was suddenly put out of circulation it was always referred to as 'he's gone to Rose Cottage for a while'. What a name for a VD clinic.

He changed the subject. 'We'll be going into Sicily soon. They say that troops and landing ships are massing everywhere.'

Frazer said bitterly, 'I don't see Prothero's Navy doing much, do you?'

The tent flap cracked open and Lieutenant Commander Goudie stepped inside. He looked as if he had been walking for miles and his khaki shirt was black with sweat.

They had not seen much of him except for matters of briefing and daily routine. He looked strained and his temper was constantly on a short fuse.

He regarded Frazer's nakedness with a wry smile. 'Better get dressed. Otherwise some of the lads will think you're both having it off.'

Allenby blushed and Frazer said evenly, 'It's just a little joke, Dick. You're full of them, aren't you, sir?'

Goudie sat down on a box. 'Give me a drink, will you?' Allenby poured him a glass full of neat gin. He was astonished the way Goudie could knock it back.

Goudie said at length, 'Get your gear packed. All of it. We're moving out.' He held out the empty glass for a refill.

Frazer said, 'Is it all right to ask where to?'

'You're leaving in two hours, so it's safe to tell you.' He

looked at each of them in turn. 'We're going to Gib. The Yanks are flying us there.'

Frazer sat up. 'You as well?'

Goudie drank the gin almost savagely. As if he loathed it. 'There's something big on. Must be.'

Allenby said, 'Good.' His gaze dropped as they both stared at him. 'I – I quite like Gib.'

Goudie threw back his head and laughed. 'Don't get too fond of it, my lad. I doubt if we'll be there long. In this regiment we tend to move a bit sharpish when the word is passed.'

The mood changed again. 'Anyway, have your stuff packed and ready. I'll get some hands sent over to shift it when the truck arrives.' He wiped his neck and stared at his wet fingers with distaste. 'Bloody heat. I'll bet the Afrika Korps are bloody glad to be out of it. Poking all the Eyetie maidens in Naples by now, I shouldn't wonder.'

Allenby kept his mouth shut. There was not much humour in Goudie. Not any more.

Goudie said, 'I'll go and tell Archer the good news.'

Frazer groaned. 'Must you?'

'I'm short of good officers.' Goudie smiled, his teeth very white in his tanned face. 'And he's not as squeamish as some.' His shadow withdrew down the tent as he strode out into the hard sunlight.

Frazer touched his burned side without realizing what he was doing.

'Bastard,' he said calmly. 'What makes him tick?'

'He tries to get under your skin.'

Frazer smiled, 'He does that all right.'

Allenby looked around at the small tent and remembered the moment below the power-plant wall when he had never expected to see this place again. He watched Frazer jamming things into a case, his tousled hair falling across his forehead. They would still be together, no matter what else might happen to them.

*

They arrived at Gibraltar just before sunset. In spite of the fading light the sight was impressive as the overcrowded aircraft turned and plunged steeply towards the runway, which from the air looked no bigger than a plank.

The harbour and the bay was so crammed with shipping the hulls and superstructures seemed to overlap. There were several troopships which had once earned their keep as proud ocean liners, transports and repair vessels, landing craft of every class and size, and anchored and moored around them were the familiar dazzle-painted shapes of their escorts.

With its rugged crest touched with bronze in the dying sunlight the Rock looked what it had become, a symbol, something unbreakable. The streets were packed too. Khaki and blue, a great aimless press of figures taking their ease before the next offensive, and the one after that. Apart from a few muffled Moorish women there did not seem to be many of the opposite sex, although Allenby had heard there were some Wrens. They would have the pick of the whole place, he thought enviously.

Goudie banged out of a small office and watched as some seamen picked up their bags.

'He's here. We're to join him at once.'

Allenby asked, 'Who, sir?'

Goudie shrugged. 'The Boss.'

They followed him to a small khaki truck.

Frazer said, 'Prothero must have had a plane all to himself, eh?'

Allenby grinned. 'He's big enough.'

Frazer, who had visited the Rock several times to refuel when he had been part of a long-range escort to Ceylon, pointed out the fortifications and heavy guns to Allenby, but he had to admit to being completely lost as they were driven deeper into the defences. Eventually, on foot, they were led down one of the many passageways, tunnels which over the years had been carved deep into the Rock itself.

It was cool after the sweat and dust, the discomfort of the

plane whose pilot must surely have been a stuntman in happier times.

Passes were examined repeatedly, faces watched them curiously, and Frazer found himself wondering how many others had come here like lambs to the slaughter.

They were shown into a brightly lit office, its crude walls bedecked with maps and aerial photographs.

Commander Aubrey Prothero strode across the floor and shook their hands in strict order of seniority.

He was dressed in white, and his shorts around his massive girth looked as if they could have been used as a tent.

There was a second officer present, a full captain with a DSO and other decorations on his immaculate uniform. He was thin and hawk-faced, pale beside Prothero, as if he rarely saw the light of day.

Prothero introduced him gravely. He was Captain Jocelyn Heywood, Chief of Staff to the Flag Officer in charge of Special Operations.

Frazer studied him. He was important, so whatever they were going to attempt was equally so.

He wondered how Prothero felt about serving under a peacetime regular, about whom he had been so scathing at their first meeting.

They all sat down, Prothero on the edge of a desk. He probably mistrusted the canvas chairs.

Captain Heywood said, 'I have read all the reports on your recent operation. For some of the people it was a first time,' his eyes rested on Allenby but only briefly. 'The results for the most part were satisfactory, our casualties minimal.'

Allenby listened to the captain's cool, unhurried voice as he went over the main features of the raid, but in his mind's eye he saw the sapper as he fell dead amongst the rubble, the enemy engineer being stabbed by the partisans on the catwalk. And the two marines who had died on the pier. Minimal. But only just.

'However,' Heywood glanced at Prothero, 'there are a

few points I must mention. You, Lieutenant Frazer, were reluctant to get under way without waiting for Mr Allenby to join you. Your stubbornness could have jeopardized the whole operation. Loyalty is the finest quality in any man. Personal relationships that become too strong are something else. Remember that, will you?'

He did not wait and turned to Allenby. 'You disagreed with Major Thomas, I believe.'

Allenby flushed. 'I thought he acted foolishly, sir. I could not just throw a switch and blow down the whole village. There were people in those houses – ' His voice trailed away.

Heywood nodded. 'As I thought. But you were there to do a job. What you have volunteered to do.' He darted a glance at Goudie and added sharply, 'Major Thomas has made a full report too.'

Goudie met his gaze angrily. 'I don't give a fuck what Thomas said!'

Prothero lurched forward. '*What* did you say?'

Goudie said abruptly, 'I'm sorry, sir. But that man Thomas is bad all the way through. He's a killer. I've been with him enough to see the pleasure he gets from it.'

Frazer looked at the captain, expecting him to explode or have Goudie arrested for his outburst.

Instead Heywood asked, 'How long have you been with Special Operations? Eighteen months, I believe. And before that you proved yourself a brave and resourceful officer both here and in the Channel. Very demanding of any man.'

Goudie stared at him blankly. 'If you're saying I need a rest, sir, that I'm over the hill – '

Heywood said, 'I shall decide what is or is not to be done, *right?*' He leaned forward, his voice still very calm. 'I like initiative. Beyond that it becomes insubordination or worse.'

He nodded to Prothero. 'Carry on, if you please.'

Prothero looked at the three officers, his tiny eyes glinting dangerously in his ruddy face.

'Next month the Allies will invade Sicily, Operation

Husky.' His eyes flickered momentarily to his superior as if
he expected him to challenge his show of confidence.

Or maybe, Frazer thought, he was trying to repair the
damage of Goudie's outburst, or of Thomas's handling of
the raid itself.

Prothero continued in his resonant voice, 'The Germans
will contest every foot of the way, as they always have. Their
allies, however, no matter what Mussolini may think, will be
eager to change sides once the line of battle moves forward.'

Frazer thought of the young Italian officer they had buried
at sea. There would be many like him. And the girl in the
photograph, what would happen to her?

'It will be the example of leading politicians and staff
officers that will point the way. They need to be brave as
well as convinced that we shall win the final round. For if
their German masters discover what they are about, their
punishment will be swift and terrible, the Gestapo will make
sure of that.'

Captain Heywood crossed his legs as if he were growing
impatient. Prothero took the hint. 'There is one such staff
officer who even now is said to be under Gestapo obser-
vation. He is a well-respected officer of a fine old Italian
family, General Gustavo Tesini, whose division was one of
the only ones to distinguish itself in the early North African
campaign, before Rommel appeared on the desert scene.'

Frazer found himself frowning. The war in the Mediterranean, especially the army's part, was only something he
had read about. And yet, the general's name seemed to strike
a bell in his mind.

Prothero's eyes shone like chips of glass.

'I *thought* you might remember. General Tesini is or was
a friend of your father's. They used to race against each
other, I understand.'

Frazer nodded, amazed at Prothero's store of knowledge.

'Yes, sir. I met him twice, when my old man was racing

the *Onondaga*, couple of years before the war, I think it was.'

Prothero beamed so that his pointed beard jutted forward like a grey tusk.

'That's the one. If he openly displays his mistrust of the Germans the whole Italian army will desert to our cause whenever the moment offers itself. It would be like Rommel turning aginst Hitler!'

Heywood said, 'Reliable sources have informed me that he is prepared to come over. But it has to be before, er, Operation Husky, otherwise it would be seen as prudence by the general and nothing more than a self-motivated act.'

Prothero grunted, annoyed at the interruption. 'General Tesini is far too important for the Germans to act against him. Yet. He owns a small island off the nor'east coast of Sardinia, for he is a rich man, and has estates and houses elsewhere in Italy. But the island had always been a retreat for him and his family. That is where he will be, *must* be if you are going to take him.'

Goudie sat bolt upright. 'It's a hell of a long chance, sir.'

Heywood said smoothly, 'Here at Gibraltar two motor gunboats have been prepared for the Special Boat Squadron. They were intended for another task, but this is the more pressing. They are fitted with extra fuel tanks, and each crew is handpicked. Once you are fully briefed you will take the two boats to Tunis. At an economical speed you should be there in around two and a half days.' His eyes moved across their set faces. 'It is all the time I can spare for you to familiarize yourselves with the craft and their crews.' His glance rested on Goudie. 'You are the most experienced MGB commander we have. It will be up to you.'

Frazer looked at Goudie's tense features. Heywood might have thought differently had he known about Goudie's bitterness, and the fact that he was obviously driven beyond the limit.

Heywood added, 'The general has made just one stipulation. You bring off his family and some personal items, or it's not on, right?'

Goudie looked at Frazer and grimaced. 'Why not, the more the merrier.'

Heywood said quietly, 'If anything goes wrong while you're there, the general is not to be taken by the enemy alive, do I make myself clear?'

Goudie said, 'You do, sir.'

Heywood stood up for the first time. He was very tall.

'Any other comments?' He glanced at a wall clock. 'I have a staff conference in fifteen minutes.' He saw Allenby hesitate and asked, 'You wish to ask something?'

'The village, sir, were the Sicilians there safe after the explosions?'

Heywood eyed him impassively. 'For a while, Allenby. Then the SS arrived there and executed fifty males, men and boys.'

Allenby stared round the brightly lit room.

'Oh my God.'

Frazer said, 'They had nothing to do with it. Not a damn thing.'

Goudie picked up his battered cap and stared at it.

'It'll make the Sicilians and Italians hate the Krauts all the more, won't it, sir?' He smiled bleakly. 'Or was that the whole idea in the first place?'

Heywood walked to the door. To Prothero he said, 'Ten minutes then.'

Prothero waited and then said to the two lieutenants, 'You carry on. I've detailed a rating to take you to get cleaned up and fed.'

They walked out but as the door swung behind them they heard Prothero bellow, 'I'll not stand for that kind of behaviour, do you understand? I don't give a toss if you are a bloody hero, it cuts no ice with me! If the raid had gone wrong Major Thomas could have got all of you to a safe place in the hills – could *you*?'

The rating coughed discreetly and Allenby and Frazer followed him down yet another crudely hewn tunnel.

'Is Commander Prothero finished yet?'

They both stopped dead and Frazer exclaimed, 'I know that voice!'

She came round a bend from a smaller passageway, her white shirt ghostly against the rock wall.

She held out her hand. 'What a way to meet!'

Second Officer Lynn Balfour looked from one to the other, her white-topped tricorn hat barely controlling her short auburn hair.

Frazer said, 'I should have thought of that.' He felt suddenly clumsy and awkward. He had not expected to see her here, although it was quite obvious she was not surprised at this meeting.

She said, 'Must get on. There's a lot to do. You people keep us busy at HQ.' She became serious. 'I'm glad you're safe. Both of you.'

Frazer asked, 'Any chance of taking an hour off? A meal, maybe?'

She eyed him thoughtfully. 'I doubt that. I could try.' She seemed to become confused. 'But I'm not really sure, there's – '

Frazer said, 'Well, think about it, will you?' He wanted to touch her, to protect her from whatever it was that was tearing her apart.

Allenby asked quietly, 'How is the Leading Wren I – '

She looked at him and then replied, 'Joanna? She's fine.' That was all she said.

Allenby said, 'I'll go on ahead, Keith.' He smiled at the Wren. 'It's nice to see you again.'

She stared after him. 'Poor chap. He still feels it badly.'

Frazer smiled. 'You made him feel much better.' He saw her guard drop instantly and added gently, 'You told him her name, don't you see? She's real to him now. Someone to care about if he gets home again.'

She stepped back slightly, her lips parted as she said, 'Don't say it! Please don't speak like that!'

Frazer said, 'I'm sorry. Really. But I'm also a realist.'

Voices echoed along the passage, Prothero and Goudie apparently laughing together.

Frazer said, 'They must have had a drink.' He did not see the sudden anguish in her blue eyes. Then she said, 'I really can't make that date tonight.' She watched his face feature by feature as if searching for something. Or someone. She tried to laugh. 'Anyway I'm engaged. What would people say?'

Prothero's gigantic shadow flowed around them and he boomed, 'Ah, here you are, Lynn. Where would I be without you?'

Frazer watched her small, slim figure merge with Prothero's shadow as they turned down the passageway where the conference was to be held.

Frazer said, '*Damn!*'

Goudie fell in step beside him. 'Fouled it up again, have you?'

Frazer said, 'Second Officer Balfour's engaged. Who's the lucky chap?'

Goudie glanced at his profile. 'Got to you, did she?' He relented. 'That was two years ago. He was one of my blokes at Felixstowe. Bought it one night off the Hook of Holland.'

Frazer swung round. 'But she just said – '

Goudie said harshly, 'I was there when it happened. E-Boat's cannon shell cut him in half. Don't tell her I told you.'

They saw Allenby waiting for them and Goudie quickened his pace. Frazer stared along the other passageway, but it was deserted. Two years. Living a nightmare. Clinging to the memory that had gone with all the others.

He had pushed it to the back of his mind since that day in Portsmouth. But he knew he had been deceiving himself all the time. She was not just another attractive girl, nor was

it an idea of conquest because she did not even appear to like
him. She was different. And now this. How could he expect
to compete with someone she loved as if he were still alive
to share her hopes?

Sub-Lieutenant Archer's tall shadow loomed along the
wall, his face alive with questions and curiosity.

Frazer said, 'Oh, Christ.'

Goudie did not seem to notice. 'Well, well, Sub. Just in
time to buy us all drinks.'

Archer looked quickly at Frazer. 'All set up, is it, sir?'

Goudie said, 'Wait and see. Drinks first.'

He sounded quite cheerful and it was hard to see him as
he had been earlier.

Frazer said, 'I am going to hang one on tonight, *all* night
if necessary.'

Goudie smiled. 'Good show. For tomorrow, who knows?'

The hammering seemed to be crushing Frazer's skull as he
fought off a tangled sheet and prised open his eyes in the
glaring overhead light.

He had been enduring a nightmare, flames, men shouting
and dying. He groaned. That was no nightmare.

He stared dazedly across the small room and realized for
the first time what had wakened him; it also explained the
banging in his skull.

The door was wide open, and a dishevelled figure in a
dressing gown peered around the room like a terrier after a
rat.

The man said angrily, 'I thought you were all bloody dead
in here!'

Frazer looked at Allenby who lay face down on his bed.
He could well be dead, he thought, and he remembered
vaguely how he had half carried him here to their temporary
billet and then undressed him. He doubted if Allenby would
remember anything in the morning.

He groaned and tried to moisten his lips. His tongue tasted like a piece of dirty felt.

The man in the doorway persisted, 'Which one of you is the Canadian?'

Frazer tried to work it out. Goudie getting terribly drunk, and Archer picking an argument with one of the garrison officers who had seemed intent on killing him.

'I am.' Another great effort. 'Why?'

The man glared at him. 'Telephone. Down the passageway. Right outside my cabin, that's why.' He strode away, adding, 'Pity some people can't show some consideration for the watchkeepers!'

Frazer got to his feet and for a moment he thought the awakened officer was back again, but this time the banging was inside his head.

He dragged his reefer jacket over his shoulders and lurched out into the passageway. Nothing moved except for the telephone which swung slowly from its flex.

What the hell was wrong, he wondered. Goudie had gone off his head, or maybe Archer was in trouble again.

His bare feet slapped on the tiled floor and he shivered. Strange on the Rock, how it was blazing hot by day and could feel like ice during the night.

He groped for the telephone and said, 'Lieutenant Frazer speaking.' It was what he intended to say, but his voice sounded thick and unreal, like someone else's.

He steadied his gaze on the wall. Telephone numbers and names, doodling as a thousand men had waited for a reply.

'It's me.' Her voice was right in his ear, and he realized she was half shouting, that there was a roaring sound in the background. An aircraft.

'Where are you? Are you in trouble?' He was wide awake now. When she said nothing he thought she had rung off and he added, 'Please, tell me?'

She said slowly, 'Had to call you. To tell you –' Her voice almost trailed away and the drumming engines intruded again. 'Wanted to apologize. Bloody rude. You weren't to know.'

Frazer pressed the phone to his ear and covered the other one with his palm in case he missed something. She was either in tears or ill.

She said, 'Couldn't let you go like that, now could I? Not the thing, is it?' She laughed, but broke off in a fit of coughing.

'Tell me where you are.' He made himself speak slowly and calmly. He was anything but calm. 'I'll get to you somehow.'

There was another long pause and he thought he could hear her breathing, pulling herself together.

'Can't be done, *Mister* Frazer, I have to go. Can't say any more. You know, the war and all that – '

He said, 'Take care of yourself.' He hesitated. 'Lynn. I'd like to see you again, I really would.'

'Yes.' She sounded confused. 'You take care too. Oh, God, I'm going to be sick.' The line went dead.

Frazer rattled the telephone repeatedly before a disgruntled switchboard operator said, 'I can't get it back, sir.' It sounded like 'even if I wanted to'. 'The call came through the priority line. Bit of influence.'

Frazer put it down and walked slowly back along the passageway. To his surprise he found Allenby sitting on the edge of his bed, rubbing his eyes with his knuckles.

He looked up and stared. 'Is there a flap on?'

Frazer shook his head. 'Phone call. Lynn Balfour.' She must have been drinking one hell of a lot to get like that.

Allenby said, 'Lucky she was on the end of a telephone, Keith.' He grinned and Frazer realized that he still wore only his reefer across his shoulders. It hid nothing.

Frazer looked at the window and saw the grey line of dawn around the heavy curtain. He pulled it aside and saw some lights shining weakly in the dockyard. It was the hardest thing to get used to in Gib, the lack of proper blackout.

She had telephoned him. To wish him luck, or to say goodbye? What had he expected? She had lost the love of her life. She was hardly likely to lay herself open to that pain again.

Allenby said, 'Will you be seeing her?'

'I hope so.' *I must.*

He dragged the curtain aside and watched as a small aircraft lifted above the sleeping ships and the old walls of the dockyard.

He was glad she was with Prothero. He would take care of her. She was one of his own. He let the curtain fall. Prothero's Navy.

He dropped back on the bed and groaned as he realized he had left the light on.

The first bugle shattered the stillness. *Wakey, wakey, lash up and stow!* The call that had been cursed and blasphemed at by generations of sailors.

Allenby stood up shakily. Not once had he remarked on the fact someone had undressed him.

'I'm hungry,' he said.

Frazer thought of the girl in the deep corridor, the way she had looked at him. Seeing her dead lover, or was it that she knew something about the next raid? The margin of survival.

Allenby watched his friend's anxiety and dismay. He had known how Frazer had felt about the girl, almost from the start. He sighed and looked around for his towel. Then it came back to him. As if he had heard someone say her name aloud.

'Joanna.' He repeated it aloud and then darted an embarrassed glance at Frazer. But he had fallen asleep again.

It must have been quite a night, he decided.

7

Jupiter

Lieutenant Commander John Goudie stood in the forepart of the motor gunboat's tiny bridge and looked at his three officers. In company with the other craft they had left Gibraltar before dawn and now in the bright sunlight the Mediterranean had offered them its other face. The sea was flat and deep blue, and only an uneven purple line to starboard betrayed the nearness of land.

Frazer watched Goudie: like the sea he seemed to have changed too. He looked cheerful, even elated. Perhaps this motor gunboat was what he needed, what he did best. The other officer was a sunburned youngster of nineteen, Sub-Lieutenant David Ryder, one of the few members of the boat's original company. He seemed very pleasant, and Frazer was thankful that Archer was over in the second boat, some two cables to port.

The motor gunboats made a fine sight, he thought. They displayed no pendant numbers and their rakish, seventy-foot hulls were painted black, giving them the appearance of pirates rather than warships.

Frazer looked across towards the land; somewhere over there was the unmarked frontier between Morocco and Algeria. It could have been anywhere.

So far they had sighted a whole flotilla of destroyers heading east and a few patrolling aircraft. The latter had swept above them, probably to report their progress as much as to verify who they were. Frazer hoped that not too many people knew about Force Jupiter as Prothero had named them.

Goudie said, 'These MGBs handle well.' He was hatless and his sun-bleached hair rippled in the breeze like corn in a field. 'If any boats can do the job, they can.'

Frazer looked over the glass screen below which a whole line of swastikas had been painted out. The boat's previous kills, battle honours. She was not very large, and had only a crew of twelve, but she bristled with guns, power-operated to give the full effect at close quarters, a two-pounder forward, a double Oerlikon mounting aft and four heavy machine guns. Her firepower plus an impressive maximum speed of forty-two knots made her a deadly adversary.

Tunis first to top up the tanks, then north to the Tyrrhenian Sea between Italy and Sardinia, one of the few areas which had not so far been fought over. It was just as well. They needed all the surprise on their side this time, and luck.

He glanced at Ives, who stood at the wheel, easing the spokes gently this way and that as he got the feel of the powerful hull beneath his straddled legs. He looked content, as if he were riding the boat, testing her response. They were making a good sixteen knots. It would be different when the three big Packard engines were given full throttle.

Ives was unaware of Frazer's scrutiny. He felt at home here. What he had always wanted. A small boat, a sense of purpose as well as comradeship. In his view it had been wrong to abandon the Siebel ferry, to use the vessel merely as a bomb to demolish the enemy's installations. A boat was a boat. Something to care for. He listened to the sweet growl of the engines. The dockyard had done a good job on them.

He had heard Goudie speaking to his officers and put the pieces together for himself. Frazer was said to be a superb small-boat man and navigator. From what he had picked up, Ives knew that navigation was of paramount importance on this job. With luck they could use the islands around their destination to mask the enemy's radar and other detection devices, if they had any. But they had controlled the whole of that area for so long, it could be their weakness. On the other hand, it was good to know they had a first-rate pilot. He liked Frazer, the first Canadian he had ever met. Allenby was on the opposite side of the bridge watching the other boat with his binoculars. Ives had decided that he liked him as far as he could tell. He doubted if anyone would ever really know Allenby, not in a thousand years.

The two-pounder gun on the forecastle swung suddenly in its mounting and Ives watched as the gunlayer, Leading Seaman Sullivan, made a few small adjustments.

He bit his lip. Sullivan was a Londoner like himself. The one fly in the ointment. He was aggressive, loud-mouthed, a real Jolly Jack. Apart from the stokers and an artificer, Sullivan was the only other leading hand aboard. He had been brought up in Bethnal Green, not far from where Ives had once walked the beat. That last night in Gibraltar as they had crawled through the boat, checking ammunition, stores and food, Sullivan had made a few remarks about the police in general, and those in London's East End in particular.

He must have discovered about Ives's background, not that you needed to be a genius to guess that. Ives was used to it anyway and took most remarks in good part.

But Sullivan's were different. He had said in front of the others, 'They're all bent on our manor, ain't that right, 'Swain?' He had grinned at Ives, but his eyes had lacked humour. 'My old man's a street bookmaker in the Green. Many's the time I've seen the copper on the beat take the drop to turn a blind eye!' When Ives had remained silent Sullivan had persisted, 'I bet if I'd said that when you was a copper you'd 'ave said summat, eh?'

Ives had had enough. 'I don't know what I'd have said *then*. But if you keep this up I'll break your rotten arm, right?'

Sullivan had stared at him, and at Ives's obvious strength, which seemed at odds with his mild manner.

They had barely spoken since. Ives decided he must do something about it. It was bad to go into action when you held grudges in your midst. He swore to himself and eased the spokes. He had allowed the boat to stray off course. Fortunately the officers had not noticed.

Allenby watched the other boat with something like wonder. He had often heard the sailors aboard his minesweeper hurling insults when the MTBs and MGBs had cut past them in a welter of spray. The Glory Boys they had called them. The usual service rivalry, and not a little envy.

It was exciting, breathtaking. The stealth and the danger would come, but the feeling of exuberance was as real as it was infectious.

He thought of his father. Perhaps he needed building up. It could be no joke, *managing* on their meagre rations, he thought. Time and time again his mind returned to the Leading Wren in Portsmouth. Frazer at least had made contact with Second Officer Balfour, whereas – He shook himself. What was the point anyway? It was likely they would never meet again. She might get a draft chit, or he could get his head blown off. It was pointless to fret about it. But he could still see her eyes, hear her voice, the bitter words. He could explain nothing. His memory was wiped clean for those vital seconds before the mine had exploded.

The telegraphist, their only one, who did the duties of signalman, coder and radio operator, poked his head through the hatch and called, 'R/T from Able Two, sir. Aircraft at Red four-five, closing.'

Goudie nodded and jabbed the button by his elbow. As the bells jangled through the hull and men in various stages of undress ran to their action stations Goudie said calmly, 'Alter course, steer southeast. Signal Able Two.'

The Aldis clattered briefly and the telegraphist called, 'Acknowledged, sir!'

Goudie raised his glasses. 'There they are. Two of the buggers.'

Allenby moved his binoculars, the reflected glare making his eyes fill. How did Goudie know they were hostile? Instinct, the sixth sense born of tough experience.

He blinked and held the glasses steady on the two tiny shapes. The sun touched their perspex cockpit hoods, so that they appeared to be burning. It made sense now, the way Goudie had ordered his two gunboats to take station abreast. It gave a far wider span of vision, less chance of being jumped.

Goudie said, 'Tell the Chief. Be ready for maximum revs.' He moved his glasses carefully. 'Sod it! I could have done without them!'

'They're turning, sir. They're going to pass astern of us.'

'Having a look-see.' Goudie allowed his glasses to drop onto his chest.

Sub-Lieutenant Ryder reported, 'Boat at action stations, sir.' He raised his glasses and watched the two aircraft pass into a shallow dive towards the water.

'Me 210s, sir.' He sounded preoccupied and Frazer guessed he was probably worrying about the new men. All were veterans although few were more than nineteen years old. But in every ship, even a tiny one, the hands had to know each other, their strength or lack of it. But as Goudie had said often enough, there was never enough time.

Goudie said, 'Fighter-bombers but used more out here for reconnaissance.' He bit his lip. 'How the *hell* did the Brylcream boys let them slip through?'

Allenby asked, 'What's their firepower?'

Goudie lowered his glasses and wiped his eyes. 'Heavy. Four twenty millimetres, and some other cannon. Can be nasty.' Goudie added, 'Clear the bridge, Sub, you too, Mr Allenby'. He turned his back deliberately on the twin-engined aircraft. 'Don't want all our eggs in one basket.'

Ryder was very young but he had done this sort of thing often.

'Come aft with me.' He grinned at Allenby. 'We might bag one of them with the Oerlikons.'

As they walked carefully along the vibrating side deck Allenby saw that one pair of machine guns was manned by Able Seaman Weeks. Weeks was squinting through his sights, but said as they passed, 'I had a notion you might need me, sir.'

Allenby touched his arm. 'I thought you were a torpedoman?' It was good to see him, no matter what the impassive Captain Heywood had said about friendship.

The deck was bucking when they clawed their way aft amongst the racks of depthcharges. The stern was sinking as propellers and rudders dug deep into the wall of dazzling spray while both boats began to work up to full speed.

'Here they come!' Ryder paused only to make certain the Oerlikons' slim barrels were already tracking the leading fighter-bomber.

Allenby turned to look at the bridge but the glare was hard in his eyes and it was just a vague outline.

Ryder shouted, 'The bastards are flying into the sun! They'll be sorry!'

Reconnaissance, Goudie had said. They probably carried cameras and even now were photographing the two alien craft in their black livery.

Prothero would not be pleased, he thought. Perhaps the raid would be cancelled. Even as he thought it, he dismissed the idea. Captain Heywood would not be in the habit of visiting the scene of his operations unless it was important, maybe even vital to the invasion.

He thought of Goudie's sudden outburst, the way Heywood had ignored it. Perhaps they were more like weapons than people to the hawklike Chief of Staff. Expendable.

The leading Messerschmitt had levelled off and was tearing

up from astern, just a couple of hundred feet from the surface. The MGB's mounting wash looked as if it might reach the plane's belly as it tore towards them.

A bell jangled tinnily above the throaty roar of engines.

'*Open fire!*'

The Oerlikons and one pair of machine guns clattered into life, the tracers almost blind against the clear sky.

They did not hear the aircraft's guns, but saw the shots ripping across the water, heading straight for the boat's stern. Allenby almost fell as the helm went hard over and the sea surged over the low side like a millrace.

Ryder shouted at the gunlayer, 'Follow him. Taylor! Hit the bastard!'

It was just wild excitement, the madness of danger that made him yell out. The gunfire, the plane's engines and their own made talking pointless.

The plane banked away and Allenby saw tracer from the other MGB lifting with the usual deceptive slowness like lazy scarlet balls before streaking towards the tilting plane and crossing it in a fiery mesh.

Ryder yelled, 'He's hit!' He waved his cap as a long greasy trail of smoke marked the plane's unsteady progress.

The second one attacked from the starboard quarter, and this time Allenby felt some of the shots hammer against the hull and clang into one of the gunshields.

Goudie altered course again and the two-pounder joined in the fight, moving easily on its powered mounting as the gunlayer tracked the aircraft until the sights could no longer bear.

Allenby had once known an overenthusiastic gunner shoot off half of his own ship's bridge as he concentrated on their attacker.

Allenby listened to the men calling to one another. There had been no casualties. A man ran to fit new magazines to the Oerlikons but paused to thump the gunlayer on the shoulder. They beamed at one another like schoolboy conspirators.

'Stand by!'

Ryder watched the fighter-bomber as it climbed up and away in readiness for another run. The sunlight glinted on the cockpit, and Allenby imagined he could see the heads of the crew turning to watch the two fast-moving hulls.

He saw the black crosses on its wings, the strange green camouflage on its body. Probably from Sicily. He thought of the pylon toppling across the railway track, the stammer of machine guns, the sapper falling dead.

The guns wavered and then held steady as the plane began another shallow dive. If the pilot tried to fly higher there was a good chance he would be raked by several guns at once. Allenby heard the mounting roar of the German's engines, the harsh rattle of cannon and machine guns. The air was full of shrieking metal, and he heard several cracks and clangs as the steel found a target.

Then tracer licked up at the plane's belly as it tore overhead, its shadow trailing across the deck like a cloak.

The pilot was either wounded or raving mad, for in spite of the cone of tracer which came from both boats he flew straight on towards Able Two, almost at right angles.

'*Hit him!*' Ryder was almost sobbing as he grasped a stanchion to stop himself from pitching overboard as the helm went over again. Allenby pictured Ives at the wheel. He at least would be enjoying this.

Able Two was twisting frantically as the enemy's intentions became clear when, like hungry jaws, its bomb bay opened.

Tracer was exploding all over the wings and belly, like droplets of bright blood in the glare.

Allenby gripped a guardrail. 'Christ Almighty.'

The other MGB was making a sharp, desperate turn as the bomb dropped with deceptive slowness and hit her amidships. It seemed as if nothing had happened, or that the bomb was a dud.

Then came the explosion. Allenby felt it kick the deck beneath him and watched stunned as the MGB staggered but continued to turn, the sea boiling over the side and not receding. A great fountain of flame belched from the broken hull, and Allenby guessed that the fuel had gone up. It was spreading across the sea in neat, fiery arrowheads, while fragments of the boat rained down in a great circle of spray.

A voice shouted, 'Aircraft! Bearing Green four-five!'

The guns swung on their mountings but the bell rattled again and all firing ceased as three Spitfires ripped overhead with their familiar whistling roar.

In the sudden silence as the engines slowed again Allenby heard Goudie shout, 'You're *too bloody* late, you bastards!' Allenby saw him shaking his fist at the three fighters as they planed after the enemy. They had no need: the fighter-bomber dived wearily and then more steeply and hit the sea with a vivid flash.

Allenby heard himself murmur, 'Brave man.'

The Spitfires altered course and were soon dots against the sun. From their altitude they could probably see the first enemy plane and its telltale smoke. If so, the German's life-line was very short.

'Fall out action stations! Stand by scrambling nets!'

They climbed to the bridge where Allenby saw the telegraphist tying a dressing on Ives's wrist which had been cut by flying splinters.

Frazer saw Allenby and grimaced. They both turned as Goudie yelled, 'Get those men aboard!' He was almost screaming. 'Chop, bloody chop, Sullivan!'

There were only six of them. Allenby thought it was a marvel that any had survived. The engineroom crew had gone up with the explosion, and the others had died either from the bomb or burned alive by the fuel. The boat's skipper, whom Allenby had met only once at the last briefing in Gibraltar, did not survive. Sub-Lieutenant Archer did, and was the last to leave the water as the MGB cruised slowly amongst the grisly flotsam.

Frazer opened and closed his hands as some of the drifting fuel reached a floating body. It was near enough to see the man's hair on fire. But he did not protest or try to escape. He was past that.

Frazer saw his own corvette. A different sea, the same fearful death.

Goudie massaged his neck and waited for the survivors to be hauled aboard.

Archer climbed onto the bridge, his face and hands black, the sea pouring unheeded from his clothing as he stared around.

Goudie said, 'Get below, Sub. See what you can do for the others. I'll be down myself in a minute.' He looked over the screen and saw that the scrambling nets were already stowed against the guardrails again.

'Cruising speed, Pilot, work out the course to steer as soon as you can, and let me know.'

The telegraphist asked huskily, 'D'you wish to make a signal, sir?'

Goudie turned on him angrily. 'Who to, for Christ's sake? *God*?' He seemed to regain control with an effort.

'We make no signals. I hope to blazes those high-fly idiots remember that!'

Allenby looked at Archer. 'I'm glad you made it, Sub.'

Archer stared right through him, his eyes completely empty.

Frazer said, 'Take over the con, Dick. I'm going to look at the chart and my notes.' His eyes shifted astern, toward the widening circle of boat and human flotsam. Some gulls were already cruising above it, waiting for the flames to die. It made him feel sick.

Allenby asked, 'Will we go on with the raid now?'

Frazer tore his eyes away. 'If you'd been up here with me, Dick, and seen the way he behaved, you'd not have to ask.'

He lowered himself through the hatchway to his chartroom. 'I think he's round the bend. *Kaput.*'

Ives heard his comment but did not glance at him. He raked over his feelings instead, his reactions to what had happened. No matter whether or not they continued with the operation, there would be others, all at high risk. His mouth lifted in a sad smile. *Never volunteer if you can't take a joke.* But throughout the brief, savage action he had never doubted himself or the boat. Round the bend or not, Goudie had trusted him, had barely given a direct order but for the first violent turn. He looked at the bandage on his wrist and grinned at the young telegraphist.

'Thanks.' He thought of the Master-at-Arms at the detention barracks. 'My son.'

In the motor gunboat's tiny wardroom where the officers had their makeshift meals, slept and pondered over their fates, Allenby sat alone, his elbow on the folding table.

The cabin was very dark, partly because it lacked proper scuttles and also because it was moored alongside a destroyer. It was obviously intended to dissuade anyone from trying to get ashore to see the sights of Tunis, or let something slip out about Force Jupiter.

He frowned. It was not so much of a force now.

Goudie was ashore somewhere, and Frazer was aboard the destroyer, using the facilities of her large chart space. He glanced round the wardroom. Large by comparison anyway. It was amazing how much they could cram into such a small place. Long padded seats which folded into bunks and could be used as life rafts if things went badly wrong. He thought of their bombed consort. No one had found a chance to use them then.

The hull nudged against the fenders and Allenby heard music coming from the forecastle, the messdeck, which was even more cramped. They seemed carefree enough. It did not take sailors long to learn that the important thing was to survive, no matter what risks you took. *Pull up the ladder, Jack*.

He looked at the letter he had just written to his mother. God alone knew when she might get it. Allenby was twenty-five, old by some standards in wartime, but his handwriting was that of a schoolboy.

It was always hard to know what to write about. The important things were secret, and personal feelings became more private with each succeeding risk. His father would love to hear about it. He had been through hell but he never interrupted his son when he described a ship or his companions.

Allenby sometimes wondered if his mother was proud of him. Once, when he had been describing his fellow officers aboard a minesweeper, she had said, 'They sound a toffee-nosed lot.'

His father had sighed. He often did. 'Our boy's as good as any of them.'

He licked the envelope and wondered if some censor would read it on its long journey.

Then he looked at his writing pad, holding back what was really uppermost in his mind. She might never see it, or if she did she might think him ridiculous. Worse, it might bring back the pain again.

To give himself time he addressed the envelope. Leading Wren Joanna Hazel.

How should he begin? He bit the end of his pen and toyed with the idea of asking Frazer. He frowned more deeply. No, that was stupid.

In his round, careful hand he wrote, *Dear Miss Hazel* – it did not look very exciting, he thought, but it was the only way he knew.

When Frazer came aboard Allenby did not even hear him. As the tall lieutenant ducked through the entrance and tossed his cap onto a bench Allenby looked up and then tried to cover the letter with his forearm.

Frazer sat down and laid some charts beside him. 'You did it then? Good show.'

Allenby coloured. 'I wanted to. Keith. I – I'm not sure if – '

Frazer watched him, but his thoughts were still with Lynn Balfour. 'It's the only way, Dick. What can you lose?'

They both turned as someone fell on the upper deck and voices filtered through the open bridge.

Frazer grimaced. 'Goudie's back. Sounds smashed to me.'

Goudie entered the wardroom and very carefully laid a canvas bag on the deck. His eyes were red-rimmed and he looked exhausted.

Frazer asked carefully, 'Anything I can do, sir?'

Goudie looked at them vaguely. 'I've sent Sub-Lieutenant Ryder for some gin.' He reached down and lifted the bag with elaborate care. 'Some *more* gin, that is.'

Able Seaman Weeks, who combined the duty of messman with all his other expertise, entered with some clean glasses. He said nothing, and left after placing a jug of water on the table.

Goudie grinned broadly as Allenby poured the drinks. It made him look incredibly sad.

He said, 'Poor old Weeks. He stopped me from falling in the harbour just now. Lucky it wasn't our gallant Killick Cox'n. He'd probably have marched me off to the nearest police station!'

The others watched him in silence. Goudie was going through torment which was terrible to see.

Goudie swallowed the neat gin without apparently noticing it. He said abruptly, 'You once asked me about your predecessor, Lieutenant Bill Weston, *right*?'

Frazer nodded as he watched the gin overflowing Goudie's glass as he refilled it.

'Might never have happened. But for two things.' Goudie

took some deep breaths. 'Weston had landed some agents and was waiting to pick up some others. The other reason was that Weston thought he was bloody good, Christ in uniform.' He fell silent and they wondered if Goudie had said all he intended to say.

But Goudie continued, his voice slurred. He must have been at it all day. 'Major Thomas was handling the operation.' His eyes fixed angrily on the rack of pistols as if he were counting them. 'Everything went wrong, the Krauts got wind of it and jumped the agents who were supposed to be lifted off. Thomas and his own men vanished, and Weston, who was a brave officer with the mind of a halfwit, stayed put and waited, the stupid bastard. He got a bar to his DSC, or rather his parents did. It said that he acted over and above the line of duty. Nice, eh?'

Allenby swallowed hard. The gin made his stomach feel raw. What must it be doing to Goudie?

Frazer asked, 'Archer got the boat out, did he, sir?'

'Right. Archer should have got another ring and a medal, but he didn't.'

Frazer said, 'I'm sorry, sir. I seem to have misjudged him.' He watched the bottle shaking against the glass. The first bottle was empty.

Goudie squinted as if to recall Frazer's words. Then he shook his head. 'Oh no, Archer's a top-class shit. You were right.'

Ryder climbed down with some difficulty, two cartons of bottles under his arms.

He was young but a quick glance at their faces told him more than words.

Ryder asked gently, 'It's on then, sir?'

Goudie glared, or tried to. 'Speak when you're spoken to.' He saw the cartons. 'I see the supply officer did as I asked.'

Ryder looked unhappy. 'Not exactly, sir. He made me write a chit for the lot.'

Goudie chuckled. 'He would. Another bloody desk warrior, that one.'

Eventually he said, 'Yes, the operation will go ahead as planned – well, almost.' He saw Allenby's two letters for the first time. 'Good idea. I trust you've made your will too? It may be your last opportunity.'

Goudie fumbled in his canvas bag and pulled out a bulky envelope. 'An' here's some light reading for you, Pilot.'

Frazer opened the package and laid it on the table, his eyes skimming over the dates, times, recognition signals, everything much like the original plan, except they were going in alone. What the hell would happen if Goudie was like this? His eyes settled on the date. Three days from now. Just like that. He looked at Goudie, but he seemed to have fallen asleep, an empty glass still grasped in one hand. His face was relaxed again, youthful.

Allenby asked quietly, 'Anything new, Keith?'

Frazer pushed the bottom sheet towards him. Once at the rendezvous, the operation would be under the overall command of Major F. Thomas of the SAS.

Frazer said, 'I wonder what the "F" stands for?'

Goudie opened his eyes. 'You should be able to guess!' He waved his glass. 'Three days' time.' His eyes were closing again. 'If he tries anything this time, I'll kill th' – ' His head lolled and he was asleep.

Ryder took the empty glass and remarked, 'I sometimes wonder if we're going about this war the right way.'

Frazer laughed. 'Tell the War Cabinet, Sub!'

Allenby picked up the two letters and looked at them again. He studied the last one. Leading Wren Joanna Hazel. What would she say? She was probably out with a boyfriend right now.

He saw Frazer watching him. Ryder had gone and Goudie was snoring gently.

Frazer smiled. '*Send* it, Dick.'

Allenby picked up his cap. Perhaps he had really intended to tear it up.

He went on deck and climbed up the destroyer's side where the quartermaster and armed sentry watched him with mild curiosity. Beyond the ship was the town, the inevitable dust drifting everywhere.

The orders had arrived. There would be no more runs ashore. He wondered if these two tanned sailors would stop him if he attempted to cross over to the brow. They would probably call the OOD.

'For the postman, sir?' asked the quartermaster politely.

'Yes.' Allenby watched the man drop them into a sack beside his lobby. It was done.

Allenby turned aft and saluted the quarterdeck.

Despite everything, that letter had made him feel better.

8

Not for King and Country

It was dusk and the sea unbroken but for a slow regular swell, as if the black water was breathing. On deck and inside the small bridge the guncrews and watchkeepers swayed with the hull, conscious of the stillness beyond their little world, of a great sense of loneliness.

In the wardroom the air was humid and sour with the filtered stench of fuel as the boat ploughed very slowly closer and closer to their objective.

Allenby sat with his back to the side, exactly where he had written to Joanna Hazel. Like the others, he was dressed in light khaki shirt and slacks, with just his lieutenant's shoulder straps to mark him out as an officer. It was one small comfort, he thought vaguely. At least he could not be shot as a spy or partisan. Or did the Germans make such fine distinctions? Did anyone? He felt his shirt and skin sticking to the padded support and longed to be on deck in the air.

Goudie stood by the entrance and eyed them bleakly. He looked strained but showed no signs of his previous drinking. He was quite amazing, Allenby thought. The way he changed as the mood commanded him.

Sub-Lieutenant Ryder sat with his arms folded, his eyes shaded by the peak of his faded cap. Opposite him was Archer, tense as he listened to Goudie's final briefing. Allenby noticed that Archer occasionally opened and then closed his fingers into tight fists, as if he were still going over his terrible ordeal. Apart from that he was no different from usual.

Goudie said, 'Our first objective is a yacht haven on the southeast corner of the island. It's small and natural, as you can judge from the chart.' They all looked at the folded chart with its pencilled lines and crosses where Frazer had translated the secret orders into bald facts. 'It will be a good place to lie low while negotiations are taking place with General Tesini.' His eyes moved restlessly in the yellow glow. 'We shall rendezvous with Major Thomas's party as soon as we enter. One sign of a cockup and we run for it.'

Allenby considered the chart again, the distance they had come since Tunis. To run for it would merely delay their complete destruction if the Germans already knew about Jupiter. He watched too for some sign of resentment when Goudie spoke of the SAS major. But there was nothing. Goudie was different. On the job. Weighing their chances. Making alternative plans. He had had enough practice. Allenby found himself wondering if this raid or any of the previous ones which Goudie had led with such skill and courage would make even a fragment of difference to the war.

He heard the scrape of feet from the bridge and guessed Frazer was moving about, checking and rechecking their position and progress.

Goudie said, 'We go in just before dawn. Thomas's party should be in position about an hour earlier.' He did not elaborate and Allenby guessed that Thomas had been transferred from a submarine to some local craft. It implied that Thomas already had collaborators on the island. General Tesini must be important. It would have been far easier to kill him from Thomas's point of view.

It was as if Goudie was reading his thoughts. He said quietly, 'The invasion of Sicily has to be done perfectly. It is our first step back into Europe. If we fail or are badly delayed the Italians may stand firm with their German allies.

To win, we require the Italians to throw their lot in with us.' He added wryly, 'In other words, we need their treachery. That is the grand plan, fashioned in far-off places by those who are better informed than we are.'

He cocked his head as a man coughed on the bridge and then said, 'To those of us who actually have to carry out these missions there is only one sure guide. In this sort of warfare you are not fighting for King and Country, you are doing it for your own small team. There's no rulebook, and no room for the squeamish.' His eyes rested momentarily on Allenby. 'It's not a game, and we must win. General Tesini is important to the cause.' His eyes hardened. 'But not vital. If he changes his mind, or tries any sort of treachery, shoot him. Do I make myself clear?'

They nodded in unison.

'Good.' Goudie opened his holster and dragged out a heavy Luger. 'Go round the boat and check everything again. We will remain at action stations until I say otherwise, right?'

Allenby stayed for a few moments after Goudie and the others had gone. He patted his pockets and examined his revolver. It was like going to a mine. There was no time to go and look for anything when the action began.

He saw himself reflected in the glass of the keys' case on a bulkhead. Even in this light he looked pale. His hair protruded from either side of his cap, too long by naval standards. His mother would be shocked.

He tilted his cap to a rakish angle and forced a smile.

'Piece of cake.'

Frazer bent over the compass and studied the luminous points with great care. He thought of his last ship, the graceful *Levant*, with her up-to-the-minute chartroom, gyro compass and all the latest radar to make navigation easier. But his father's voice seemed to push the thought aside as he had once said scornfully, 'One shot through their wiring systems and they're as helpless as mice in a trap. Give me an old magnetic compass and a quick mind any time.' The old man had trained him well and it was standing him in good stead now.

Frazer straightened his back and looked at the sky. Still a lot of cloud about. It had made fixing their position difficult. But with luck they should be ready to alter course for the little island yacht haven bang on time. He examined his feelings and discovered that he was quite proud of what he had done.

He almost fell over Ives's legs as he sprawled asleep against the flag locker. Poor Ives, he had had to order him off the wheel, to hand over to a spare seaman so that he could rest. When they made their final approach the coxswain would have to be at his best. Frazer smiled to himself. Ives had made the boat something personal. Like the proper navy.

Frazer thought of Lynn Balfour and the man she had lost, whom she still loved. Why not put her out of his mind. It was more than likely she would turn away from another similar association to the one which killed her lover. But she did telephone him. She had – Frazer stiffened as he heard Goudie's footsteps on the bridge gratings. He always wore the same old scuffed sea boots. They must have seen as much action as their owner. He did not belong in this century, Frazer thought. He would have been right at home in the sailing navy, or as the skipper of a privateer.

Goudie joined him by the glass screen and peered at the thrusting arrowhead of the forecastle. Only the occasional necklace of white spray from the stem revealed the division between hull and water.

'On time, Pilot.' It was a remark but sounded like a question.

Frazer said, 'I'm satisfied, sir.'

Goudie was not listening. Frazer smiled. *As usual.*

Then Goudie said, 'I wanted a second boat to replace Able Two, you know.'

Frazer waited, and guessed that was why Goudie had gone ashore immediately they had moored in Tunis.

Goudie said, 'Needn't have bothered. Lot of bloody fools, mental pygmies. You'd think I was trying to arrange a pleasure cruise the way those staff wallahs carried on.' His fist beat a slow time on the screen and Frazer could feel the driving power of the man. Like a fever.

'Prothero's gone back to the UK and Creeping Jesus with him.' Frazer hid a grin. That must be Captain Heywood. 'If I could have raised the Boss he might have fixed something.'

Frazer asked, 'Is he that good?'

Goudie shrugged. 'He still wants to play it all by the rules. Like cricket. But then he's always been like that.'

Frazer was lost. 'You knew him before the war, sir?'

Goudie turned and stared in the darkness. 'He used to write boys' adventure yarns, didn't you know that? Called himself Spindrift.' He shook his head with mock sadness. 'You colonials have sadly neglected your education!' His mood changed again. 'I shall be in the chart space if you need me. Change the lookouts every half-hour. Eyes begin to accept danger or imagine things after a stint of this stuff.' He strode away, pausing only to examine the compass. He had said nothing about Ives asleep in one corner of the bridge. He delegated his authority, Frazer thought, and set the same standards as he accepted himself. What had Goudie been or done before the war? He chuckled and saw a lookout turn his head. Prothero, *Boys' Own Paper*. It fitted him like one of his own characters.

Shadows moved on the cramped deck and around the gun mountings. Archer up forward with the two-pounder, Ryder aft with the secondary armament and depthcharges, with Allenby ready to take over from any of them. Four officers and twelve hands. All chiefs and few Indians.

He heard Ives give a gentle snore, and wished he too could flop down somewhere and sleep. But it would be a long night. There was still a chance that the plan might be changed or cancelled altogether. He wondered how he would feel if Jupiter was called off. He must be raving mad to feel disappointment, but in his heart knew that was how it would be.

He stretched and groaned. Time to make another check.

He came up with a jerk as he recalled the Italian general who had met his father, who had sailed with him aboard the *Onondaga*. Goudie had told him what would happen to Tesini if the plan went wrong. But suppose Goudie ordered him to pull the trigger, how could he?

He was still brooding over it when Allenby mounted the ladder to relieve him for some hot cocoa.

Frazer's head jerked up and he realized with disbelief that he had fallen asleep on his feet. In spite of the slow, unsteady motion, despite everything that experience and the navy's discipline dictated.

A seaman said, 'W/T, sir.'

Frazer lurched to the voicepipe. It must have been that which had roused him.

'What is it, Sparks?'

'Picked up a transmission, sir. Couldn't make it out. German I think. Quite close.'

'Bloody hell!' Frazer grappled with the news, his mind clear and icy again. 'Keep a good listening watch, I'll tell the CO.' He did not need to, Goudie was already there.

'Sparks has picked up – '

Goudie nodded briskly. 'Yes. I heard. So much for intelligence reports.' He was thinking aloud. 'How far now?'

'Should sight the island in forty-five minutes, sir. Sooner if the clouds clear.'

Goudie's shadow leaned back as he stared at the sky. 'They won't. Pass the word. Absolute silence on the upper deck, and tell the Chief not to fling any spanners around. Not like the Krauts to poop off signals even in these waters. They must feel pretty safe, wherever they are.'

Their eyes met in the darkness and Frazer said, 'They must be there on the island.'

Goudie rubbed his chin. 'If so, they could have the jump on us. On the other hand, that's a double reason for their not transmitting on W/T.'

The voicepipe squeaked again and the lookout said, 'No more signals, sir.'

Goudie grunted. 'That settles it. We'll go straight in.' Frazer waited. Goudie had intended to lower their one small boat with Allenby aboard to sniff out the land and lead the way. 'The yacht haven was reported clear, but the enemy may have mined the area since the last report.' Goudie continued in the same unemotional tone, 'Issue extra automatic weapons immediately. We may have to fight off an attack, or shoot our way out of the place.'

Frazer saw Ives's powerful shoulders silhouetted against the clouds. Back on the wheel. Ready for anything. It was strange when you thought about it. Ives had had less seatime and experience of this kind of thing than anyone. And yet he seemed to radiate a sort of confidence that was infectious.

Goudie said softly, 'It may mean that General Tesini has been a bit dicey if the Jerries are already onto his little game.' He did not sound troubled; it was just another problem to be solved.

Frazer considered what would happen if the enemy knew exactly what was going on. They would all be dead within the next few hours.

Every movement and sounds of feet had stopped on the bridge and each gun mounting. They all knew. Guns would be cocked, ears straining to catch the first hostile sound.

Goudie said, 'One thing, Pilot, we've got to knock out that radio, chop bloody chop.' He lapsed into silence again.

The deck yawed and plunged and Frazer knew they were barely able to keep steerage way with the engines throttled down to their minimum revolutions. In open sea they could outpace any other vessel, even the deadly E-Boats, but here, inshore of an invisible landfall, they were like a cripple.

He peered over the screen and saw the nearest machine guns moving warily from side to side. That was Weeks. It seemed a lifetime since he had met him and Allenby with his jeep. In the gloom he could see the trailing snakes of ammunition belts, with more close by for instant reloading. Up forward the slender two-pounder was also training slightly from bow to bow. That was Leading Seaman Sullivan. What was it between him and Ives? Their dislike for one another was almost physical.

Archer was there too, hidden in the shadows, using his glasses to watch for the first hint of land. If they got into the yacht haven without trouble Archer was to remain with the boat. Goudie had mentioned it casually although he had previously detailed Ryder for that. Ryder was after all more used to the MGB than any of them. Goudie knew Archer's qualities and his failings. Did he see something different in Archer? Perhaps the air attack and the suddenness of the other boat's destruction had been one load too much for him.

'Bridge! Land in sight, port bow.'

The night glasses lifted as one and Goudie said, 'Good navigation, Pilot.' He sounded husky, but Frazer was more surprised by the compliment. Goudie must be slipping.

All at once the island was upon them. It seemed incredible that it could be so near and yet remain unseen until now. Frazer knew it was a normal trick with night vision but it made the closeness of danger all the more stark.

'Stand by all guns.' Goudie stood on the gratings with both hands gripping the screen. 'Not a bloody sound from anyone, right?'

'Signal, sir!'

Goudie gave what sounded like a sigh. 'Wait for repeat.'

Frazer listened to the growl of the engines and their echo

thrown back from the land like another vessel. It sounded deafening, but again he knew it was the usual illusion.

He saw the short stammer of Morse from a torch and heard Goudie say, 'Seems all right. Acknowledge.'

Frazer flashed his torch briefly over the side of the bridge. It was wrapped around with a piece of bunting, but quite bright enough. Too bright if there were any sentries about.

Goudie said, 'Very well. Stop main engine. Slow ahead port and starboard outer. Stand by with heaving lines, but *don't drop your guard*, any of you!'

Two seamen vaulted over the side as a wooden jetty loomed out of the blackness, their rubber shoes soundless as they ran to secure a mooring line. The two-pounder and several light automatics covered their every move, but apart from a motionless figure in battledress they might have had the whole island to themselves.

Goudie with Frazer beside him climbed down to the pier. After all the hours of creeping progress and the sickening motion it took both of them several moments to get their balance.

Goudie peered at the man who had signalled with his torch. He was hung about with ammunition, and carried a German sub-machine gun in the crook of his arm. It was just possible to see a corporal's chevrons on his battledress blouse.

'Is everything all right?' Goudie sounded very calm, but Frazer had come to know it was a carefully rehearsed act.

The soldier nodded. 'Major Thomas is with the Italian general now.'

The soldier had a slight accent, not unlike Thomas's when he had lost his temper on Sicily.

He added, 'There are Germans here. They have a boat on the other side of – ' He struggled for the right word and then pointed vaguely into the darkness where a jutting headland was still in total darkness.

Goudie snapped, 'What kind of boat, man?'

The soldier looked at him but his expression was invisible.

He replied coldly, 'Transport,' the slightest hesitation, 'sir. They are here to remove some of the general's things.'

Frazer gave a silent whistle. This was cutting things a bit too fine for comfort.

Goudie said, 'Well, this boat has a radio. It must be silenced. Right now.' He looked at Frazer. 'Clear the boat, all except for the engineroom chaps. Tell the Chief to make certain his men have their Stens with them at all times. Archer will remain in command. He can keep three ratings. I want the rest up here double quick. Tell Allenby to bring his bag of tricks.'

The soldier watched impassively as the seamen scampered along the pier. He said, 'There is a telephone in that hut. It connects with the general's house.'

Frazer's eyes were growing accustomed to the gloom and he saw the long, pale outline of a motor yacht, covered from stem to stern with a tailormade tarpaulin. The general was a rich man still. Influential too, not to have had his boat commandeered by the navy.

Goudie tapped his boot impatiently as Ives marshalled his small landing party into order.

He asked, 'What is Thomas doing?'

'*Major* Thomas is explaining matters to the general, sir.'

Goudie unbuttoned his holster. 'What country do you come from?'

The soldier shrugged. 'I am sorry, sir. I am not allowed to reveal that.'

Goudie swung away. 'Bloody cloak-and-dagger heroes!'

Frazer could not help grinning even though his heart was pumping against his ribs. Goudie sounded just like *Levant*'s skipper.

Goudie led the way along the pier. From what the taciturn soldier had said it seemed as though the Germans were uninterested in anything but collecting Tesini's personal belong-ings. Either he had fallen out of favour or more likely he was needed on the mainland in the event of an Allied invasion.

Goudie said quietly, 'Hardly anyone lives here. Just a few peasants on the other side of the island, and the rest work for Tesini and the estate. All right for some, eh?'

The house was easy to see despite the surrounding darkness. It was white, with a long driveway which was as straight as a ruler and lined with matched trees like ghostly soldiers.

One of Thomas's men lay beside a marble statue, a Bren gun covering the gardens. He did not look up as they passed. There was something unreal about Thomas's raiders. Frightening and somehow alien.

The Germans had overrun and enslaved so many countries, these men could be from any one of them. They had good cause to fight this secret war. To hate.

Nearer to the pillared entrance lay another figure. It was a dead German, some broken plates and dishes scattered around him. An army orderly probably, Frazer thought. Killed like an animal as he had been going about his domestic duties. He could smell the blood, and wanted to soak his hands and face in one of the nearby fountains.

Frazer stood by the door and felt Ives close behind him. Their guide stood aside and Frazer pushed open the double doors. More darkness, although he did not know what he had been expecting. Suddenly a gun barrel jabbed hard into his ribs and a hand deftly removed his pistol from its holster.

Then Major Thomas's voice said, 'Close the doors. Put the lights on.'

The sailors crowded into an ornate hallway, and the soldier who had removed Frazer's gun so easily stood grinning at him.

Thomas said, 'Give it to him.'

Frazer took the revolver and said, 'Try that again, and I'll flatten you.' He was surprised that he sounded so calm.

Thomas looked at Goudie. 'Only one boat?' It sounded like an accusation.

Goudie nodded. 'We'll manage.'

'You know about the Germans?' Thomas glanced up at the ceiling as someone dragged furniture across a room.

Goudie said, 'Lieutenant Allenby will deal with them.'

'Allenby, eh?' Thomas raised his eyebrows. 'A strange choice.'

Frazer shifted restlessly. Why didn't they get on with it? Someone from the German boat might come to the house at any moment. Even if they could outfight them, they could not prevent a signal from being sent. It would be a hornets' nest in a matter of hours.

Thomas continued, 'It seems that the general is being recalled to some new post. He may suspect that he is mistrusted. He will not say. But he remains firm about his conditions.' He watched one of his men carrying a satchel of papers towards the door. 'There were three Germans with the general. One you probably passed. The second was killed as he tried to reach the sea. The third is being questioned. There may be things we should know.' He straightened his belt. 'Come, meet the general.' He gave a brief sardonic smile. 'He imagines he can give us orders.' It seemed to amuse him.

General Gustavo Tesini made an imposing figure. He was tall and heavily built but because of his height looked perfectly proportioned in his immaculate green uniform. His hair was grey, and his small pointed beard was white-tipped and looked as if it was regularly combed to keep it perfect. When he spoke his voice suited him. Deep and resonant. He was even jovial as he said to Frazer, 'Just like your father!' He shook his hand warmly. Frazer noticed that his eyes were small and sharp, like Prothero's. There was no other similarity.

Goudie said, 'I have only one boat, General. You had better take only essential possessions with you. How many people do you have?'

The general looked at him gravely. 'I am speaking to your lieutenant.' It sounded like a reprimand.

Thomas snapped, 'I shall be with the other prisoner.'

He went out, deliberately turning his back on the general and slammed the door behind him.

Tesini said slowly, 'A coarse fellow.' He gathered his thoughts again. 'My wife is here, and my youngest son. A few servants, but they are of no account now. They will remain here.'

Frazer watched him curiously. A friend of his father's. He doubted very much if Bill Frazer would care much for the man now. He recalled suddenly what Allenby's father had said when they had been talking together. War brings out the best and the worst in people. But it doesn't change them. Whatever it is has always been there, waiting for the right moment.

God, it was true enough of the people he had met in the past months, he thought.

Goudie asked, 'The German prisoner, is he an officer?'

The general shook his head. 'Unhappily no. It is in fact a young woman from the army secretariat. She is an interpreter, among other things, and was sent with me to select certain papers that might be considered secret.'

Frazer looked away. What could she know which would be of any use? He thought of Thomas's face and guessed it would make no difference what she knew.

The general leaned backwards and his beautiful polished boots squeaked on the carpet. 'A distasteful affair.'

Goudie said, 'We shall remain here throughout the day. But first we must get rid of that damned radio. Then at dusk we leave.' He looked at Frazer and said, 'Go and see if Allenby's doing his stuff.' His eyes said that, as far as he was concerned, the general was not worth the risk and the loss of Able Two.

Frazer gestured to Ives and they left the house, pausing by a trickling fountain to get their bearings.

Ives watched as Frazer soaked his handkerchief in the water and dabbed it on his face and throat. It was getting light already and he could see patches of paler sky between the low clouds. This was harder to get used to than danger, he thought. Surrounded by trees and sweet-smelling flowers, statues and fountains, while two Germans lay dead and others were aboard their boat no more than a hundred yards away at a guess.

Frazer said, 'No sign of Lieutenant Allenby. He must be near the boat by now.'

'Rather him than me, sir.'

Frazer said, 'He'll be all right. He's a real wizard.'

They both spun round as a piercing scream cut through the damp air to be cut short as if someone had slammed a soundproofed door.

Frazer whispered, 'God Almighty!'

Ives looked at him. 'Look, sir, we can't just stand here and do nothing?' He was pleading.

Frazer wiped his mouth with the back of his hand. He felt clammy, unclean.

'No, we bloody can't.'

Frazer dragged out his revolver. 'Can you use one of these things?'

Ives followed him through some bushes. There was no time to tell Frazer that he had twice been pistol-shooting champion in the Job. The revolver, which looked like a toy in his fist, was much like the one he had trained with in the Met. You could not trust automatics. They jammed. With a revolver you just kept pulling the trigger. Crude but efficient.

He replied, 'Yes, sir. I've done a bit.'

9

Friends or Foes

Allenby removed his cap and very slowly raised his head above some ragged bushes. It was difficult to fix your position in the darkness, he thought for the hundredth time. The ground sloped towards the sea and was rough and uneven underfoot. Almost volcanic. The occasional clump of bushes afforded some cover and he heard Weeks sucking in air after their sprint from the MGB.

'Jerry's not too bothered,' he said softly.

Weeks crawled up beside him and they both listened to the sad, lilting voice of a German singer. Either a gramophone or one of the boat's crew must have tuned into a friendly station on the radio.

It seems so strange, almost more unnerving than what he had to do.

He glanced at Weeks. 'Ready?'

The seaman nodded. 'We stick 'em up, and then truss 'em like chickens. I've got some cord with me.'

Allenby raised his head again. He could see the faint shimmer of the sea, and a sturdy black shadow beside the little landing stage. Not a warship anyway. That would have finished everything. He felt the explosives in his pockets. Like fat cigars. But deadly.

There were no sentries, unless someone was lying down and that seemed unlikely. They obviously felt pretty secure, he decided.

A slow breeze rustled through the bushes and stirred a

great carpet of wild flowers. Millions of poppies, like Armistice Day in England.

He screwed up his face to gather his thoughts. He must be more tired than he had thought to allow his mind to wander, now of all times.

Weeks hissed, 'What was that?'

Allenby turned his head. Someone crying out? He replied, 'Disturbed gull, I expect.' He made up his mind. 'Let's go.' He drew his revolver and heard Weeks cock his tommygun. He said, 'Keep close to me, and try to stay on the hard ground.'

'Something wrong, sir?'

Allenby bit his lip. *Edgy.* Or was it the old instinct which had saved his life more than once in those abandoned buildings with their telltale parachutes.

'I'm not sure – ' They both turned as feet grated on the rough ground and a running figure hurried towards them. It was Ryder. Allenby had purposely left the young sub-lieutenant in the rear. He was their only link with Goudie, and if things went wrong like the last time, Ryder's reactions might be vital. Allenby had also left him behind for another reason. He had had plenty of experience with the Special Boat Squadron, but not at this kind of thing.

Allenby called out as loud as he dared. 'Get back, you bloody idiot!'

Ryder exclaimed, 'A scream! Did you hear – ' He got no further. There was a gentle click and something shot into the air from a clump of poppies where Ryder was crouching.

Allenby threw himself against Weeks and together they tumbled headlong into the bushes.

The bang was earsplitting and Allenby held his breath as steel fragments cut above their bodies and cracked into the ground. It had been only seconds and yet Allenby found he could recall each horrific detail. There must have been a wire, and Ryder had triggered it with his foot. The bomb was probably like the 'butterflies' as they were nicknamed. They could even be dropped from aircraft, but once they touched the ground they opened their wings and lay in wait for the merest touch.

Ryder writhed on his back and sobbed, 'Oh God! Oh God, *help me*!' Each word was torn from his lips as the agony mounted.

Allenby said, 'Come on, Weeks. Our only chance, *now*!' Weeks stared at Ryder, unable to move.

'Leave him.' Allenby pulled out one of his explosives and ripped off its safety tape. 'They'll do for all of us otherwise.'

He hated his words and shouted, 'We'll be back, David!' Another figure ran down the slope and Allenby sobbed with relief. 'Put a dressing on him!' Even in the gloom he knew it was Leading Seaman Sullivan.

Then with Weeks close behind him he bounded towards the landing stage.

Sullivan watched them go and then crouched down beside the groaning officer.

Ryder gasped, 'Hit my leg.' He clenched his teeth to hold back a scream. '*Oh my God!*'

Sullivan tugged out his pack of dressings and felt the young officer's body with his hands. He was bleeding from at least two bad wounds. Sullivan swallowed hard and retched as he touched Ryder's leg. Except that there was no leg. Just a mangled stump which pumped out blood in time with Ryder's desperate cries.

He would not last long, Sullivan thought. But he said, 'There, sir, nice an' comfy. That should do it.'

Then he held Ryder tightly in his arms until he died.

With the explosion still ringing in his ears Allenby dashed onto the landing stage and heard shouts from the moored vessel's deck. The boat had a heavy-looking hull and tall funnel. An old tug, or perhaps a pilot cutter, he thought wildly.

Two heads appeared above the bulwark and Allenby flung

his cigar-shaped bomb over the rail. There was a short, vicious explosion and the heads vanished.

Allenby ran up a short brow and fired his revolver as a another figure moved in the shadows. Instead of hiding the man threw up his hands in surrender.

Weeks was aboard now, his tommygun swinging round to cover a hatchway.

Even as they stood stockstill facing their first prisoner Allenby heard the sudden stammer of Morse.

'This way!'

He slammed through a screen door and saw a strip of light beneath an inner compartment. It was the radio room.

'Keep clear.' He ran forward and tried the door but it was locked. How urgent and threatening the Morse sounded. Allenby took a small bomb from his other pocket. No bigger than a packet of duty-frees with just a three-second fuse. He triggered the plastic catch and tossed it to the bottom of the door and ran. He was almost lifted from his feet by the blast as dust and smoke funnelled out across the deck.

Weeks peered at him anxiously. 'You OK, sir?'

They turned and waited for the telegraphist to stop screaming, then Allenby made himself walk back to the radio room. The set was smashed, and its operator, who had lost his life trying to summon aid, had been hurled against a bulkhead. The white paint was smeared with blood where he had slithered down to the deck. Allenby looked at the man's bulging eyes. It was as if they still lived. There was not much left of him below the waist.

Weeks said, 'Two dead on deck, sir. What do we do with Jerry here?' He moved the muzzle of his tommygun. 'Shall I –'

'No. There must be others.'

They found a German petty officer and three more sailors hiding in the forecastle. They seemed too old for the German navy, and Allenby guessed they were probably the boat's original crew, in uniform for the duration of the war. They obviously thought that the boat was under attack by a much larger force. For them the war was over, unless Goudie decided to leave them behind. Or to kill them as Weeks had been quite prepared to do if so ordered. They found a boatswain's store with a steel door and herded the small crew inside. As Allenby snapped a padlock in place he said, 'If they've any sense they'll stay quiet until their chums get here.'

Weeks watched him curiously. 'I hope the bugger didn't get a signal off, sir.'

They left the boat, now deathly quiet, but taking on shape and personality in the growing light.

Sullivan was still on the hillside with Ryder's body nearby. In the uncertain light Allenby saw the darker patch of poppies where Ryder's blood had made a wide stain.

'We'll take him to the house.'

He picked up Ryder's cap. The stained seagoing one with the tarnished badge of which he had been so proud.

'Sorry, David.' He started as the other two looked at him. He had imagined he was speaking only to Ryder and himself.

Nearer to the fine house, where the rough ground submitted to green lawns and terraces, Allenby turned and looked at the sea. It could have been a beautiful view, he thought.

Today I killed three human beings. He thrust the revolver into its holster and gave a deep sigh. Aloud he said, 'So what?' but the first thought remained like an epitaph.

As Frazer kicked open the door and burst into the room the group of figures froze motionless like some terrible tableau.

Several of Thomas's men in their unmarked battledress were standing around a chair beneath the only light in the room. The girl was tied to the chair, her arms pulled back so tightly that her wrists were raw. She was completely naked, her face and body bruised, a bright thread of blood running from one corner of her mouth.

Ives held his revolver ready to fire, but his eyes recorded everything. The girl was young, her hair dark in the hard glare. There were smears of blood on her thighs; she had very likely been raped as well as beaten.

Major Thomas glared at them. 'What the *hell* do you think you are doing?' He jerked his head. 'Get on with it.'

One of his men was smoking a black cheroot and suddenly reached out and seized the girl's right breast with his hand. He squeezed it so hard that she squirmed with agony, her eyes rolling up to the ceiling. With the nipple pinched out between his fingers and thumb the man held the cheroot's glowing end within an inch of it.

'She knows something.' Thomas watched as another of his men screwed his fingers into the girl's hair to force her to look as the cheroot moved slowly onto her nipple.

Frazer bounded across the room and brought the barrel of his revolver down with such force on the man's wrist that the bone snapped like a carrot.

Frazer's sudden move broke the spell. The girl's head fell forward and she gasped repeatedly, as if she was sobbing without making a sound.

Frazer said, 'Release her, Now.'

Thomas snapped, 'What the hell do you expect? My men know what the Germans do to their prisoners. This Nazi bitch probably knows something. I will bet you she is quite used to writing down confessions of our people as they are interrogated'.

Frazer tried to keep his voice level. He was shaking with anger and disgust. He knew he would have shot the torturers if Ives had not intervened.

'You make me sick. You wear our uniform, but you foul it with your cruelty, your hate!'

Ives had untied the girl and caught her as she fainted. With

infinite care he carried her into an adjoining room and then
stopped dead as an explosion shook the building.

Frazer exclaimed, 'That's too loud for Allenby. Too near!'

Ives laid the girl on a bench and then went back to pick
up her uniform jacket. The rest of her clothes lay in a pile.
They looked wet and stank of urine. Thomas stared at him,
his face expressionless. Minutes passed in an uncomfortable
silence. Then suddenly the doorway filled with faces. Goudie
said, 'Go and help the others. Allenby's knocked out the
boat's crew, but Archer phoned from the yacht haven to say
the bastards got off a W/T signal.'

He watched Ives and looked at the girl in the other room.

'Christ, Thomas, you've gone too far.' He swung round.
'Ryder's bought it, by the way. Loosed off a mine of some
sort. It seems as if Jerry intended to mine the whole coastal
strip above the landing stage and the beach.'

Thomas stared at him, his eyes blazing. 'You see? She
probably knew. I would have got it out of her!'

Goudie pushed his pistol into its holster. 'Doesn't make
much difference now, does it?' He looked round the room
as if seeing it for the first time. The blood on the chair, the
fouled uniform and the girl's underwear. 'You enjoy your
work, don't you, *Major*?'

Allenby came into the room. He looked tired and even
paler than usual.

'The boat's out of commission, sir.' He saw where the girl
had been tortured and said dully, 'Ryder heard a scream. He
was coming to warn me when he set off the bomb. But for
that he and three German sailors would still be alive.' He
looked at Thomas and added unsteadily, 'If you are an ally
I think maybe I'm on the wrong side, you bastard!'

Goudie snapped, 'That's enough from all of you. Post two
sentries, one on the top of the house. Good view from there.
We shall lie low today and leave at dusk, maybe earlier. I've
told Archer to camouflage the MGB with yacht tarpaulins
in case some spotter plane comes looking. Thank God they

can't land here. There'll be ships soon enough if the signal
was understood.' His face lost some of its sternness and he
said, 'You did well, Allenby. You all did.' He looked at Ives.
'Get one of the maids to help you with the German girl. I'm
putting you in charge of her.'

To Frazer he said, 'Return to the boat and see that the
general's gear is stowed where it will not be in the bloody
way, right?'

He looked at Thomas's men. 'And get these vermin out
of my sight until we leave.'

Able Seaman Weeks asked, 'What about Mr Ryder, sir?'

Goudie pulled out his tobacco pouch and pipe. 'Bury him
in the garden. It's the best we can do for him. Some part of
a foreign field and all that stuff.' He looked at Frazer. 'I
could do with a drink.' He tried to smile. 'I think we all
could. Tell Archer to break out some tots for the chaps, and
gin for us.'

He strode away without even a glance at Thomas.

Frazer looked at Allenby. 'Glad you made it, Dick.' The
grin would not come. 'Again.'

In the next room with the door tightly closed Ives took a
warm facecloth and began to wipe away the smears of blood
from the girl's limbs while the Italian maid watched from a
safe distance.

The girl groaned and then opened her eyes. Ives saw the
instant terror as her memory returned. She looked as if she
would have a complete collapse. She saw what he was doing
and her hands darted down to cover herself.

Ives laid her uniform jacket across her thighs and said,
'You have nothing to fear. Trust me.' His voice was low and
somehow soothing. He felt her flinch as he reached up to
dab away the blood from her bruised mouth. He did not
hesitate but kept dabbing and then wringing out the cloth in
the maid's bowl of warm water. Slowly, very slowly he
sensed that she was relaxing although her eyes remained wide
and desperate.

Ives had dealt with dead and injured women before. Road accidents, air raids, or after pub brawls, but nothing like this. She had a lovely face, and her body, in spite of the cuts and angry bruises, made his stomach turn over.

He made himself keep talking, 'Sorry I don't speak German, miss. But you're an interpreter, I believe?' He felt her quiver again as he brushed the hair from her eyes. She made him feel clumsy and helpless at the same time.

'I'll get you some food presently, but first you must try and rest.'

She leaned forward and covered her breasts with the towel.

'Don't leave, *please*.' She glanced at the door, her eyes filled with fear. 'Those men – '

Ives said, 'They'll not harm you again. I'll see to that.'

She studied his features and then the ribbon on his cap with its lettering HMS upon it. 'Navy,' she said.

Ives nodded sadly, 'S'right, miss. Long way from home.'

She frowned. 'Please?'

'Just a joke.'

The door opened and Allenby entered, a mug in his hand. 'Here, 'Swain. Some brandy from the general's cellar.' He tried not to look at the girl's naked limbs and was ashamed of his embarrassment. He saw the bruises and had heard one of the seamen saying the girl had been raped. She had dark hair, something like Joanna's. How would he feel if she had been tortured and violated?

Ives held the mug to her lips. 'Drink on this side, miss, I'll keep it away from the cut.'

She looked at Allenby. 'Thank you, Herr Oberleutnant.'

Allenby remained pale but could feel himself beginning to flush. Then he hurried from the room.

'You work with him?'

Ives wrung out the cloth and nodded. 'Yes, miss. He's not a bad sort. For an officer, that is.'

She reached out impulsively and touched his wrist. 'Thank you for what you did. I was very afraid. They hurt me. So

much they hurt me. I have never been with a man before,
you understand? They laughed at me, held me while they
took me.' She began to sob, the tears running down her
throat and breast.

Ives covered her with a blanket and pulled it up to her
chin.

He said, 'I'll be over there in the corner if you need me,
see?' He saw her nod and gave her his handkerchief. 'Have
a good blow.'

She did not understand his words, but her eyes showed
she knew what he meant.

As Ives slumped down in an armchair she added softly, 'I
shall never forget. *Never*.' But Ives was already fast asleep.

The day was the longest Frazer could remember. Although
Ryder and the dead Germans had been buried the place
seemed to smell of death.

He had seen the general several times and had been
incensed by the man's total lack of regret or uncertainty. If
his German allies arrived and prevented his escape he would
probably proclaim he was being kidnapped, taken prisoner.
The dead German sailors would give weight to that. If he
survived, he would not lose either.

There were several false alarms during the day. Aircraft
had been sighted, but they had passed well clear of the islands
and were obviously not searching or patrolling.

As the afternoon arrived and Archer reported that all the
general's valuable possessions had been loaded into the
MGB's hull where even the smallest space could be found,
Allenby joined Frazer in one of the well-furnished rooms
which overlooked the terrace. Beyond it lay the sea. Blue
and sparkling, full of invitation.

Allenby said, 'I'll be glad to leave this place.' He looked
round t' e room and added bitterly, 'This is one target I
wouldn't mind blowing up!'

Frazer tried to break his despairing mood. 'Can't do that, Dick. One of our own brasshats will probably want to move into it shortly!'

'You really think so, Keith?' Allenby's eyes were rimmed with fatigue. 'I keep thinking about David. I should have guessed, warned him.'

Frazer eyed him anxiously. 'How could you? You know the score, David knew it too. It was *his* turn.' He shrugged. 'Let's just concentrate on getting out of here.' He turned as the sound of a piano filtered through the door. The general was playing, and Frazer had to admit that he was good at it.

Goudie banged into the room and hurled his cap onto a chair.

'We'll prepare to slip in two hours. Get General Tesini and his wife and son aboard thirty minutes before that. Put them somewhere safe, wherever that is. He's also decided to take a couple of servants after all.' He had a crumpled signal flimsy in his hand and he added savagely, 'There'll be no rendezvous with the submarine. We just had a signal. So it will be hell for leather all the way. Air cover will be provided as soon as possible.'

Frazer made a quick calculation. It would mean that Thomas and his men would be crammed aboard too. It would not be a happy trip, he thought.

Allenby asked, 'What about the prisoners, sir?'

'Leave 'em. It makes the whole thing look more convincing. They'll probably say they were outnumbered ten to one.' He grimaced. '*I* would in their position.'

He crossed to the window and stared emptily at the blue sea. 'By the way, the invasion is on. Operation Husky will begin the day after tomorrow.'

Allenby looked at Frazer. No wonder the high command did not want a submarine in the area as well. Any additional activity might delay things and prevent General Tesini from calling on his men to change sides.

Goudie said, 'The rest of the Italian servants will remain here. They will be no trouble.'

Allenby asked, 'And the other prisoner, sir?'

Something in his tone made Goudie stare at him. 'We'll leave her too. I know how you feel, but she *is* the enemy. She must be tied up securely when we leave, right?'

Allenby said, 'If I get out of this –'

Goudie smiled. 'Not if, *when*. Then you can do what you bloody well like, but we have a job to finish.' He clapped his cap on his unruly hair and marched out into the sunlight.

The withdrawal from the house and grounds was done in twos and threes. The servants had vanished into the kitchen and cellars, and the house assumed an air of tense expectancy.

Goudie stood by a telephone and spoke only briefly. Then he put it down and tore the wires from the wall.

To Allenby he said, 'Frazer's aboard. He's ready to proceed.' He sounded relaxed, as he had when they had left Gibraltar. He understood the sea. To him it was a friend.

Goudie saw Leading Seaman Sullivan by the door. 'Call the lookout down from the roof.'

Sullivan nodded. 'Aye, aye, sir.' He cocked his head to the passageway which led to an adjoining wing. 'Shall I tell 'Swain too, sir?'

'Yes. He's to tie up the prisoner right away.'

Sullivan hurried along the passageway, pausing only to snatch up a small silver clock from a little table. He glanced at it and decided it was worth a bit. He thrust the clock into his first-aid bag. There were bloodstains on it. Ryder's blood. He pushed open a door and saw Ives looking down at the girl as she drank from a cup.

Sullivan said curtly, 'The guv'nor's orders, 'Swain. Truss 'er up. We're leavin'.' He took a pace towards her. 'I'll do it.'

'Keep your hands to yourself! I can manage here!'

Sullivan peered at him and bared his teeth. 'Oh yeh?' But he recognized the danger and turned on his heel. He called, 'Don't know wot you're bothered about. She's a Kraut, like the others!'

The door slammed and in the sudden silence Ives could hear her forced breathing. She had fallen asleep on several occasions during the day. But each time she had awakened violently, as she had relived the nightmare of what had been done to her. Even when she slept, she had cried aloud in short anguished sentences. Ives wished he could understand German so that he could have helped in some way.

He asked, 'You heard what he said?

She stared up at him, her eyes searching his face. 'Yes. Must you tie me?' She was shaking again as if she had a fever.

He stopped beside her. 'I will not make it tight. But it will be better for you.' She did not understand and he persisted. 'If your people come, and they will very soon, they might think we had treated you better than the others. They might even believe – '

She nodded slowly. 'That is what they *will* believe.'

Ives picked up a length of cord, hating it and what he must do.

He said, 'The general's servants will take care of you. They are frightened.'

He knelt at her feet; the bare ankles were raw from being lashed to the chair in spite of the ointment he had got from the general's wife. He took one ankle in his hands. It felt smooth and cool although the air in the room was hot and oppressive. Or was it? *Is it me?* The general's wife had told him that the girl's name was Christiane. It seemed important that he should know it. What was the point? She probably believed that her country would win the war anyway. They might at that from some of the cockups he had seen. He tightened the cord and pushed his fingers between it and her leg, leaving it as loose as he could without making it obvious.

Once when she had been asleep she had almost rolled of her makeshift bed. It must have been a nightmare. Ives had eased her back again and had adjusted the blanket. But before he had done so he had seen her breasts again as the tunic had parted across them. He had wanted to touch them if only to wipe away the memory and ease the pain of the bruises.

As he got to his feet she held out her hands for him to tie them, but her eyes never left his face. She must have understood his indecision; perhaps she even knew what he had been thinking.

Ives stood back and looked at her. 'That should do it.'

She nodded. 'It does not hurt. Thank you.' Her eyes followed him as he put on his cap and buckled on his belt and holster.

Ives heard Goudie talking to Allenby and the clink of a glass. God help us if Goudie gets pissed now, he thought vaguely. That's all we need.

He made up his mind and returned to the chair. 'I – I'd like to ask you something.' Already he was feeling lost, stupid. 'It's just that I – '

She asked quietly, 'What is it? Tell me.'

Ives said desperately, 'I'd like to kiss you, Christiane. Before I go.'

She stayed quite still and silent, her lips slightly parted as she stared up at him.

Then she began to cry, her eyes shining with tears as she looked at him.

When he made to comfort her she said between sobs, 'Don't you see? You *asked*! You did not steal!'

Ives bent down and touched her cheek with his lips. She turned her head and their mouths came together for just a few seconds.

Ives touched her shoulder. 'Maybe one day – '

She shook her head. 'I shall not forget you.'

The door closed behind him and Ives strode past Sullivan without seeing him.

Alone in the room the girl called Christiane lowered her head and cried without restraint. Ives had saved her sanity. And now he was gone.

Allenby watched Ives as he walked along the passageway. He had never seen him look so grim and the realization pushed his own despairing thoughts aside.

'All right, 'Swain?'

Ives looked at him, his face slowly clearing, like a cloud passing away.

'Yes, sir. I suppose so.'

They both turned as Goudie clattered down a narrow stairway which led to a terrace on the roof.

'I've been shouting for you, Allenby!' He recovered himself and added in an almost matter-of-fact tone. 'We've got company. Come and see.'

They followed him up to the terrace. It was evening but the flagstones were still hot from the sunshine. The sky had changed again, more clouds, but tinged with pink, like fluffy lumps of coral.

Allenby hesitated as Goudie said, 'Stay where you are, both of you.'

Allenby saw the moored German vessel and thought suddenly of Ryder's terrible screams, of the faces above the boat's bulwark before they were blasted away by his bomb. He saw the black cross painted on the boat's foredeck, but nothing different.

Goudie said quietly, 'Not there. Look below the headland.'

Allenby felt his stomach muscles contract. Two black shapes motionless on the carelessly ruffled sea They must have come round the other side of the island, keeping inshore and out of sight.

Allenby found he was whispering. 'What are they?'

Goudie gave a short laugh. 'Oh, they're old friends of

mine. E-Boats.' No one would know that better than
Goudie. Allenby watched his profile to gauge his reactions
and their chances. If any.

Goudie said, 'They've anchored. It's very shallow there.
If they intend to enter the yacht haven or move closer to the
landing stage they may prefer to wait until daylight.' He
glanced at the clouds. 'It'll be dark soon anyway. My guess
is that they intend to stay where they are. They can cover
the landing stage as well as our hideout around the headland.
They won't know fully about us until they land a party to
investigate. But my guess is that they got the emergency
signal.'

He looked at Ives, his mind busy. 'Get back to the boat,
Cox'n. Tell Lieutenant Frazer we're leaving immediately.
Prepare the depthcharges, minimum setting.' He smiled
crookedly. 'Even with that it may blow our arses off.'

He watched as Ives strode away. 'Good hand, that one.'

Allenby said, 'Shall we fight them, sir?'

'If we do we'll lose, believe me.' He clapped Allenby's
shoulder, the first time he had offered such a gesture. 'We'll
catch them on the hop. Our only chance. They're anchored
half a cable apart. I intend to pass between them at full
throttle. How does that suit?'

Allenby shrugged. 'It'll be lively.'

'It will that.' He touched his holster. 'That girl. She can
tell the Germans everything about us.' He saw Allenby's face
and said quietly, 'No. Not my style.' He gave his sad grin.
' 'Sides which, Ives would never forgive me!' He quickened
his pace down the stairs and through the deserted house.

'Pity Creeping Jesus isn't here. It might do him good to
be around when one of his pet schemes falls apart!'

They saw the shadowed yacht haven and the motor
gunboat's black outline by the pier.

Allenby looked back but the house was hidden by the
sloping land. He thought of Ives and the girl, an enemy, he
was leaving behind. Of Major Thomas and of David Ryder

buried with only a muttered prayer in the general's garden. Of all the others who would die the day after tomorrow whether their scheme worked or not.

Goudie said sharply, 'Well, let's see what the little lady can do, eh?'

10

Last Chance

Lieutenant Commander John Goudie stood at the rear of the MGB's bridge, hands on hips as he watched the final preparations for leaving their mooring.

Frazer climbed to the bridge and saluted. 'All stowed, sir.'

Goudie smiled. 'Such formality all of a sudden.'

Frazer said, 'Force of habit, sir.' He thought of the packed hull beneath his feet. One burst of cannon shell through that lot and it would be like a slaughterhouse. 'I've put the general and his wife and son in the W/T cabin. I've crammed in the servants as well.' He tried to smile. 'No room for dancing, I'm afraid.'

Goudie watched him impassively. 'Makes sense. They'll have the galley directly forrard of 'em, the officers' heads and then the engines just abaft with the bridge right above. The wardroom isn't much but they're inboard of it, so they are as well protected from flying bits and pieces as they can be in this boat. Good show, Pilot.'

Frazer added, 'Major Thomas's men are mostly on the messdeck, although I put their Bren gunner down aft. We may need a bit of extra firepower.' He recalled the soldier with his wrist bandaged and tied to his chest, the one he had smashed down with his revolver such a short time ago. In his heart Frazer knew he would have shot him but for the need for silence. Poor David Ryder had made even that unimportant. The soldier had turned to look at him as a seaman had bustled him below. Frazer could not recall seeing such hatred on a man's face before.

Well, they all need *us* now, he thought.

A light blinked from the opposite side of the haven. Goudie had sent Archer and a seaman across to the headland with their tiny dory to keep an eye on the anchored E-Boats. He had already reported that the Germans had been calling up the transport vessel at the landing stage with a signal lamp. They must surely be wondering what was happening.

The telegraphist read the hesitant signal and said, 'Dinghy putting off from one of the E-Boats, sir.'

Goudie rubbed his chin. 'One of those rubber things. It'll take all of fifteen minutes.' He saw an overalled figure on the bridge ladder and snapped, 'All set to move, Chief?'

'Shiner' Wright, the ERA who controlled the MGB's power and machinery nodded. 'As I'll ever be, sir.'

Frazer had rarely seen the ERA, and wondered how it could be possible in such a small vessel.

'We'll go straight out as soon as Archer's aboard. We'll ditch the dory, there's enough bloody weight already.'

They had offloaded spare mooring wires, fresh water, canned food, anything that might knock a knot off their speed if they managed to get past the E-Boats.

Goudie eyed the Chief calmly, 'Good luck.'

Paddles splashed in the evening shadows and Frazer saw the dory coming alongside. There was a different mood in the boat, he thought. Subdued, even angry. It hung over them like a cloud.

Goudie said, 'Put your tin-lid on, Cox'n!'

Ives reached down for his steel helmet. He hated the thing, it reminded him of the Blitz on London. He was about to point out that nobody else was wearing one when Goudie added dryly, 'You are important and you won't be able to duck and dodge like the rest of us, right?'

Ives pulled the chinstrap into place. 'Right, sir.' His fingers brushed across his cheek as he recalled her tears, the taste of

salt on their lips when they had kissed. If anyone knew they
would laugh their heads off.

Goudie clambered over the forepart of the bridge and
stood on top of the small chartroom.

He did not have to raise his voice, it was like a tomb.
Anyway, the Germans were on the other side of that dark-
ening finger of land.

Allenby stood beside Frazer and watched as the dory was
kicked away from the side and Archer walked forward to the
two-pounder.

Goudie said, 'We will go out at full speed. Within minutes
after that we shall be in action. Now, gun crews, listen to
me. I know you've all been in combat several times, but in
the heat of battle even the veteran can forget. Remember
that E-Boats have steel hulls, not like our wooden jobs. So
concentrate on their upper decks and bridges. Maximum fire
to starboard as we shall be closing as near as possible to the
E-Boat on our port side.' He glanced aft, his calm features
and folded arms somehow impressive against the pink clouds.

'Depthcharge party, don't drop them until you get the
order.' He hesitated. 'That's all, lads. Good hunting.'

Frazer watched the faces of those nearest him. The
youthful telegraphist, Ives and the machine gunner below the
starboard wing of the bridge.

They couldn't have looked much different at Trafalgar or
Jutland, he thought.

Goudie's scarred boots landed on the gratings and he said,
'You go aft with the depthcharges and Oerlikons, Allenby.
And don't forget, they'll be feeling a bit low and thinking
of Ryder who would have been there with them.'

Frazer looked at Allenby. Was he noticing the astonishing
way Goudie seemed to be able to think of even the smallest
detail?

Allenby smiled. 'I'll see you later, Keith.'

Frazer touched his cap. 'You'd better. Keep your head
down.'

Goudie looked around the bridge. 'Let go forrard. Let go aft.' The lines snaked aboard and Goudie said, 'Bear off forrard!'

The MGB moved slowly away from the pier, pushing the abandoned dory and a drifting boathook aside as the gap of water widened between hull and land.

Frazer watched, waiting for the moment. It would be just their luck if the engines failed to respond in this unorthodox departure.

To Ives Goudie said, 'If the bridge is knocked out, take over until Mr Allenby can come from aft. This has to be done exactly right. There'll be no second chance.'

He took his unlit pipe from his slacks and jammed it into one corner of his mouth.

Frazer glanced at the land already in deep shadow by the slope which led to the general's house. He thought of the general's son as he had last seen him in the W/T cabin. A good-looking boy with dark, frightened eyes. One thing, he thought, if the worst happens they'll all go together. He heard Ives testing the helm and recalled the tender way he had picked up the girl's naked body and carried her away from her torturers' eyes. Protective. Or had it hit Ives so deeply that he would not get over it?

Goudie peered at his watch. Then he leaned over the central voicepipe.

'Chief? *Start up!*'

The engines roared into life as one, the air cringing to their din in the confined moorings. Petrol vapour fanned over the bridge and made one of the seamen burst into a fit of coughing. The hull was shaking wildly, ammunition and loose gear joining in the chorus with their vibration.

Goudie stared hard at the pointer of headland and waited until the drifting hull moved into line.

'Full ahead!'

The motor gunboat seemed to leap forward as if some invisible leash had been severed.

Within seconds the hull gathered speed, the bow waves surging away on either beam, the wake frothing from the triple screws in an angry furrow.

Frazer gripped the rail below the screen and felt the hull rise like a seaplane as the revolutions mounted and sent them hurtling towards the open sea. Spray deluged over the bows and rattled against the bridge like pellets.

Goudie did not turn his head and seemed to be yelling into the spray itself, 'This is more bloody like it!'

They tore as close to the headland as they dared and then swayed hard a-port as with startling suddenness the anchored E-Boats burst into view. Their dark silhouettes appeared to overlap, like two basking serpents on frosted glass. All these wild thoughts flashed through Frazer's mind as a solitary thread of red tracer tore across the sea towards them.

'Open fire!'

Goudie's voice was drowned by the instant rattle of Oerlikons and the heavier crack of the two-pounder. Then the pairs of machine guns added their earsplitting rattle, the tracers cutting across the surface and reflecting on the surging water like blood.

A voice yelled, 'Somethin' in the water! Port bow!'

Frazer tensed for a collision. At this speed anything solid could rip out the bottom.

It was the Germans' rubber dinghy, paddles stilled in mid-air as the armed sailors stared with horror at the onrushing MGB.

They hit the rubber dinghy a glancing blow but it was enough to capsize it in a welter of foam and staring faces, mouths like black holes, the screams drowned by the roaring engines.

Bullets raked across the hull and Frazer heard the windows of the chartroom shatter to fragments. A burst of cannon fire added to the bombardment and Frazer felt the deck jump as some of the steel hit home. The nearest E-Boat was end-on; she must have cut her cable and was already swaying in pale foam as her big Daimler Benz engines coughed into life.

Goudie yelled, 'Depthcharges! *Ready!*'

Shots cracked around the bridge and the White Ensign floated down like a ghost as tracer ripped through the halliards. The telegraphists ran to replace it, but Goudie seized him by the arm, 'We can fight without it, you young maniac!' But he was grinning. His face like a mask changing in colour in the reflected tracer and shell bursts.

The E-Boat came looming at them and Frazer saw several figures running to take cover as the little MGB tore alongside.

Goudie jabbed at the bell button by his elbow and they heard the metallic clatter as the depthcharges went over the side. There was a vivid flash on the starboard side and the barrel of a machinegun flew overhead before splashing into the sea. The remaining gun pointed at the sky, and pieces of the seaman who had seconds earlier been firing at the other E-Boat hung from the harness like bloody rags.

Two shining columns of water shot skywards as the depthcharges exploded.

One must have been really close, Frazer thought, and it looked as if the E-Boat had swayed almost onto her beam ends before she floundered upright again in a welter of spray and smoke. Frazer ducked as more tracer thudded into the mahogany planking. The MGB had been shaken like a rat when the charges had exploded. The E-Boat must have been badly holed at least.

But the other one was turning now, her moorings cast adrift as she swung in pursuit, her forward cannon pivoting to keep the MGB in its crosswires.

Goudie swore as more shots beat into the hull. 'He'll knock out the engines in a second!' He jabbed the button again and seconds later two more depthcharges exploded astern. But the German captain was an old hand at this

Coastal Forces trick. The big E-Boat rolled from side to side as she zigzagged around the telltale cascades of water.

'The after guns are out of action, sir!'

Goudie shouted, 'Get Weeks off the MGs and send him aft. It's our only chance.'

Frazer peered astern. 'He's not overhauling us, sir!' He was hoarse from shouting and from tension.

'Doesn't want to! He'll stand off until he lands a lucky shot.'

The twin Oerlikons opened fire again and Frazer pictured Weeks down there with Allenby. He was glad they were together.

The bridge screen appeared to jump over the side and bright starlike holes punctured the thin plating as a fresh burst of firing raked the upper deck like a bandsaw.

Ives yelled, 'Skipper's down, sir!'

Frazer leapt across the madly swaying bridge and caught Goudie around the shoulders. There was a lot of blood on his shirt, but his eyes were wide open as he gasped, 'Leave me! Get the boat out of this mess!'

Frazer propped him against the side and wondered briefly how he had escaped. Then he saw the young telegraphist sitting in the opposite corner by the ladder. His legs were thrust out and he appeared to be staring at his hands, which like red claws were clutching his stomach as if to contain his intestines. Mercifully his head dropped and he was dead. A shell must have passed right through him before cracking around the bridge in a whirl of splinters. But for him, Goudie would have taken the full impact.

Frazer reached the voicepipe and had to repeat himself twice before Wright answered him. God alone knew what it must be like down there. Every explosion, no matter whose, would sound like one about to burst in on them as they crouched between their thundering engines.

'Chief! I'm going hard to starboard! I need to bring her round in a tight turn!'

Wright replied, 'Ready when you are.'

Frazer looked around the bridge. Goudie was still conscious, his ears and eyes trying to guess what was happening. The telegraphist swayed with the boat, as if he were asleep, and the one remaining seaman was trying to bandage his knee where a flying sliver of wood had plunged into him like an arrow.

'Turner! Go aft and tell Mr Allenby I'm going to turn and engage! Drop the smoke floats!'

The man seemed to forget his pain and stared at Frazer before he staggered down the ladder. He had nearly cracked wide open, but the fact that Frazer had remembered his name in spite of everything seemed to steady him.

A chip of metal clanged away from Ives's helmet. He eased the spokes again, hating what was happening to the boat. He knew Goudie was staring up at him, remembering perhaps that but for his insistence that bit of German steel would be firmly inside his skull.

It could not last much longer. No boat could take this sort of punishment. The survivors might be landed back on that same island. Would he have to face the girl like that? Himself a prisoner?

With the sea surging across the narrow afterdeck whenever the boat changed course it was difficult to think as well as stand. Allenby clung to the injured seaman, their faces inches apart as he listened to Frazer's instructions.

The deck was shaking wildly and the screws were hurling great banks of water away like a gigantic fishtail. Allenby stumbled to the smoke-float release, and as it fell astern dipping and rearing in the wash he freed the second one and saw the vapour rise immediately in a ragged screen.

'Depthcharges! Cease firing, Weeks, and give me a hand! You too, Turner, you're not dead yet!'

Allenby tried to swallow but his mouth was raw from

gunsmoke and yelling orders. 'We ditch the lot! It's our last chance!'

Weeks stared past him at the great wall of smoke. They were moving so fast through the water it was difficult to accept that the sea and wind were so calm. The clouds were much darker now; within the hour it would be pitch black.

Weeks said aloud, 'Might as well be a bloody year!'

But Allenby was clinging to the depthcharge rack, his eyes watering as he peered at each setting. It would be a big bang. It might do for their own boat if she was not already sinking, he thought. She must look like a pepperpot.

He heard Frazer's voice carried aft from the bridge, the immediate change of sound as the starboard outer engine was stopped and then flung full astern as the rudder went hard over. Allenby held on with all his strength, with the injured seaman clinging to him and gasping with pain as the wood splinter caught against the rack.

Over and over, they would turn turtle, Allenby thought wildly. He saw the sea surging past the deck and then rising above it to sweep around their legs and the abandoned gun mounting. When he looked up the smoke had vanished and he stared at Weeks with utter disbelief. They had done it and were now tearing headlong towards the smoke.

The enemy captain might think they were trying to slip away with the smoke's aid in the hope of finally shaking him off in the darkness. If so, he was in for a shock. Surprisingly, Allenby threw back his head and roared with uncontrollable laughter. We shall all be in for a shock if we meet bows-on.

The others peered at him anxiously and probably thought he had gone round the bend.

He was still laughing as they plunged into the smoke, dazed and blinded as they waited for the first contact.

A flat-trajectory burst of tracer shells passed down the starboard side, bright fiery balls in the swirling smoke.

If he had wanted to the German captain could not have revealed his position better.

The bell jangled beside Allenby and he jumped, his laugh dying away as he and Weeks flung themselves on the charges. He found a split second to wonder if but for this he would not have been able to stop his crazy laughter.

The charges rolled from their racks; it took only seconds to release the others. Whoever had fitted the racks to the MGB must have known exactly what was expected of her.

Allenby's mind cringed as a towering white moustache of a bow wave rose out of the smoke, the E-Boat's forward cannon still firing on the same bearing. Where they would have found a ready target if Frazer had stayed on the same course. All caution was gone. The E-Boat was charging towards them at full speed. The MGB tilted over again and Allenby fell to the deck choking beneath a ton of water.

Pressed to the deck, his hands scrabbling for a grip, he felt the charges explode. Like hitting a mine. The hull seemed to leap beneath him and he heard a sudden high-pitched metallic whine from one of the shafts. If the Chief didn't stop it, the screw might chew its way through the bottom.

Weeks was shaking him, his face and body streaming with seawater.

The E-Boat was slowing down, and as she turned away from her enemy Allenby saw that she was beginning to list over, smoke pouring from her bows.

Weeks waved his hands in the air and cheered. Even the soldier with the Bren gun staggered to his feet and grinned at the E-boat with a mixture of disbelief and amazement.

Frazer's voice came aft to make everyone realize that it was not over.

'Come to the bridge, Dick!' Then to the boat at large he added, 'Bloody good show, lads! But Jerry will have screamed for help on his radio by now, so we must make tracks fast!'

Allenby reached the bridge and stared with dismay at the bullet and splinter holes, the great pattern of blood which even in the gathering darkness seemed to ripple in the deck's vibration. Someone had covered the telegraphist with some of his signal flags, and Allenby saw Ives on his knees putting a dressing on Goudie's shoulder while a spare seaman stood at the wheel. The first time Ives had left the spokes since their mad dash for the open sea.

Frazer wiped his face with a filthy handkerchief.

'Chief's had to stop the starboard outer. Something's running hot. He can't do otherwise.'

He watched his friend's pale and smokestained features.

'Are you OK?'

Allenby nodded. He felt light-headed. Sick.

Frazer said, 'We lost three killed, Dick. Three wounded, including the Skipper.' He hesitated. 'Archer's going round the guns and checking damage up here. Will you – ?'

Allenby nodded. 'Yes. I'll go below.' He glanced at the flag-covered body. 'Poor little Sparks,' he said absently.

He groped his way below, his ears picking up the uneven growl of engines. Their speed would be badly reduced, and Ives would have a hard job to hold them on course. Did this mean they would be caught and destroyed after all they had done? It was wrong. Unfair.

The ERA had got the pumps going and as he stopped at the foot of the ladder Allenby saw water trickling from the diagonal planking where shots had raked the side.

The W/T cabin was so full of people Allenby was moved in spite of his anger.

The general was jammed in one corner, his arms around his wife and son. The boy smiled at Allenby and then burst into tears. The servants stared at him as he clung to the doorway and Allenby guessed he must look like something recovered from the sea itself. He forced a smile. 'No one hurt?'

It was amazing how his smile and the sound of his voice seemed to restore them. They all began to speak at once, not that Allenby could hear much. His ears were still throbbing from the persistent gunfire.

He said, 'We'll try and get something hot to drink, eh?'

He saw them nod happily, accepting at last that they were still alive. Allenby had seen it so often. The carnage left after a stick of bombs or a mine that had exploded when someone like him had forgotten about the boobytrap.

A cup of tea. It always seemed to work like magic.

He pushed his way forward and peered into the galley. It had received a direct hit from a cannon shell. There would be no tea this time.

In the entrance to the messdeck he saw Major Thomas speaking with his corporal. It sounded like Polish, but they both changed to English as he appeared.

Thomas snapped, 'Is it finished?'

Allenby eyed him with dislike. 'Both E-boats knocked out, sir. Maybe one of them will sink.' He noticed the sudden pride that had crept into his voice. For the first time he realized what they had done together.

Thomas's expression did not alter. 'There are three dead here.'

Allenby passed him and saw the bodies by the mess table. There were several holes in the boat's side just above them through which water spurted like jets each time the bows dropped into a trough.

Most of the lights had been shaken into broken glass, but Allenby saw that one of the dead soldiers had his wrist in a bandage. Perhaps Keith Frazer would not have to face a court of inquiry after all. Considering what he had done he should get a bloody gong, he thought.

Thomas said, 'I should like to see the general.'

'I'll tell the bridge, sir. But everyone is to stay put until we've rearmed. When daylight comes I doubt if we'll be alone for long.' Thomas's curt indifference filled him with a new wave of anger. 'I suggest you put your men to work plugging holes. It's bad enough without having the bilges full of water.'

He turned his back and went back to the bridge. He had

purposely not told Thomas that Goudie was too badly hurt to continue in command. Thomas was insufferable anyway, without knowing he was in the charge of two lieutenants.

Frazer listened to his report and said, 'It's a bloody miracle that anyone made it.'

They turned as a halliard squeaked and saw a seaman hauling up the White Ensign again to the gaff.

The seaman looked at the two officers and shrugged. 'Sparks wanted to do it. Seems proper.'

Archer appeared and said wearily, 'The two-pounder's on manual control. It took a lump of steel as big as your fist.'

Weeks clambered onto the bridge with a tray of mugs.

Frazer asked, 'How did you manage it?'

Allenby took one of the mugs. 'It's not tea.'

It was neat rum which Weeks swore had been broken open from its store by a cannon shell.

Goudie opened his eyes and stared up at them. 'Tot for everyone, Weeks.' He tried to smile but the pain froze it on his lip.

Weeks got down beside him and said, 'You next, sir.'

Goudie coughed as the neat rum ran down his throat but managed to gasp, 'Just the ticket!'

The hands worked in silence throughout most of the night. The dead were tied in canvas and lashed to the empty depth-charge racks. As Leading Seaman Sullivan remarked, 'They won't feel the wet, not any more.'

Ives stood at the wheel, his eyelids sticking together with fatigue, his mouth still sore from the smoke. It was like being only part alive, he thought. Like an onlooker outside himself. Even when Goudie managed to speak to him he felt he could see himself too as he answered.

Frazer remained in the forepart of the bridge and sent Archer to the chartroom every so often to check his original calculations. In spite of all his grumbling Shiner Wright was working wonders. Even with only two screws in use they were making good, about eighteen knots. By first light they would be passing the final piece of Sardinian coastline. He thought of his last desperate attempt to knock out the E-Boat, his astonishment when she had swerved away, listing and probably damaged beyond repair. No matter what happened when daylight laid them bare, nobody could say they had not done the impossible. He grinned, his face cracking; miracles take a bit longer however.

He thought of Lynn Balfour. She would know about this. Perhaps she had been in the Operation Room with Prothero and the urbane Captain Heywood, the one Goudie disrespectfully referred to as Creeping Jesus.

Yes, she would be wondering about them. Fingers crossed. About him in particular perhaps.

Goudie's voice cut through his aching mind. 'Don't doze off, Pilot!'

Frazer nodded and thrust himself away from the screen. He had been nearly asleep standing up.

Allenby found an unopened case of dressings and did his best to patch up the wounded and to remove the vicious splinter from Turner's leg. It kept him busy and away from the dread of the dawn. He thought of the Wren called Joanna. When would she get his letter? Would she care?

As the first hint of light touched the clouds the weary, depleted company stood-to at action stations again.

Goudie seemed content to allow Frazer to rearrange his handful of men, but said, 'Put the wounded to work too, and bring one of the stokers up from the engineroom. They can all manage something, even if it's just praying!' It seemed to tire him and he fell into a restless sleep.

The sun showed itself for the first time and the eastern horizon was revealed like a bright steel tape.

The seamen fingered their weapons, and Archer stood very upright beside the two-pounder.

The growing light revealed the extent of their damage. Splinter holes and punctures in the bridge plating. There was also a lot of blood; it looked pink in the scuppers as the spray drifted back from the stem.

Above it all the ensign rippled in the breeze, clean and unnatural.

'Green four-five!' Weeks's voice made them jerk out of their thoughts. 'E-boats, three of 'em.'

There was a gap in the clouds and part of the sea was suddenly very bright and clear, like metal.

Goudie croaked, 'Get me up!' He twisted his head as the bells jangled through the boat. 'Give me a hand, damn you!'

Frazer raised his glasses and blinked as the glare came back from that patch of bright water. Then he saw them. They were moving slowly, in line abreast. Even as he refocused his glasses the other craft began to turn into line. They had sighted the MGB.

Frazer said, 'They're coming.' He felt Allenby move up beside him. There was no point in sending aft to the Oerlikons. It would soon be over.

Allenby asked quietly, 'Will you fight?' He saw the look of wretched uncertainty on the Canadian's face.

'It would not be a fight, Dick. And with those helpless people below – ' He shook his head. 'If it had been just one E-boat, but it isn't.'

Goudie lurched against the side, his teeth gritted against the pain as Able Seaman Turner tried to support him. He too was weak from loss of blood.

Allenby looked at them sadly. 'How could we let them die, Keith?'

Goudie took a deep breath and then yelled, 'Look again!' He shook Frazer by the shoulder until his wound made him release it. 'They're ours.' He lowered his head so that they should not see his face. 'They're bloody ours, the Dogs.'

Frazer watched the oncoming silhouettes. Of course, the Dogs. The name given to the biggers MTBs and MGBs, Fairmile Ds. They had often been mistaken for E-boats.

Frazer lowered his glasses, but he knew there was nothing wrong with them this time in spite of the mist.

Allenby said in a whisper, 'Tell the engineroom. Wright should know.'

The three big Dogs swept down protectively on the little gunboat. Frazer could see their crews staring in utter silence, and then heard the leader's loudhailer echo across the water. The most beautiful sound he could ever remember.

'We are to escort you back to father unless you need a tow, or wish to abandon?'

Goudie gasped, 'Cap! Get my cap!' He jammed it, blood-stains and all, on his head and then dragged himself along the rail until he was up on the forward gratings.

'*Tow? Abandon?*' He peered at Frazer. 'Tell that ass, Able One will proceed to base as ordered.' He relented slightly. 'Add, thanks for your company.' He slumped down and muttered, 'Told you these were good little boats.' Then he fainted.

An hour later the promised air cover arrived.

Frazer, Allenby and Ives solemnly shook hands as the planes tore overhead, so close that they made the ensign flap as if in a gale.

It was over.

11

Faces of War

Commander Aubrey Prothero leaned on his desk and stared at the big map on the opposite wall. Somewhere above his head the usual din of rivet guns and machinery would be deafening as Portsmouth Dockyard continued its work of repairing ships of every kind, survivors from a dozen battles. They never stopped, not even for air raids, not any more.

It was January 1944 and as he studied the large map he could follow the extent of the Allies' success to their point of present stalemate. Six months ago they had invaded Sicily. Operation Husky had had its shaky moments but it had been an overall success.

Then, in September, Operation Avalanche, when an even greater combined army had hit the Italian beaches; the operation had been aptly named, he thought grimly. But it was not another Sicily. The enemy had fallen back, but time and time again they had launched counterattacks of unbelievable ferocity. Now, with winter bogging down the Allied armies there was little real progress. The Eastern Front was the same, where millions of Russians and Germans fought, froze and died.

Prothero's thoughts returned to Sicily. He was proud of what his Special Operations Section had achieved. Like sharp prongs of the advance which goaded and harried the enemy whenever possible. On the whole, Prothero decided, the Royal Navy had done rather well. In September, for instance, midget submarines, X-Craft, had penetrated a Norwegian fjord and placed explosive charges beneath the enemy's biggest warship, the battleship *Tirpitz*. Intelligence had reported that she would be out of the war, probably for ever.

And just a week or so ago the news of another victory. Admiral Fraser's flagship *Duke of York* had fought and destroyed the battle cruiser *Scharnhorst*. The last of Germany's big ships. It was odd when you thought about it. *Scharnhorst* had been the enemy's most successful warship and had earned true admiration from the Royal Navy. Sailors were a strange crowd, he thought.

Prothero glanced at the clock and then pressed his buzzer. The clock was still hung about with paperchains, reminders of Christmas, but hanging limp in the damp atmosphere.

Captain Heywood would be here soon. He was never late or early, but exact. He was that kind of man.

The door opened and Leading Wren Hazel looked at him questioningly. 'Sir?'

She was very attractive, Prothero thought, not for the first time. Lovely eyes and nice legs which even the regulation stockings could not spoil.

'I want to make a couple of signals. Got your pad?'

She sat down and crossed her legs, her dark hair shining in the hard lighting.

A very self-possessed girl, Prothero thought. Even before her brother had been killed in that explosion. He pictured Allenby's pale face that first day, and what he had done in Sicily. General Gustavo Tesini had played his part as promised, and as the Allies advanced so the Italian armies deserted to their side, a direct response, some said, to Tesini's broadcasts.

The little depleted team that had been Jupiter had scattered for a while after the two invasions. The boat had been taken to Gibraltar for temporary repairs and was now on her way to England again in the care of a passage crew.

Frazer and Allenby had moved about in various craft, dropping or recovering agents, running guns – battlefield clearance stores as they were known – to Yugoslav partisans under their inspiring leader, a man called Tito.

Goudie had been flown home after a brief stay in a field hospital. Prothero had visited him in the naval hospital here at Haslar. He had received a bad wound but was still as uncompromising and outspoken as ever.

Now all anyone could talk or think about was the inevitable invasion of Europe. It would have to be Normandy. If it was so obvious the enemy must surely think the same.

He straightened his back and felt his uniform protesting. He did not eat much and was not a heavy drinker. He loathed his girth, the discomfort of every movement.

He dictated his signals with his usual brevity, his small eyes half closed in concentration.

'And I want a copy to go to Flag Officer, Plymouth.'

She looked up at him, her pencil poised above the signal pad. 'Does that mean Lieutenant Allenby and the others are coming home, sir?'

Prothero grunted. 'Yes. Any hour, convoys permitting.' He studied her thoughtfully. She had large brown eyes. If only –

He asked, 'Why the interest?'

She coloured. 'They've been through a lot, sir.'

It was no answer, but Prothero knew it was all he would get.

'Tell Second Officer Balfour I'd like to see her, will you?'

'I forgot to tell you, sir. She's off sick. Third Officer Manners is in temporary charge of Ops.'

'I see.' He discarded the idea of sending for Manners. A cold fish of a woman. A very suitable mate for Heywood.

The telephone rang and Prothero picked it up instantly.

Then he said, 'Captain Heywood is here. Show him in, please.'

She had a nice smile too, he thought wistfully. It never occurred to him that it was because they all liked him despite his bluff and sometimes blunt manner.

Captain Heywood entered and sat down. He shivered. 'Blowing like the Arctic up top,' he said.

Prothero handed him his file of notes and watched his superior for any reaction as he read them.

Heywood said eventually, 'You seem to have thought of everything, Aubrey. Their lordships have agreed that you can begin moving your operational HQ to Cornwall without delay. There'll be a holding staff left here, of course.'

The move to the West Country had been Prothero's idea. Their preparations and regrouping would be less obvious down there, lost amongst the gathering armada of ships and landing craft which were filling every harbour and creek as far as Land's End and around into Wales.

They had been offered a small hotel right on the River Fal. It would make a nice change. Prothero thought it might give his team of helpers a welcome release.

Heywood said, 'The good news is that I've got two more motor gunboats for you. They're being refitted for Special Ops right now. As soon as they're ready they can begin training together.'

Again Prothero thought of the near disaster in the Med when one of his boats, code-named Able Two, had been lost. He had always wanted three boats. A better set of odds.

A new HQ and better weapons. What of the people?

Heywood said, 'Their lordships have also given their approval to your suggestions. A half-stripe for Frazer, and a second one for Archer for obvious reasons. There'll be some decorations too. A DSO for that lunatic Goudie, and a DSC for Frazer. Perhaps a couple of medals for the others.'

'What about Allenby, sir?'

'He has the George Cross, for heaven's sake.'

Prothero smiled. 'So has Malta, sir.'

'Yes, well, we'll have to see. When they get back you can arrange some leave for them.' He frowned. 'You're sure you want Goudie to remain in overall command?'

'No question about it, sir. He's a natural. A bit of a rebel, but damn good.'

'I had thought you might say otherwise. Major Thomas seemed to think Goudie was, well, not to put a point, round the bend.'

Prothero shrugged. 'Thomas had his own views, so do I, sir.'

Heywood pressed his fingertips together and eyed him severely. 'I know how you feel, but you're wrong. To beat the enemy we have to use his own weapons and his own methods, no matter how ruthless they may appear. If the Germans terrify people, we must do it better. We need the Thomases of this world.'

Prothero sighed. 'If you say so, sir.'

Heywood had already dismissed the matter. Like Sicily. It was all so much history now.

He said, 'I'll inspect your HQ as soon as you say the word.'

Prothero tried to contain his feelings of uneasiness. The three boats would be safe and snug on the River Fal, but moorings everywhere were at a premium because of the growing invasion fleet. Just a few days ago the naval berthing officer there had telephoned him to complain about the lack of notice. He was not a bloody magician, as he had put it angrily. Prothero had smoothed things out eventually. But he knew that he had told Second Officer Balfour to complete those same arrangements weeks ago. She knew her job, and anyway the officer in question would want to make a pass at her, even on the telephone. Now she was sick. He would have to look into the matter, and fast before Heywood suspected something. He had about as much sympathy as a brick.

Heywood said, 'We'll have the three boats repainted and given new pendant numbers. To all intents they will be part of a new flotilla.' He tapped his nose. 'Top secret as always.' He stood up. 'Must dash.'

'Drink before you go, sir?'

Heywood consulted his watch. 'Sun's not over *my* yardarm yet. I've not time anyway.'

Prothero smiled. It was a game he liked to play. Heywood never got too close to anyone, he had noticed that. Afraid of soiling his reputation perhaps if someone else blundered.

He accompanied the captain through the adjoining rooms, their ceilings covered with droplets of condensation.

Prothero thought that some of his girls were looking distinctly pale. Cornwall would be better all round.

Leading Wren Hazel was already typing out his signals ready to pass them through the SDO.

Heywood did not seem to notice any of them.

The Leading Wren glanced up as Prothero made his farewell. She thought of Allenby and his letter which was carefully folded inside her paybook.

Frazer and Allenby entered the Special Operations Section and stared round with astonishment. There seemed to be very few people working in the cellarlike offices and the passageway was strewn with crates and steel cabinets. It looked as if a bomb had gone off. But Prothero was there, waiting for them, as if he had never moved.

Prothero wasted no time. He glanced first at Frazer. 'You'll all be going on leave, and you will get your uniforms made up *first*, right? I suppose you do know about your half-stripe?'

Frazer grinned. 'Yes. Thanks a lot, sir. I even feel different.'

Prothero smiled. 'Possibly.' He turned to Allenby. It was strange how Frazer was so tanned and yet Allenby seemed to remain as he was.

'I expect it was all a lot different from what you expected. You did well, very well.'

Allenby asked, 'What's happening here, sir?'

'We are in the process of moving house to Cornwall. You'll get your orders while you're on leave.' He hesitated and glanced at Frazer again. 'There is something I should tell you. As a Canadian you are entitled to transfer back to general service, or in fact to the RCN itself. I've read between the lines and I feel bound to tell you that if you went back to the Royal Canadian Navy you'd most certainly get your own command, probably one of the latest corvettes.' He watched Frazer's features and saw the sudden indecision where before he had obviously been so glad to be home in one piece. 'But I have to know before we begin working up the new boats.'

Allenby suddenly felt deflated. He had been expecting to see Joanna Hazel; he had thought about little else once they had been put aboard a fast convoy from Gibraltar. Now she was gone; she might have changed anyway. Here, in this dismal place, he would have felt more confident. And now Frazer was leaving. He'd be a damned fool not to, after what they had just gone through.

Frazer's mind was in a whirl. Promotion, talk of getting a decoration, and now the chance of a command. He could barely take it in.

Prothero said, 'Anyway, get off on some leave as soon as the Intelligence people have done with you.' He had already spoken to Archer who had arrived back a day earlier. He seemed quite different, Prothero thought. Withdrawn, even morose. They might have to have a second think about him.

Frazer said suddenly, 'I've decided, sir. I'd like to stay.'

Prothero beamed. He was glad he had been right about Frazer in the first place.

Prothero said, 'You both see now why it was hard to make the best selections from all the volunteers. Being good at your work is essential, but in Special Operations we need that bit more.' He rocked back onto his desk and added gravely, 'But you know that now, eh?'

Allenby saw Prothero glance at a pale outline on the wall

where his clock had once been. He had to say something before Prothero dismissed them.

'Will you have all your same staff with you in Cornwall, sir?'

Prothero's bright little eyes settled on him. So that was it. Allenby was a brave lad and his record was blameless. But he was no use at all at hiding his feelings.

'There'll be more of them this time. We shall have our own flotilla, so to speak. You, Frazer, will be second-in-command under John Goudie, so you may yet be sorry you turned down that transfer.'

Frazer was pleased about Goudie. He had all but recovered, he had been told, and had been sent to a recuperation hospital, then on leave. Frazer had never believed he would come to like Goudie, let alone miss him.

He asked casually, 'Is Second Officer Balfour still your first hand, sir?'

Prothero was about to end it, to shut them up on grounds of secrecy. But there was something about Frazer. He might be just what she needed. Lynn Balfour had gone to the new HQ in Cornwall as soon as she had recovered from her illness. The PMO had described it as strain and overwork. Common enough.

He replied, 'Yes, she's there already.' He waited, judging the moment. 'Cornwall's a bit bleak at this time of the year. My PO writer is Cornish. She'll buff you up on where to go.' He controlled his sudden envy with an effort. 'But get that half-stripe stitched on before you do anything. Now, wait outside, I want to speak to Allenby.'

The two officers glanced quickly at each other and Frazer winked.

'Stay with it.'

As the door closed Prothero said, 'You get on well together.'

'Yes, sir.' What the hell was wrong? His father, or had the house been bombed?

Prothero said, 'I have to ask you something, and it's important.'

Fifteen minutes later Allenby joined his friend in the passageway.

'I shall have to call you *sir*, now.' Allenby smiled, but it did not reach his eyes.

Frazer watched him thoughtfully. 'Anyway, three weeks' leave is not to be sneezed at, is it?'

Allenby looked away. 'One week.'

Frazer faced him. 'What d'you mean, *one* week?'

'I shall be recalled to do another operation.'

Frazer stared. 'So soon? Who with, for Christ's sake?'

Allenby walked along the littered passageway, his mind still reeling with shock.

'On my bloody own, Keith, that's who with!'

The next day Allenby stood in his own bedroom at home and stared out at the small back garden. The apple trees, his father's pride and joy, were jet black against a thin layer of snow. It was cold. The whole house seemed chilly in spite of the fire blazing in the room below him.

He was sure it was imagination but his parents seemed so much older. He touched a pile of magazines on his chest of drawers. Stories he could repeat almost word for word. It would be funny if Prothero had written some of them. Tales of valour and war. Not like anything he had seen since he had joined the navy.

He tried to put the operation to the back of his mind. His father had already noticed his nervousness, an inability to sit still.

Like the time spent in convoy when he had tried to sleep. He had drawn the curtain to try and find privacy and seclusion. Not easy in a cabin you shared with five other young officers. And when he did sleep the pictures began to rise through his thoughts. The vivid flashes from the explosives he had hurled onto the transport's deck, the solitary sailor who had surrendered, who Weeks would have shot down without barely considering it. And the girl who had tried to hide her nakedness from him, his own inability to deal with the matter, whereas Ives had been like a rock.

He sighed as he heard the clatter of cups and saucers. Tea. He went slowly downstairs and saw his mother's surprise as she finished laying the table with her best plates.

'Your uniform, Dicky! What have you done?'

Allenby had changed into some old flannels and a sweater. Funnily enough, they seemed too big for him. Like Alice in Wonderland, he thought. The house got smaller with every visit, and his clothes got larger.

'You look a mess. You'll have to change again. The Mannerings are coming round this evening.'

Allenby hated the Mannerings almost as much as he loathed being called Dicky. But they lived in the same road, always had, like his own parents. The male Mannering was a self-taught expert on the war. Neither of the Mannerings seemed to have first names. It would be a difficult evening. But it was his first. He would do what he could.

His father removed his pipe from his mouth and said, 'Leave the boy alone, Mother. He's had a hard time.'

Then she did something that was far worse than any complaint. She crossed the room and laid one hand on his cheek.

'I know. You don't have to tell me. Look at him.'

Allenby sat down and said, 'Different sort of war, that's all.'

As his mother left the room for the huge teapot his father said, 'Bad, was it?'

Allenby nodded, his eyes suddenly smarting. 'Bloody awful.'

His father moved his artificial leg and smiled. 'Don't let your mother hear you swear.' He added, 'How's your Canadian chum?'

'Fine.' Allenby took a firm grip on himself. What was the matter with him? He had nearly cracked over nothing. He pictured Frazer in Cornwall, trying to decide how best to see his Wren officer.

His father said, 'Seven days' leave. It's not much in my view.'

'Oh well, you know how it is. We're doing something new. All hush-hush. We shall be pretty busy.'

'Did you lose many, Dick?' His eyes were very steady. 'You can tell me. You know that.'

Allenby found he was on his feet although he did not recall getting up.

'Not many, Dad. But there weren't a lot of us at the beginning.'

He looked at his father. How could he have stood his war? Months in stinking, waterlogged trenches. Hundreds, thousands being killed in suicide charges over the top. The wire, the gas, the machine guns. It made capturing an Italian general seem simple.

His mother entered and stared at them. 'Up to the table, Dad,' but she was watching her son.

'Mr Mannering says that we should have taken the whole of Italy by now.'

Allenby smiled at her. 'Why don't they send him? I'm sure he would frighten the Germans no end. He does me.'

His mother poured the tea and asked, 'Met a nice girl yet, Dicky?'

'Yes. I have as a matter of fact.' It was only a part lie. He could see her right now. Her eyes and her dark hair, and her voice, he would never forget that.

He said, 'She's a Leading Wren.'

She looked at him searchingly. 'Not an officer then?'

'No.'

His father took a piece of cake. Homemade. It would be, for his son's return.

'What's her name?'

'Joanna Hazel.' It slipped out just like that and he saw the sudden anxiety in his father's eyes. His mother did not seem to have noticed. As she left the room saying, 'Joanna? Nice name,' his father said, 'The same as your chap who got killed.'

Allenby nodded. The room seemed to be closing in, stifling him.

'His sister.'

'What's she like?'

Allenby described her as best he could, bringing the unknown girl into the room with its dusty blackout curtains and the ration books on the mantelpiece. He did not even realize his mother had returned with some more food on a dish.

His father said at length, 'You must bring her home, if you can.'

Allenby looked at his plate. 'If I can.' He stood up suddenly. 'I must go upstairs.' He saw their expressions, concern and hurt. He tried again. 'I'll put my best uniform on.'

She smiled at him. 'That's better. But you must eat. You're like a stick.'

As he closed the door behind him Allenby could feel the sweat on his forehead like ice.

He heard his father say in reply to something she said, 'Leave it alone, Mother. Can't you see? He's been through hell. He's been pushing himself into the flames ever since he joined up. No wonder he wants to dress all anyhow. To hold it at bay just a bit longer.'

Allenby returned to his room and stared out of the window. The darkness had closed in again. *Seven days*. He lowered the shutter across the window and then after a few moments sat on his bed and buried his face in his hands.

Frazer looked around the small but comfortable room which,

like the old pub with its thatched roof, looked pleased with itself. He must remember to take a photo of the little pub, the King Charles Inn, for his mother. She'd like it.

It was the only available room and he knew why it was vacant. He must be directly over the main bar and he could hear the jangle of a piano, the roar of voices mingled in song, laughter and beer.

Frazer had begged several different lifts to reach here. Army lorries and once a staff car with a very senior Royal Marines officer who chatted to him about fishing and shooting grouse before he apologetically dropped Frazer while he turned farther south to Plymouth.

The last free ride was from a local doctor who asked him about the war. As the car tore along winding, narrow country lanes Frazer could understand how it must sometimes seem far away down here. Every town he had been driven through had been filled with uniforms – British, American and a lot from his own country. It made him feel uneasy to hear their familiar voices and accents, as if he was on the outside.

The doctor had been the one to guide him to the King Charles Inn. Perhaps to make amends for his remark when he had first picked Frazer up.

'You an American?'

Frazer had grinned. The perfect way to make enemies. 'Canadian.'

'Don't often see officers thumbing a lift,' he had commented.

The woman on the desk had given him a map of the area. Frazer had thought about that. The place was already filled with troops, weapons and vehicles, exercising and preparing for the greatest invasion of all. He could have been an enemy spy for all anyone seemed to care.

He was wrong. A local policeman pedalled up to the inn on his tall bicycle and very politely asked to see Frazer's identity card and leave pass. He managed to do it without causing offence, and to down a pint of cider at the same time.

Frazer had, of course, been given the telephone number of the new HQ. Tomorrow he would try his luck and attempt to speak to her. Why was he so unsure, so nervous? It was ridiculous, and he would probably make himself more so.

He took the framed picture of his mother and father out of his case and propped it on the bedside table. Then he thought of Allenby and wondered what the hell he was getting into. Then, with a brief glance at himself in the mirror, he picked up his cap and made his way towards the noise. He would take a walk before he turned in. Catch again some of those rich, country smells he had noticed when in the doctor's car. The rain had stopped and he had enjoyed the feel of the land which seemed to have altered little for centuries.

But first a pint. He thrust his way through the khaki and RAF blue until he reached the bar.

A jovial man with a face like an apple beamed at him.

'Yes, zur, what'll it be?'

'Large Scotch and – ' Frazer broke off and grinned awkwardly. 'Sorry, I forgot. I'll have a pint of that – ' He pointed at a barrel behind the bar.

'Scrumpy,' said the landlord, apparently satisfied, like the policeman, that he was not a spy.

Frazer sipped it and wondered how many of these powerful local brews it would take to knock a man down.

He edged into a corner, away from the piano and two argumentative soldiers, and thought about tomorrow and how he might spend his leave. She would probably regret ever telephoning him at Gib. She had only done it because she had known what he was being ordered to do. No more than that. And in any case – he turned as someone dropped a glass on the stone floor, and saw her sitting on the opposite side of the bar in conversation with a young naval officer.

Even as he stared at her, caught entirely off balance, his carefully prepared speech blown to the winds, she looked up and saw him. As he pushed through the crowded figures he kept his gaze on hers. It was like an awareness, something that had been there for years when he knew it had not.

He reached the table and the young officer, a RNVR sub-lieutenant, sprang to his feet. He was brand new, his uniform barely used. Frazer realized with a start that the subbie was staring at his sleeves. He was impressed, just as Frazer was still unused to his sudden promotion.

He said, 'Hello, I was going to try and ring you tomorrow.'

She was still looking at him, as if she was searching for something.

'Now you don't have to.' She patted a chair. 'Join us.'

Frazer looked at the young sub-lieutenant. It must have ruined his evening.

She said quietly, and for an instant there was pain on her face, 'Meet Alex.' She watched them shake hands. 'My brother.'

12

Beginnings

The King Charles Inn seemed totally different in the daytime. The landlord had guided Frazer to a small, darkly panelled bar named the Snug. He obviously did not approve of officers sharing the place with other ranks. Frazer smiled and tried not to glance at his watch.

It was well past noon, when she had said she would be here. Frazer had slept badly on his first night at the little thatched pub, and now as he tried to remember everything that they had said he began to wonder if he had heard only what he wanted, no, needed to hear.

Then she had left with her brother. Frazer thought that he was something like poor Ryder. It was to be hoped he lived a bit longer. Frazer put down his glass and looked out of the nearest window. How the weather could change. It was bright and clear, and the occasional passing serviceman or civilian gave off a cloud of breath in the crisp, cold air.

He had telephoned the new HQ and after identifying himself had explained where he would be staying for his leave. The voice at the other end had been polite. Disinterested.

The landlord glanced in at him. ' 'Nother gin, zur?'

Frazer pushed the empty glass across. 'Thanks.' The gin was about all the pub had apart from beer and scrumpy and rum. It reminded him of Goudie.

The landlord owned a large fat labrador called Hector who spent most of his time sprawled in front of the fire in the main bar. He seemed to manage to avoid being trodden on when the place was crowded and scrounged titbits of food whenever possible. He had been lying by the fire and as Frazer took his drink he saw the old dog perk up and stare at the door, then very slowly begin to wag his tail.

The door opened and she stood framed against the washed-out sky and a squad of bare trees.

She crossed to the Snug but paused to pat Hector's head. The dog did not get up. He did not know her well enough yet it seemed. Her skin was glowing from the cold and she offered Frazer her hand in an almost formal handshake. Then she tossed her bag onto a chair and pulled a packet of cigarettes from her reefer jacket.

She looked at his glass. 'I'll have the same, if you were about to ask me.' She exhaled a stream of smoke and unwound very slowly. 'Sorry I'm late. There's a flap on. Usually is with the Boss away.' She eyed him gravely. 'What sort of day are you having?'

Frazer said, 'Went for a walk.' He hesitated. 'You look marvellous.'

She showed neither surprise nor approval. 'How's your war going?'

Frazer sat back and watched her eyes. Blue like the sky. 'It's different. I've grown used to seeing ships sink, to chasing Jerry submarines all over the ocean, only to find they've slipped past us and are mauling the convoy again.'

'That's different?'

'You never see the enemy, you accept the losses of friends and ships. Now, I know the enemy is real, human. Flesh and blood.'

Frazer changed the subject. 'Alex is easy to talk to. How long has he been in the navy?'

She looked past him, her eyes troubled, like the previous night. 'He left *King Alfred* six months ago. He did a bit of time in an escort destroyer, then he volunteered for Special Operations.' It sounded as if she had repeated it word for word to someone else, or to herself. 'I blame myself. If I'd not been involved in Ops, if I'd been a quarters officer in some nice quiet Wrennery, it wouldn't have happened.'

Frazer watched her, afraid to break the spell. That she would get up and leave.

'He doesn't have much experience, that's true.'

She looked at him. 'He's a bright lad. Speaks fluent German and French for one thing. Can't you see how the minds of the top brass work?'

She glanced at her watch. It gave Frazer a few moments to study her, her hair, her small, well-shaped hands. He had to stop her leaving.

She said, 'I shall have to dash in a moment. I'll have another drink though.'

Frazer said, 'I'd like to see you again, in fact – '

'You're on leave, I'm on duty around the clock getting my section organized. And even if I was free I'd – '

He put his hand on her sleeve, very gently, and could feel her tense, as if to pull away.

'I know that. But I want to see you. Very much. I've thought about you a lot.'

She watched his hand but did not draw away. 'It's not good to get too close. Not in wartime.'

Frazer said, 'My mother always said that holiday romances never last. I expect she thinks that about the war too.' He added suddenly, 'Tell me about Paul.' He saw her flinch as if he had sworn at her. 'If you like.'

'Who told you?' She shrugged. 'No matter. I can guess.'

Frazer felt that his grip on things was falling apart but he persisted. 'How long had you known him?'

'Six weeks.' Her head dropped. 'It may not sound much, but, you see, we – '

She broke off and stared at him angrily. 'You wouldn't understand! A few kisses and your North American charm and I'll leap into bed with you, is that it?'

'You phoned me at Gib.'

'I was worried about you. Now you know why I want to keep Alex out of the dirty war. I don't know what I'd do if anything happened to him.'

Frazer watched her as she glanced at herself in a gold compact and then reached for her bag. He had blown it.

'Don't leave like this, Lynn.' He saw her surprise at the use of her name. 'And it's not the way you said. After all, I may not have seen you, but I've known you for *over* six weeks.'

She regarded him thoughtfully, weighing his words or her own. 'Well, so long as it's understood – ' She faltered. 'I'm not sure.'

'You've been ill. They told me at Portsmouth.'

'Ill?' She turned as two army lieutenants clumped into the other bar, calling for drinks and laughing over some joke or other. The old dog did get up for them.

Then she said, 'I suppose I was in a way.'

'Phone me in a day or so.' She stood up and straightened her tricorn hat. 'But my advice is to go somewhere else to spend your leave.'

Frazer walked with her to the door. 'I suppose. You never know when it may be the last one.'

She swung on him angrily, her eyes flashing. 'Don't ever say that! Not to me!'

She was oblivious to the landlord and the two soldiers who were staring at them transfixed.

Frazer said, 'Paul was a lucky man.'

She recovered immediately. As if the use of her lover's name was a talisman, something to hold on to.

'No. I was the lucky one.' She looked away to hide her face. 'And I'm sorry for what I said earlier. It's not your fault.'

Frazer said, 'What about tomorrow, right here? Just for a few minutes if it's all you can spare.'

'You are persistent.'

'I'm afraid you'll change your mind and not come if you

have time to think about it.' He smiled and added, 'What d'you say?'

'I can't promise.' Then she smiled. 'If I can make it.'

Frazer said quietly so that the others could not hear. 'You should smile more often. You're lovely.'

She did not reply, but looked at him for several seconds, her eyes holding that same awareness that he had seen in the bar. Then she was gone.

She was exciting and very desirable despite her aloofness. That was her protection, and it might still act against him. But she had agreed to see him. It was a beginning and Frazer was conscious of a great happiness.

The seaman, protected from the cold in a long watchcoat and wearing white belt and gaiters, examined Allenby's identity card and special pass.

Allenby looked along the neat driveway and saw a sprawling, two-storeyed building which had once been a hotel for people who liked the country, walking and fishing. The navy was doing its best to change all that. Neat, white-painted stones lined the driveway, and a White Ensign flapped damply from a newly erected mast.

The sentry shifted the weight of a Stirling sub-machine gun on his shoulder and said cheerfully, 'Commander Prothero's expectin' you. Th' first door, you want.'

He had a twangy northern accent. It seemed out of place, Allenby thought. Devon and Cornwall were the farthest he had been for his prewar holidays with his parents. He felt vaguely at home here.

It had been a long journey from London. Changing trains and several holdups because of work on the line, and an air raid that lit the darkness like a far-off electrical storm. A jeep had awaited his arrival at Truro. The new HQ was situated some four miles from there, and about five from the main port of Falmouth. As the crow flies, that is. He smiled as he recalled the narrow, twisting lanes in which he had hiked, dreamed and imagined what he might become one day. You had to double every distance if you were going by road in Cornwall.

His driver called, 'I'll take your gear to your quarters right away, sir!' He revved his engine.

It was his quiet way of telling the lieutenant that Prothero was not in the habit of waiting. Even if Allenby was worn out and needed a bath, the moment was now.

Allenby walked up the driveway and returned the salutes of two sailors in oilskins. They too looked as if they should be at sea dressed like that, then Allenby realized that the river was right there below the hotel. Even here it was not secluded. Landing craft, fuel and ammunition lighters, and others which appeared to be carrying mobile cranes and lifting gear lined the opposite bank. It would be like that all the way downstream to Carrick Roads and Falmouth itself. No wonder there were so many checkpoints and wire fences. But how could they keep such a massive build-up a secret? Surely the Germans must know what was happening.

As he trudged up the driveway he thought of his seven days' leave. It had been strained, and they had all been cut off from each other. The Mannerings had dropped in as promised. Threatened, more likely, he thought. Mr Mannering had gone on about Salerno, the losses of men there during and immediately after the landings. At one point he had said, 'I'd have thought the navy would have been better prepared. It's the same with everything we do.'

Allenby had seen his father's sudden apprehension and had said, 'When I was sweeping mines I was one of the lucky ones. My ship was a proper sweeper. There were peacetime paddle steamers, clapped-out fishing drifters and trawlers doing the toughest and most thankless job there is.' His voice had risen as he had exclaimed, 'We have no say in the ships and weapons we receive. We just have to get out there and fight the bloody war!'

His mother had exclaimed sharply, 'Dicky, *please!*'

Mannering had said in an almost forgiving tone, 'Never mind, I've broad shoulders, what?'

Allenby had been about to say 'and a big mouth too,' but he had desisted. But the evening had not been a happy one.

In some ways he was glad to be back. It was the life he had come to understand like no other. He belonged. He paused and glanced up at the empty sky. Empty except for several barrage balloons. Like a school of flying whales.

He entered the door and saw the bustle of figures in every direction. Empty boxes to be removed, full ones to be opened and sorted into the various offices. There was nobody he recognized. His heart sank. What was he expecting?

A squat, elderly Chief Yeoman of Signals was peering at a clipboard, his red face screwed up with concentration.

Allenby said, 'Good morning, Yeo. Can you tell me where I can find Commander Prothero?'

The Chief Yeoman looked at him and sighed loudly as a Wren dropped a packet of papers on the floor so that they scattered in every direction.

He said with feeling, 'Gawd, what a bleedin' potmess!' Then he grinned. 'Still, worse troubles at sea, they tells me!' He pointed across the entrance hall where visitors had once gathered to sign the register.

'Through there, sir. 'E's a bit peeved today.' Allenby was wearing his raincoat and displayed no rank, and the Chief Yeoman was obviously offering a friendly warning.

'Thanks, Yeo.' He bit his lip. 'Is Leading Wren Hazel about?'

The man eyed him impassively. 'She 'ad the forenoon, sir. She's gone to 'er billet. You just missed 'er.'

Allenby walked into the office and felt the Chief Yeoman staring after him.

Another Wren he did not know ushered him through the outer office to another, grander one which was already lined with maps, aerial photographs and clips of signals. Some

Wrens and a petty officer writer were putting files into order, and a torpedoman was testing the newly installed telephones. There was a sense of urgency about the place, as noticeable as the strong smell of pusser's paint.

Then into another office and the Wren announced, 'Lieutenant Allenby, sir.'

Prothero was drinking coffee from a huge cup and waited for Allenby to reach him before he offered his hand.

'Good to see you.' His bright little eyes searched Allenby's face. 'Fit?'

'I've seen the PMO, sir.' It was not what Prothero meant, but Allenby was too strained to play games.

Then he realized that there was another officer in the room, partly concealed by a high-backed leather chair. One of the original hotel's, he thought.

The officer was a lieutenant with the interwoven gold lace of the Royal Naval Reserve on his sleeves. He had a round, competent face, the look of the professional seaman like most of the RNR.

Prothero said, 'This is Lieutenant Quinlan. He did not elaborate. Prothero settled himself uncomfortably on a chair.

'No one was sorrier than I that you had to cut short your leave after what you had been through.'

Allenby felt like smiling. You would think that he had offered to forgo his leave.

'But this is an important mission and I want to keep it in the family. The Admiral agrees that it is a job for my section.'

The same Wren entered the room and put a cup of coffee beside Allenby's chair. As she left, Allenby saw the Boss watching her legs. His expression made him look suddenly vulnerable.

Prothero said, 'I'm sending you to the Channel Islands, Jersey to be exact.' He watched Allenby, his eyes mild again.

Allenby stared at him. The Channel Islands had been occupied by the enemy since the fall of France. They were the only part of Britain under the German jackboot. He knew little about them, other than the travel pictures and brochures he had read before the war. Hardly a top-line military objective.

Prothero said, 'Amazing isn't it? Jersey's only one hundred and fifty miles from your chair. But it's so well defended it might as well be on the moon.'

He heaved himself up from his seat and crossed to the nearest wall map. The south coast of England and the Western Approaches. France and the Cherbourg Peninsula, and nestling just below it that small group of islands.

Prothero said, 'The Germans have thrown up some impressive fortifications, gun sites and an anti-tank wall above the beaches that would stop just about anything. The garrison, however, is not the best in the Wehrmacht. Mostly older men, reservists, and others sent there to recover from wounds and illness received on the Russian Front. But there are plenty of naval patrols, some based on the islands, and of course there is a flotilla of E-Boats just over the water in St Malo. Impressive, eh?'

Allenby got to his feet and walked to the map. From the way Prothero described the place it sounded like a one-way exercise.

Prothero said slowly, 'The Allies will be invading Normandy eventually. Sooner rather than later, and *we* shall be playing an important role. My sources tell me that the enemy has built a completely new radar complex and erected it on Jersey. In the event of an attack it will protect their flank and monitor all surface and air movements. It's very advanced, I'm given to understand. It must be destroyed.'

Allenby looked across to the windows, his mind grappling with the simple statement.

Prothero added, 'The Channel Islands are British. They have managed to exist under the German occupation with minimum persecution. There is no Resistance as we know it in France and Scandinavia. Occasionally a few reckless individuals have carried out acts of defiance. If caught they have been harshly dealt with. And that is how it must remain. The war will end one day. I don't want us to be the cause of savage reprisals in those islands as carried out elsewhere.'

Allenby thought of the raid on Sicily. He had heard that when the SS and Gestapo had arrived at that fishing village to investigate they had executed even some of the women.

'So you want me to do it, sir?'

'You'll be met when you land. One of the people there has formed a small group. He helped design the structure, and he also has access to some of the equipment. Our Intelligence and radar advisers would give their teeth to have a look at it. It may have to be jammed before the invasion. We shall need to know how.'

'Why can't this local man do the job, sir?'

'It's got to look like a raid from outside. We shall create a diversion while you get on with the mission. Well?'

Allenby knew it was useless to ask about his chances.

'When do I start?'

Prothero beamed. 'Good lad. It'll be a day or so. But it's all laid on.' He frowned. 'You're not bothered by submarines, I trust?'

He gestured to the other lieutenant before Allenby could reply. 'Quinlan here will be your taxi driver. He is captain of a midget submarine X-19, one of those sent to attack the *Tirpitz*. He had to pull out at the last minute with some mechanical trouble.'

Allenby saw the round-faced lieutenant through new eyes. Like most of the navy, he had been excited and astonished by the audacity of the midgets' attack on Germany's greatest battleship. Most of the submariners had been killed or captured. Quinlan had been saved by a stroke of bad luck, or whichever way he looked at it.

Quinlan saw Prothero's impatient nod and said, 'We shall leave Falmouth in an ordinary submarine with X-19 on tow. When we get within working distance we shall board the boat and leave the passage crew in the parent sub. There is a supply vessel which calls regularly at Jersey from St Malo. Troops, fuel and rations for the army.' He glanced at Prothero, his expression cold. 'Not a target we would normally risk an X-Craft for, but it may make the Germans believe it was a fullscale raid.'

Prothero glared. 'They *must* believe that!'

Quinlan looked at Allenby. 'I've got my little sub hidden inside a dock at Falmouth. Flag Officer Submarines is making all the arrangements.' He studied Allenby's pale features and added, 'Don't worry. We'll manage something. I sometimes wonder what they'll think of next. And don't worry about mechanical trouble. It's been taken care of.'

Prothero folded his arms. They barely reached across his body. 'Get settled in, Allenby.' It was a dismissal. 'I have a few points to discuss with Quinlan.' Or did he merely want to separate them until the time to move?

Allenby asked, 'Can I take it that Major Thomas is not involved this time, sir?'

Prothero scowled fiercely. 'Now, just because you – ' He calmed himself with an effort. 'You are not supposed to know who is doing what and when. But no, Major Thomas is employed elsewhere. I know how you feel, but we often have to work with other sections. Thomas's is just one of them. And before you condemn him completely, just remember that his family were wiped out by the SS as a reprisal. He has no love for Germans.'

'I know that, sir.' Allenby faced him. 'But he enjoys his work too much.'

He closed the door behind him and saw the Chief Yeoman in the outer office talking with one of the Wrens.

He grinned as he saw Allenby's grim expression.

'All done, sir? I *did* tell you about him.'

As Allenby turned towards the staircase the Chief Yeoman added, 'By the way, sir.' He held out half of a signal flimsy. 'Phone call for you just now. I've wrote down the number.

Young lady it was.' He almost winked. 'The one you mentioned like.'

Allenby found a telephone and after some explaining to the operator he heard the line begin to buzz.

His mouth was completely dry. As if he was just going into battle. If only he had time to compose himself. He knew it would have made no difference.

There was a click and then she said, 'Yes?'

'This is Lieutenant Allenby, is that – ?'

He thought he could hear girls' voices and the clatter of crockery. It must be the Wrens' quarters. Her voice returned, closer this time as if she had shut a door to exclude the noise.

'I – I just wanted to thank you for your letter.'

There was a long pause while Allenby covered his ear with one hand in case he missed something. For an instant he thought they had been cut off.

Then she said, 'It was good of you, after the way I treated you.'

Allenby said urgently, 'No, it was my fault. I wanted to explain.' The words were tumbling out of him in confusion. 'You see, I can't remember.' He tried to steady himself. 'I'm sorry. It's not at all what I wanted to say.'

She asked, 'What *did* you want to tell me?'

'Please don't laugh at me, or hang up, but – ' He groped for words. 'I've thought of you such a lot. I wondered if we might meet somewhere?'

It seemed an age before she spoke again. 'Yes. All right.'

There was another pause and he could hear her breathing. Fast, as if she was nervous too. She said, 'I know what you are going to do. I have seen the signals. I wish – '

'Don't let's talk about it.' So she knew. He would not have to pretend like he did at home. 'I do so want to talk to you.'

'Yes. We are working watch-and-watch until things settle down. I could see you during the dogs. Only for a few moments. By the way, do you have a bicycle?'

Allenby thought he had misheard. She explained. 'There's a little teashop about a mile from you. We could meet there. It's usually empty. The Chief Yeoman will get a bike for you.'

'How did you know I'd arrived?'

She laughed. 'He was the one who phoned me when you were with the Boss.'

'I'll be there.'

She said, 'I must go. There's a queue outside the box.' She added, 'I'm glad you're safe – ' The line went dead and an aggrieved voice said, 'Sorry, sir, but this *is* a service line.'

At least the operator didn't say that there was a war on.

Allenby walked away, his mind in a daze. He was going to see her. Explain, or try to, what had happened to her brother. And to see her, just as he had described her to his father.

He saw the Chief Yeoman filling his pipe. There was some order amidst the chaos now and he looked almost pleased.

Allenby said, 'Thanks, Yeo.'

The man grinned. 'Now you'll be wantin' a bicycle, right, sir?'

They laughed like conspirators.

Allenby said, '*Right!*'

The little tearooms called the Marigolds were on the edge of a village called Feock. Allenby pedalling fast on the unaccustomed bicycle arrived at four o'clock, far too early as the dogwatches did not begin until then.

An old lady with her hair twisted into a severe bun eyed him suspiciously as he entered and waited for him to sit down. Apart from two women at a table by the bay window the place was empty. Again, it reminded Allenby of his boyhood. The checkered tablecloths, farming scenes on the wall.

The proprietor walked to Allenby's table and said, 'Tea?'

Allenby glanced quickly at his watch. 'I'm a bit early. There'll be two of us.'

She eyed him for a few seconds and said, 'This is not a waiting room, young man.'

Allenby flushed as the other two women turned to stare.

Perhaps a lot of servicemen came here to meet their dates, he thought. The locals probably disliked being swamped by the forces of several nations, no matter how honourable their intentions.

The woman said sharply, 'What's that?' She pointed at the ribbon on Allenby's breast.

Why did he have to get so embarrassed each time someone mentioned it? In the past he had pretended, boasted even, of the things he hadn't done. Reality seemed to render him speechless.

In a small voice he replied, 'The GC, ma'am.'

She leaned closer and he could smell lavender.

'The George Cross, eh?' She studied it and then him in silence. Then she did something as unnerving as when his mother had momentarily dropped her guard. She rested her hand on his shoulder and said quietly, 'Stay as long as you like, son.'

She turned away and vanished into the back room.

The bell above the door jangled and Joanna Hazel walked in, and then stopped to look at him.

Allenby got to his feet, the other women, everything, forgotten as he stared at her. Her jaunty Wren's cap was tilted over her dark hair and she sounded breathless from her ride.

She smiled. 'It was uphill most of the way.'

They sat opposite each other, both nervous, unsure.

He said, 'I know. I nearly fell off when two chaps saluted me and I tried to return the compliment.'

She laughed. It was a delightful sound, Allenby thought, and it made things easier.

The proprietor came to the table and regarded them curiously. She seemed satisfied and said, 'I'll bring your tea now.' She turned her head and added, 'Cream too.'

Allenby said, 'You look smashing.' He faltered. Too quick. Too clumsy. 'Sorry. I'm not used to this.'

She smiled and watched him sadly. 'You're doing fine. I just can't help thinking of the way I spoke to you, and now you're back I feel ashamed.'

Impetuously he reached across the table and took her wrist.

'We're not going to talk about that. Once I thought I might never see you again. That worried me more than anything.'

The tea arrived, and the little old lady unloaded her tray with great care so that Allenby would not have to release the girl's wrist.

Allenby said, 'I must see you again after this. If you can bear it. I need to.'

She studied his face, the lines around his mouth. He was like a lost, desperate boy.

She said, 'I was speaking to my family after you rang me.' She stirred her tea and did not look up. 'I have a week's leave. My people would love to meet you.'

Allenby watched her, the way her lashes covered her eyes. Her hair was black, much darker than he had realized. He also noticed how her spoon was still turning. It had never occurred to him that she might be as unsure as he was.

'But you know about – '

She lifted her eyes again. 'Yes. It won't be for a few days yet. It'll be easy. My home is just on the "frontier" in Devon. We can go there together. The supply officer has a van that can drop us almost at the front door. Daddy can arrange a car for you if you get a recall.' She watched him steadily. 'I'd like that.'

He squeezed her wrist. 'So would I. Very much.'

She said quietly, 'They may ask you about Tim. You know.'

Allenby had expected that. 'I'll try to explain – ' He could not continue.

Instead he asked, 'What does your father do?'

She replied, 'Daddy's a soldier.' She left it at that.

They talked quietly until the road outside was completely dark. Allenby realized that the two women had gone. He had not even heard the bell above the door ring.

Her hand was in his now, very still and warm. He could not believe it was happening.

But it was real. The mysterious mission, the X-Craft, Prothero's plan, they were without substance.

Then it was time to go. She had the first watch and needed to have a bath. She smiled as she said it. 'Baths are rationed at the Wrennery! You'd never get one otherwise with some of the girls down there!'

They stood up and Allenby said, 'I'll escort you back there, if I may?'

She picked up her shoulder bag. 'Thanks.'

The old lady came to the table and as Allenby took out his wallet she said, 'No. Not this time, son.' She glanced at his George Cross. 'Come again.'

What was it, Allenby wondered. Had she lost someone in the navy? Had the decoration sparked off some memory?

The old woman watched them leave and then said to the tearooms at large, 'Just right for each other.'

They pedalled downhill until a secluded building with a naval patrolman at the entrance loomed out of the darkness. They stood self-consciously with their bicycles between them.

Then Allenby said, 'I'd very much like to kiss you.' That he had said it was even harder to believe.

She leaned over the bicycle and he kissed her on the cheek. He could not see her expression as she said, 'That was nice.'

The tea or the kiss he was not quite sure. Then she mounted her bicycle and rode through the gates.

Allenby pushed his own cycle and turned towards the river. He did not want to get back too soon. He needed this moment to last.

13

A Place in the Country

The supply officer's van gathered speed and left Allenby with the girl at the roadside. There was nothing else there but a great pair of gates and a long, curving drive lined by trees.

She said, 'Come on.' Together they walked through the gates and Allenby saw several army ambulances parked near the house and outbuildings. There were people too. Men in blue coats like dressing gowns, some on crutches, others being pushed in wheelchairs.

It must have been a fine country house, Allenby thought. Now it was a military hospital.

He glanced at her anxiously. 'Is your father one of those poor chaps?'

She stopped and looked at him, her eyes warm. 'I never thought you might think that.' She seized his arm and squeezed it. 'No this is my home, or part of it at the moment.'

She saw his astonishment and added, 'Don't be nervous. They're just people.'

But when they reached the house and the door was opened by a maidservant Allenby began to realize the extent of his mistake.

'Why, Miss Joanna, how lovely to see you again!'

It was just like a film, he thought.

A door opened across the hallway and an imposing khaki figure strode over to greet them.

Allenby's heart sank. The soldier as she had called him was some sort of general.

He shook hands while the girl removed her hat and tossed out her hair as she watched them.

'Good of you to invite me, sir.'

The girl's father eyed him and then the decoration on his jacket. In those seconds Allenby was able to recognize the rank on his shoulders; he was a brigadier.

'Come into the study for a moment, eh?' He beckoned to the maid. 'Take his bag up to his room, Lucy, there's a good girl.'

He was not at all what Allenby had been expecting nor was he much like Joanna or her dead brother. You would have known him to be a military man no matter what he wore. Neat grey hair and clipped moustache, a man who moved and spoke with every confidence. Used to being obeyed.

The study was comfortable and lined with books. There was a big desk with silver oddments scattered on it to act as paperweights. Pieces of army memorabilia, of the brigadier's career.

The girl sat in a deep leather chair, kicked off her shoes and drew her knees up to her chin. In spite of her father's intimidating presence Allenby had to look at her. She had discarded her coat, and he saw the curve of her body which no regulation white shirt could hide.

The brigadier said, 'Your mother's in the village, Joanna. Arranging for tonight's dinner I have no doubt. We shall have a few friends along too.' He eyed Allenby questioningly. 'All settled in?'

'Yes, sir. I – I know this part of the world quite well. Before the war – ' His voice trailed away.

'Really? Which hotels did you use? I'm afraid most of them are billets for my licentious soldiery nowadays.'

Allenby looked round the room. He felt trapped and yet so conscious of the girl watching him. He was making a fool of himself. Hotels. If only the brigadier knew. At best they had managed to stay in a boarding house, or some bed-and-breakfast cottage in those far-off days.

'One was the White Horse, I think.'

'Can't say I know it.' He turned as boots thudded on the terrace outside the windows. 'I must tell the MO not to allow those damned orderlies to use this for a short cut!'

He sat down and offered Allenby a silver cigarette box. It had a regimental crest on the lid.

Allenby shook his head and wondered what the brigadier thought about having two children in the Senior Service.

The brigadier crossed his legs and blew smoke towards a lively fire.

'Tell me about my son Timothy. Anything you can remember.'

Allenby knew that the girl had another brother, the oldest one, who was a captain in the Coldstream Guards somewhere in Italy.

Allenby began to talk. It was easier than he had expected. As if he was describing somebody else.

Once or twice the brigadier stopped him to clarify a point. But otherwise he listened intently.

Allenby saw the girl watching his face, and as a log on the fire blazed up suddenly he saw that her eyes were wet. But she smiled at him. Protective, as if to encourage him.

He said, 'And that's just about all I can remember, sir.'

'He was on the other side of the door, you say?'

'Yes.' Allenby could see it, the room, the obscene parachute mine, as if it had been yesterday.

'By the time I was dug out and sent to hospital, it was all over, sir. I was going to write to you, but – but I didn't.'

The girl looked at her father. 'That was my fault, Daddy.'

'Perhaps.' The brigadier seemed to be far away. 'And you shouted a warning?'

Allenby looked down at his hands. They were gripped together although he did not recall doing it.

'I'm not sure, sir. It's all blank. Lost. I'm sorry. We were friends.'

She said quietly, 'Tim wouldn't have felt anything.' She looked directly at Allenby. It was a question.

He shook his head. 'No.'

The brigadier consulted a clock. 'I must go now.' He studied Allenby and then his daughter. 'I shall see you for a drink before dinner.' He strode out calling for his driver.

They both sat in silence for several minutes and then the girl got up and crossed to his chair. Allenby could not see her face because she stood just behind his shoulder.

She said, 'Don't mind him. I know he can be a bit forbidding.'

Allenby stopped trying to remember. It was hopeless. All he could think of was that the brigadier had not hugged or kissed his daughter. Not the thing, perhaps.

Her father was in charge of transport. He would be up to his eyes in it with plans for the invasion looming every day. That probably explained his abrupt manner. His only daughter was working in Special Operations, and his dead son, who had not even been an officer, had died doing a vital job. His other son was on active service at the front, while he, who had given his life to the army, was involved only with transport.

She said, 'Thank you for telling us. I often wondered about it. He wrote in his letters how fond he was of you, of the way you looked after him. Tim would have been a brilliant scholar so I was amazed that he went for something like mine disposal.'

'He was very brave. It would be nearer the truth to say that he looked after me, not the other way round.'

She touched his hair with her fingers and when he turned to look up at her he saw that she was smiling but her cheeks were wet. He put his arm around her waist. 'I'm in love with you. You know that, don't you?'

She did not move or speak and he could see the movement

of her breasts against her shirt which made a lie of her composure.

'You mustn't say that, Richard. You hardly know me.'

'I can't help it.' He tried to smile. 'Call me Dick. Everyone else does.' He thought of his mother. The one exception. He said wretchedly, 'I'm a fool. I don't know what's got into me. We both know what may happen.'

He made to get up but she shook her head and then put her arms around his neck and pulled his face to her breast.

'Don't speak like that. You mustn't. I *care* what happens to you. When I got your letter I felt something. Something that was different. It frightened me. It still does a bit. But love? How can you know that?'

He pulled her closer and heard the beat of her heart, felt her nearness, her warmth.

'I just do.'

Somewhere a door slammed and an ambulance drove slowly down the drive towards the gates. But its mission, even the war itself, was held at bay.

'I'll take you to your room.' She laughed shakily. 'They've given you one about a mile from mine!'

Allenby stood up and held her, her hair touching his mouth. 'I wish we could be alone somewhere.'

She prised herself from his grip. 'You be good, *sir*.' She stepped away but her eyes were bright, excited.

'Mummy will be here any minute.'

Allenby smiled. 'That settles it then.'

Later, when Allenby had shaved and taken a bath in a vastly proportioned room, she led him on a tour of the house. One complete wing had been taken over as a recuperation hospital for wounded officers. Allenby caught occasional glimpses of some of them. They did not appear to speak much and looked lost, totally separate from everything but the fate which had brought them here. Survivors, as Frazer would call them.

It was a great house, he thought. How could he have hoped to impress Joanna?

They met again for drinks and Allenby was introduced to Joanna's mother. She was extremely attractive and very like her daughter. There was the senior medical officer from the hospital, the local magistrate and his wife, a couple of army types from the brigadier's staff and a close woman friend of the family whose husband had been reported missing in Burma. She was doing her best, but looked closer to tears than to laughter.

Allenby sat down for dinner next to Joanna's mother and somehow knew that the meal was going to be a trial of strength. The magistrate was extremely boring and kept complaining about the soldiers who were camped everywhere.

Joanna looked up and smiled at him. 'But they are *our* soldiers, surely?'

The brigadier said between courses, 'I suppose you were too young to have a job before the war, eh?' He was smiling at Allenby. 'At university no doubt; what were you reading?'

Like a cat with a mouse, Allenby thought.

When he had first been commissioned he had sometimes been asked the same question by his new companions, mostly out of idle curiosity. He had usually sidestepped the matter by referring to his previous life as 'studying at college'. After all, he had told himself, a technical school was almost a college in its way.

He replied, 'I didn't go to university, sir.'

He hated to lose face in front of Joanna, but to lie to her father would ruin everything. Not that the brigadier would allow him to slip off the hook so easily.

The brigadier's eyebrows rose slightly. 'Surprising.'

The senior medical officer, who looked slightly drunk, exclaimed, 'It's the *navy*, sir, not the army, what!' and roared with laughter.

Allenby was angry with them, more so with himself for caring so much.

The door opened and the brigadier looked at the maid, 'Well, Lucy?'

Allenby saw Joanna's eyes watching him, anxious for him, defiant, it was hard to tell which.

The maid said, 'Beg pardon, sir, but there's a telephone call.'

The brigadier dabbed his mouth with his napkin. 'Duty calls, I suppose.' He looked round the table. 'If you'll excuse me.'

The maid explained, 'No, sir, 'tis for the naval gentleman.'

Allenby stood up, his mind suddenly frozen. *Not now.* Not so soon.

The maid stood by the open door as he hurried past. But he heard Joanna's voice as he left the room, as clear as if she had been speaking to him.

'He didn't go to university, Daddy. But the King gave him the George Cross, and he's down for the DSC although he doesn't know about that, or care either, I suspect!' She sounded close to tears.

The room was still quiet when Allenby re-entered. He looked at their faces and mixed expressions. Then he turned to the girl and gave a shrug.

'Recall. I have to go.'

She hurried round the table and seized his arm, oblivious to everything.

'I'm coming with you, Dick!'

He tried to laugh it off. 'Probably got it wrong. You stay here and – ' His voice trailed away.

The brigadier said, 'I'll get my driver.' For once he seemed at a loss for words.

Allenby said his farewells and took his bag from Lucy. And he had not even slept in that fine bed.

They walked out to the car. The sky was full of stars, the air like ice.

She did not put on her cap but clung to Allenby's arm, her head pressed against his shoulder as the car roared down the drive and onto the main road.

They barely spoke until they were almost at the river. Then she raised her face and tightened her grip on his arm. She whispered, 'Kiss me.' When he lowered his face to her cheek she said urgently, 'No, Dick, a proper one!'

Their mouths came together, her lips parted as he kissed with the desperation of despair and hunger.

The car swung round a bend and they saw the wire fence and the armed sentry already staring at the approaching staff car.

They broke apart, hearts pounding, eyes slightly wild. He kissed her again, hard on the mouth. 'I love you.'

She replied in a small voice, 'Come back, Dick. I'll be waiting.'

The driver opened the door and watched as the lieutenant strode towards the gates.

'Home again, miss?'

She shook her head, barely able to speak. 'No. Take me to the Wrens' quarters, please. I'll show you the way'.

She looked back but Allenby had been swallowed up in the darkness.

When Allenby awoke from a restless sleep it took a few moments to recall where he was and what was happening. He groped for the curtain which enclosed his bunk and peered into the submarine's wardroom. A small place lined with bunks and crammed with lockers, a table, even some cases of food which could not find a home elsewhere in the boat.

He licked his lips as he peered at his watch. Four o'clock in the morning. They had been at sea for two days since leaving Falmouth; now the midget submarine X-19 was towing somewhere astern in the hands of her passage crew.

What an unnatural existence, he thought. His mouth tasted of diesel, of wet steel.

Like the X-Craft's crew, he had slept as much as he could, snatching a meal when the watches changed or a sudden alarm brought the crew charging from their sleep.

He listened to the faint purr of the electric motors and toyed with the plan he had to carry out, the orders that he had done his best to memorize.

A face parted the curtains and a seaman whispered, 'Nearly time, sir. I've got some tea ready.' He vanished.

Allenby lowered himself to the deck and saw Quinlan and his first lieutenant, Lomond, already at the table, their faces deep in thought.

Quinlan looked at him and nodded. 'Pretty calm up to now, they tell me.' He sounded edgy, not nervous. He probably wanted to get into his own boat, he would be at home then.

The speaker on the bulkhead said, 'Diving stations, diving stations.' Even the man's voice was hushed, as if he was afraid someone outside the hull might hear him.

The others picked up their bags, and Allenby made a quick check on his special satchel. He remembered seeing the submarine captain's face when he had lowered himself down the conning tower with it.

Allenby had said, 'It's all right, sir. Nothing risky!'

He had known what the man had been thinking. A year or so back some agents had been taken aboard a submarine for landing later on the enemy coast. One of the agents had some small bombs in his pocket, the kind which would explode under pressure. When the boat had dived one of them had exploded. It had killed three men, but somehow that skipper had got his command to the surface.

It was not something they would forget in this exclusive service.

They moved out and into the control room. In the dulled

orange glow the place seemed crowded. It was difficult to keep out of everyone's way.

'Silence in the boat!' The submarine's captain, a big bearded lieutenant commander, seemed too large for the job he did, Allenby thought, but he moved easily, a bit like Ives.

Watches and gauges were consulted. Above and around them the sea was silent. Allenby had looked at the plot and knew that the submarine had made a wide detour of the islands to ensure they would approach in deep water.

The bearded captain joined them by the chart table.

'I have to put you over now. The forehatch will be opened, so we must get a move on. With that thing open we're very vulnerable and can't dive.' He looked questioningly at Quinlan. 'All buttoned up? Rendezvous, signals, emergency stuff?'

Quinlan said, 'Should be all right.' They all looked at Allenby. Quinlan added, 'Our chum here has got the worst job.'

The captain sensed the mood, the danger it could create. He said curtly, 'Good luck. Let's get the show on the road.'

He crossed to the centre of his world by the shining periscope standards. His eyes passing over his team, the coxswain and second coxswain watching the hydroplanes, a stoker at the periscopes, first lieutenant checking the trim of the boat, lookouts by the ladder ready to dash to the bridge. They wore dark glasses to prepare their eyes for the night sea. They looked like blind men, Allenby thought.

Throughout the submarine's hull men would be waiting and listening, very aware of any time spent on the surface. They were only five miles from land.

The captain waited for the hydrophone operator to make a final report. 'No HE, sir.' His way was clear, as far as he could tell.

'Periscope depth, Number One.'

The captain ran his fingers through his thick hair and then stooped in readiness.

'Thirty feet, sir.'

Apart from the sound of the pumps Allenby felt little.

'Up periscope.'

The captain caught the handles and snapped them into place as he made a slow circle around the periscope.

'Down 'scope. Stand by to surface. Tell the dinghy party to shift themselves, Number One.'

The lower hatch was opened, the captain moved to the ladder, his glasses slung about his neck, a towel wrapped round beneath his duffel coat to repel the spray. It will be cold up top, Allenby thought.

Quinlan gave the captain a mock salute and they began to make their way forward, to the dinghy.

Allenby heard the first lieutenant call, 'Ready to surface, sir!' He took a quick glance through the periscope, watched by the captain from the ladder.

'All clear, sir!'

'*Surface!*'

The noise seemed deafening after the stealthy silence of cruising depth. The roar of compressed air bursting into the ballast tanks, the sudden vibration as the boat was released from her hydroplanes and rolled freely on an offshore swell.

Before the forehatch was opened the captain, lookouts and gun's crew would be in position, ready to fire, ready to dive.

Although Allenby was well wrapped up in his waterproof Ursula suit he was unprepared for the icy wind which seemed to cut his face like wire. Men tumbled around him, and the rubber dinghy was in the water and being warped aft before he knew what was happening. Quinlan and his own crew went with them. They were used to it, and what seemed like sudden pandemonium was part of a practised drill.

They were still moving ahead into the darkness so that the dinghy and its towline would not foul the screws. The submarine was just a black shadow, her waterline only visible because of the small bow wave.

'*Jump!*'

Allenby jumped and was hauled breathlessly into the dinghy which instantly began to fall astern from the parent submarine. Spray swept over them from the busy paddles and then Allenby saw another shadow coming towards them, the X-Craft on her own towline.

There were brief exclamations and greetings, and Allenby felt someone slap him on the shoulder as if to wish him luck. He turned to speak but the dinghy was already moving back along the towline.

Quinlan guided Allenby to an open hatch; the other three were already below, their voices unreal as they completed their first checks after taking over.

He crouched shivering by a forward bulkhead as the hatch was held open in the bitter air. The hull was even smaller than he had expected. These little submarines were only fifty-one feet long, and most of that was machinery. The control room was so small there was no way a man could stand up except under one small dome in the deckhead.

He saw the engineer, a chief ERA, sitting at the wheel, Lomond, the first lieutenant, clung to the lowered periscope, a stick compared with the other submarine's, and the third member a young sub-lieutenant named Eastwood, who was the boat's diver, waited with the captain for the signal to cast off the tow.

There was an oval door which led to the forends of the hull. The heads were in there, Allenby had discovered, also an extra, temporary, bunk. But in action the space, called the Wet and Dry, was used for flooding and releasing their diver for work outside the tough little hull.

'Signal! Cast off!'

The hull yawed violently as the tow was released. Their umbilical cord. Allenby could sense rather than feel the sudden roar of water as their parent boat flooded her tanks and dived once more.

Quinlan glanced at his first lieutenant. 'I've got her,

Charles. You get something hot to drink as soon as we've dived.'

Allenby watched. The passenger. The first lieutenant sat aft facing to starboard. He was adjusting the pump controls. The ERA was at the wheel, his eyes alert as he watched the gyro compass. The diver had removed a spare bunk from over the chart table and was busy with his pencil and dividers.

The hatch was closed and the air became a little warmer.

Quinlan raised his small periscope and grimaced.

'Dive, dive, dive. Thirty feet, 850 revolutions. Course zero-nine-zero.'

Allenby listened to the immediate inrush of water as the vents were opened and pictured the two great crescent-shaped charges which were fitted to either side. Each was of two tons of amatol. Enough to blast a battleship, as *Tirpitz* had found out.

The small crew completed another set of checks – course, speed, depth, pumps, everything – until Quinlan was satisfied.

Allenby pictured the other submarine already running deep and away from this tiny pencilled cross on the chart.

They were completely alone.

He tried to concentrate on that day at Joanna's home. How he had thrown all caution to the winds. How he had wanted her, and had needed her to know it.

But it became more difficult to recall each sequence of events. He opened his Ursula suit and put his hand inside to make certain he had a spare set of tools. It always made him feel like a burglar. Instead, he remembered the drive back to the river. Her head on his shoulder, the words almost torn out of her when he had kissed her. 'No, a proper one!'

It seemed to steady him. He would get back from this. Somehow.

14

Cold Courage

Lieutenant Quinlan rolled back his sweater sleeve to look at his watch. 'Time for a quick look. It must be getting light.' He moved to the chart table and waited for Allenby to join him. The boat was swaying and pitching, caught in the race of currents that converge on the Channel Islands.

Allenby watched the points of the dividers touch the chart.

Quinlan said, 'This is a tough bit of coast, rocks all over the place. But thank God the Germans with their usual efficiency have built a big radio mast there.' The dividers moved slightly. 'Should get a good fix on that for the last run-in.'

Allenby's stomach felt queasy. The confined space with its clinging smells was making him retch.

'Many local patrol vessels, d'you think?'

'Not really. There's a minefield along this stretch.' He jabbed the charge again. 'See?'

'When will we reach that?'

Quinlan gave a rare smile. 'We're in it now.'

He became businesslike again. 'Take her up, Charles. Periscope depth.'

The compressed air hissed like a great serpent and the deck tilted while Lomond juggled with his pump controls.

'Nine feet, sir.'

Quinlan bent down and pressed the periscope button. Allenby watched his set features and tried to gauge what was happening. The periscope came down and Quinlan bustled to the chart table again. Over his shoulder he said, 'Alter course. Steer one-one-zero.'

The ERA turned the wheel with great care. So close to the surface it was easy to lose control of pumps and hydroplanes. If they broke surface, it could be disaster.

Quinlan stared at the chart and grunted. 'Another look.'

The periscope was raised and Allenby saw Quinlan turning very slowly. Then he stopped and snapped, 'Plemont Point and radio mast bears Green four-five.' He took another quick look around and beckoned to Allenby. 'Here. But be bloody quick.'

Allenby pressed his eye to the rubber guard and stared with sudden surprise at the land. It looked as if you could touch it. Rocky slopes and long patterns of green above. They still lacked colour in the dawn light. He saw a beach too. Spray dashed over the lens and he ducked involuntarily. It was like swimming without moving.

Quinland took over the periscope and had another careful search on both sides of the hull.

He lowered the periscope and said, 'I think we've got it right. We'll put down on the bottom now. We should be safe enough. The reef will hold off the worst of the current.'

Allenby said, 'I saw the radio mast.'

Quinlan nodded. 'Without that, well – ' He did not have to spell it out.

'Take her down, Charles. Thirty feet. Then we'll touch bottom. It seems safe according to the chart. Hard sand and – ' They all looked up as something scraped slowly along the side of the hull. Like someone feeling his way. A blind man. The noise stopped right beside Allenby and he heard Quinlan mutter, 'It's caught on the starboard side-cargo.'

Then it moved on and the sound stopped altogether.

Quinlan said, 'Carry on, Charles.'

Eventually they steadied at thirty feet.

Allenby cleared his throat. 'Was that a mine?'

The first lieutenant grinned. 'Why? Did you want to get out and defuse the thing?'

They all laughed. Quick and nervous. The sound bouncing back and forth in the damp control room which had nearly become a tomb.

They touched the seabed at exactly the estimated time. Frazer would approve of Quinlan's skill as a navigator, Allenby thought.

Quinlan listened as the motor was stopped. Nothing. There was not even a sense of being at any depth.

He said, 'We'll have a hot meal.' He watched the ERA as he knocked off the clips on the after bulkhead door and then vanished into the tiny engine and motor room. Then he said, 'We'll rest as much as we can. The air's not too bad at present, but it's sensible to save it.'

Allenby sat beside his satchel. *If I am taken prisoner*. He had thought about it many times. He had still not found an answer.

The young diver was whistling as he unpacked some mugs and plates.

He thought suddenly of the brigadier and his casual questions. Universities, hotels. They did not count for very much down here. Joanna would be getting up soon, he thought. In his heart he knew she had not gone back to her home to finish her leave. She would be at the Wrennery, maybe even on duty at their new HQ where Prothero would be fretting and waiting for the first reports to come in.

Allenby remembered how troubled Prothero had seemed when they had left Falmouth. He had spoken to him and the X-Craft crew in an old customs shed in the harbour. Looking back, he should have understood the reason. Prothero would never be able to get down a conning tower. He smiled to himself. There might be no reports at all. Just an Admiralty statement. God knows there were enough of those. 'The Secretary of the Admiralty regrets to announce the loss of HMS so-and-so. Next-of-kin have been informed.' It was probably just as well the weary, embattled British public never saw the substance of those cool statements.

He thought of Joanna again, and the way she had stood by his chair, and touched his hair with her fingers. It was not difficult to remember it, or the moment he had held her. She had pretended to rebuke him, but her eyes had said otherwise.

Or was it another delusion, one more dream in his lifetime of dreams?

The ERA bent over him with a mug. 'One lump or two, sir?'

Allenby smiled. What a pity the public never saw men such as these.

Quinlan said, 'According to my orders you will be met at twenty-two hundred exactly. It will be cutting it fine.' He glanced past Allenby, his eyes watching the instruments and the depth gauge while half his mind concentrated on his written instructions.

'I shall pick you up at the rendezvous same time tomorrow after I've done *my* job. If you miss it – ' he shrugged, 'I shall come again the next day. It's all I can manage.'

Allenby nodded. It was plain enough. The little X-Craft could not move on the surface to charge her precious batteries by running the diesel engine.

He peered at the chart. One final look. He was being met by three men. No names. Better not to know, Prothero had stressed. The radar station was about two miles inland near a place called Champ Donne. They would have to get a move on to be back in time for the pick-up.

'Stand by, everyone.' Quinlan looked at his watch again. Then he said to Allenby, 'You will take the inflatable dinghy ashore and hide it. They'll know the best place. But when you return leave it where it will be found by the patrols.

There's a bag of other gear too. This has got to look like a commando job.' He moved to the periscope.

'Two-five-oh revolutions. Periscope depth.'

Allenby listened to the electric motor, the slight vibration as the boat nosed upwards towards the surface.

As the depth needle settled at nine feet, Quinlan raised his periscope once more.

A quick look round. It would be very dark by now, Allenby thought.

Quinlan looked at him. 'Ready for the off?'

Allenby picked up his satchel, suddenly loath to leave.

'Surface!'

The boat shuddered and lurched into some short, steep waves. The hatch banged open and dead, cold air blasted away the torpor of being submerged.

The diver hauled the dinghy onto the casing and Allenby followed with his satchel. Quinlan joined him and held firmly to the small guardrail.

'Good luck.' His eyes moved along the black wedge of land. It was hard to think of it as being any other colour.

Allenby slithered into the dinghy and used the paddle to move away from the low hull.

He took a quick bearing and began to paddle strongly towards a pale line of breakers.

He soon lost sight of X-19, although he did not know if it was on the surface or had already dived. Quinlan would probably wait to the last safe moment.

The small dinghy grated on hard sand and Allenby caught his breath as some dark figures loomed up amongst the rocks. He expected a challenge or a shot. To walk into an ambush with a nightmare waiting for him.

But the first one to reach him patted his shoulder and said, 'Good to have you here.'

The second one whispered hoarsely, 'We cannot wait.' He had what Allenby guessed was a Breton accent and was obviously very nervous. They pulled the dinghy into a deep cutting between some rocks and Allenby heard them covering it with seaweed which they must have prepared earlier.

The first man, obviously the leader, took Allenby's arm and guided him up a small, shelving beach. There were traces of rusting barbed wire and some concrete 'teeth' near the one and only path, although it was unlikely that any Allied tank would ever want to land here.

One man went on ahead and the little party halted every few minutes to make certain the way was clear. They crossed a narrow road, their feet suddenly loud, and the leader murmured, 'An armoured car comes along here every half-hour.' He chuckled. 'You are not supposed to wander around here at night.'

Allenby recalled something Prothero had said. This unknown man was an engineer who worked for the Germans. He had no choice. He would certainly be able to move about freely when he wanted to.

There were three bicycles hidden in a clump of coarse bushes. Allenby felt light-headed in the bitter air. How did they know he could ride one? Joanna had not asked him either. The thought of her helped to steady his nerves, to prepare him for the work ahead.

His guide said, 'We can ride most of the way, but we must watch out. You never can be sure of the Germans!' He called to the third man who was obviously remaining by the road to warn them of danger if or when they returned. 'See you soon, Harry.'

They mounted their cycles and rode in line with Allenby in the middle.

The leader had revealed a man's name. A carefully prepared ruse, he wondered. It was more likely carelessness brought on by fear. They were amateurs and it was a dangerous game.

Occasionally they passed a small humped building or hut. Something told Allenby they were empty and deserted, the coastal strip cleared completely to prevent anyone from signalling out to sea. Sicily seemed far worse by comparison, he thought. Here there was was nothing, not even a barking dog.

They paused for a rest while the second man went on ahead to sniff out the land. He returned and murmured something to the leader.

He said, 'All clear. There is an outflow pipe from the radar station. It is not yet complete.' His teeth shone in the darkness. 'Nor will it be after tonight, èh?'

The leader knew his way and seemed to recognize every stone and bush. Once he stopped to drop a British cigarette packet which had been in the dinghy. Allenby hoped for his sake the clues would not be too obvious.

The pipe jutted out from the hillside, and it took only a few minutes to remove the protective wire grid from its gaping mouth.

The leader peered closely at Allenby. 'Can you get through it?'

Allenby shouldered his satchel. The outflow pipe was almost as large as the W and D compartment on the X-Craft, but there was no point in mentioning it.

He climbed onto the metal, feeling its chill through his waterproof suit. To have something so large installed the Germans were obviously expecting to increase their defences even more.

The slope was not very steep, but the satchel and the confining pipe soon made him out of breath. He had cut his hands and one knee, and he could feel the leader pushing up behind him. The nervous one remained in hiding to guard their retreat.

The leader flashed a small torch and grunted. 'Here. Inspection hatch. Usually locked.' He thrust at it with his shoulder and when it opened he peered through it for several seconds. He must have practised this several times before making his suggestion about destroying it. How did they keep contact with people like Prothero? Who made the first move?

'Come on.' He gave Allenby a hand to help him into the other darkness. As they stood motionless Allenby realized it was not completely blacked out. There were small pinpoints of light above, where electric cables came through an upper concrete floor.

He heard something scrape and his companion whispered, 'Guardroom above us. Just two men. Above them is the working area. I designed it.' He led Allenby across the crudely finished concrete floor and then flashed his light on a steel junction box, and behind it a partly covered girder. He stood aside, the torch level as Allenby crouched down to examine it.

The other man whispered, 'I have dynamite here. It would have been necessary to move it when the work of finishing the outflow pipe began.' He released a deep sigh which betrayed the strain he was under. 'You are just in time.'

'Fetch the dynamite.' Allenby propped the torch on his satchel. 'No need to unpack it.' He groped for his detonators and a pack of plastic explosive. 'Are you sure the Germans won't come poking around here?'

He shook his head. 'I shall report for work as usual. There are several jobs that can be done before the pipe. I have brought a Thermos and some sandwiches. It will seem like a long wait, my friend.'

Allenby moved his shoulders. He felt cold already, and the thought of staying here with the enemy above him and a devastating pile of explosives as his only company was grim.

If only he had some better fuses. Ones which would last for days if need be. It would make the job much less hazardous.

They worked in silence until Allenby was finally satisfied. The girder was one of the main supports. He recalled the pylons in Sicily, the sapper falling dead. It all seemed a long time ago.

He said, 'Fair enough then. You'd better be off.' He tried to speak calmly and hide his anxiety.

The man suddenly seemed eager to go. Perhaps he had only just realized the enormity of what he was doing.

They shook hands and the leader began to scramble through the inspection hatch, and Allenby heard the sounds getting fainter and fainter. There was a short scraping noise, like the mine along the side of the X-Craft's hull, then total silence. That must have been them replacing the wire grid.

One hour dragged after the next, and Allenby had to massage his legs to stop them getting cramped. Once somebody began to use a powerful drill overhead, and he nearly strangled himself as he tried to prevent an onset of coughing when dust filtered down in the darkness.

He eked out the coffee and the sandwiches, but by that time he was unable to tell what the food consisted of.

He tried not to peer at his luminous watch. When he did, the hands never seemed to move.

Sometimes feet clattered overhead and he pictured his night-time companion up there with the enemy. He was taking a terrible risk. If he was caught – It did not bear thinking of. The enemy would offer no quarter, show no mercy. Any more than Thomas had done. He wondered how it must feel to the Channel Islanders. Occupied by the enemy, seeing them every day, hating them and yet afraid to show it. The German troops were older men or recovering from wounds, Prothero had said. Allenby expected that they were grateful to be here. Away from the Russian Front and all its misery.

It was a long, long day.

Allenby thought of Quinlan if only to contemplate what might happen if the X-Craft's mission went badly wrong. While he was cooped up in his concrete hiding place Quinlan and his three companions would be groping their way around the southwest coast of Jersey and then down across the bay to St Hélier harbour where German transport was reported at anchor.

If the X-Craft was driven deep by patrol boats, or became

entangled in an anti-submarine net, Allenby would be left to his own resources.

But as evening closed in over the islands Allenby heard the wire grid being removed from the pipe and soon afterwards the engineer crawled through the inspection hatch and handed Allenby another sandwich.

Allenby found that he was starving despite the nearness of danger. Between gulps he asked, 'Everything quiet?'

The man nodded. 'The Germans are installing some new mobile guns farther along the coast in case of an air attack. They are too busy to bother us.' He sounded worn out.

Allenby looked at his watch. 'Let's get it over with.' As the other man held the torch he adjusted the time fuse, and a second one in case of accidents. He would look a complete idiot if the radar station was blown up and he was left on the beach with his dinghy to face the music. He felt inside his Ursula suit to make sure the revolver holster was unbuttoned. He could not help wondering if he would have the courage to use it on himself before he was caught and interrogated. In his heart he doubted it. He found that he was sweating, and he had to force himself to concentrate. He tested the wires once more then snapped down the firing switch.

Then he backed away from the neatly taped explosives.

'Let's hope it works.' It was just something to say, to prevent him from running.

He thought of the girl's face in the darkness. That last time. He would get back to her. He *must*.

They crawled down the pipe and the engineer made certain that the grid was replaced exactly as it was in case a foot patrol should appear. The enemy sometimes sent out small squads of soldiers to forestall black-market operators and generally to keep the islanders guessing.

As they mounted their cycles Allenby could sense that his two companions were half looking over their shoulders, as if they expected an explosion already.

Allenby had put some photographs and a detailed plan inside his suit, as well as some tiny metal fittings in a leather case for the Intelligence experts in England.

He almost rode into the leading bicycle and realized that the man was leaning over the handlebars, his hand in the air.

The leader whispered, 'Something's wrong.'

They dismounted and Allenby saw the first man push his machine into some bushes and then kneel beside the deserted road.

Allenby could smell the sea, sense its regular movement out there in the darkness.

The man crawled back to them. 'He is not there.'

Allenby tried to understand. That must be the one named Harry. Had he left them? Or was he captured? Either way, time was running out.

There was a slight bend in the road, although Allenby could barely see it in the blackness.

The other two whispered together and he could sense their new apprehension. The unexpected was somehow worse than a visible threat.

The leader made up his mind and after giving Allenby a pat on the shoulder he vanished along the roadside. The other man knelt in the bushes saying nothing and keeping well clear of Allenby as if it might increase his chances.

The leader was soon back.

He whispered, 'There is a German scout car less than fifty yards away. Three soldiers.' He spoke in quick, breathless sentences. 'I think their car has broken down. They are looking at the engine.'

Allenby's mind explored the possibilities. They might take ages to repair their car. If they carried a field radio they might already have sent for aid. Quinlan would surface very soon now. He had to get to the beach. It was impossible. Hide, then, with these two amateur agents? Quinlan would still surface. The Germans might see or hear the X-Craft as she blew her ballast.

The leader stood up and said, 'I can bluff them.' His fear had gone and he sounded very determined. 'They are not a patrol.' He looked towards his companion. 'Coming?'

The man shook his head and retreated into the bushes. It did not seem to surprise the engineer and he said to Allenby, 'It is time. Take good care of those plans.' Without another glance he mounted the bicycle and rode very slowly along the road.

Allenby strained his eyes but the other man had vanished with his cycle. Allenby thrust his empty satchel into a bush and walked quickly across the road, his heart pounding in time with his footsteps.

A voice yelled, 'Halt! Wer da?'

For an instant only Allenby thought the voice came from another direction, that the nervous challenge was directed at him. He quickened his pace and heard the engineer call, '*Was wollen Sie?*' He even managed to laugh although he must have been terrified.

The German shouted wildly, '*Halt!*' Then the road lit up to a savage burst of Schmeisser fire. The firing stopped and Allenby heard their voices, the clatter of a bicycle careering off the road.

Allenby found that he had his revolver in his hand and wanted to run back, to pull the trigger until they were dead, or he had fallen to another burst.

He increased his pace and was almost running when he reached the rocks. He pulled the dinghy from its hiding place and heard his revolver splash into the water as he thrust off from the beach. He was gasping and almost sobbing as he worked the paddle until his arms throbbed. He did not even consider that the X-Craft might not be there, that he could easily be floating helplessly out to sea.

All he could see in his reeling mind was the man mounting his bicycle and riding towards the soldiers. *I can bluff them.*

Now the Germans would never know the real truth.

A voice called through the darkness, 'This way! Over here!'

Then he was clawing and scrambling over the X-Craft's rounded side.

He felt hands dragging him aboard and Quinlan's voice right in his ear, 'Thank God. We thought that was you just then!'

The rest was blurred as if he was only half conscious. He heard the hatch slam shut, the increased quiver in the hull as they turned away from the land.

He could not stop thinking, it was tearing him apart. He was thankful that the others were too busy as they prepared to dive to notice his reactions. There was no relief this time. Only the steel fingers of fear that gave him no peace.

Frazer sat beside his bed and read through Prothero's latest clip of orders. It gave details of the new section in Special Operations, which would consist of the original MGB, now completely repaired, and two similar boats.

They would exercise with the military and get used to taking over from one another in any sudden emergency. They had learned something from Able Two's loss, he thought.

The small house which had been taken over for the various officers had been left bare by the previous occupants. When not getting used to their new duties most of the officers made a beeline for one of the local inns and came back too full of beer or cider to notice the cold and the bare rooms.

It was late, and they would all be back soon, he thought. How on earth could he ask Lynn Balfour to go out with him when there was nowhere to go? The place was filled with uniforms. There would be no atmosphere even if she agreed to come with him.

He had seen very little of her. Only their occasional meetings at the inn. Frazer had decided to move into his new quarters. He already regretted it, except that he felt in touch with the new HQ along the road.

He wondered about Allenby. If he was back, in some other port. Or dead. Nobody mentioned it. It was like trying to speak to a brick wall.

A telephone broke the stillness and he reluctantly got to his feet. There was nobody else in the building, nor would there be until the stewards brought the morning tea. Piping hot and orange from the tinned milk. You could stand a spoon up in a cup of pusser's tea, they said.

The telephone rang again and he hurried along the passage to answer. It reminded him of the time she had phoned him at Gib. It was a mystery, and she had never explained it to him. He recalled the irate officer who had banged on their door, the fact he had gone half naked to the telephone.

He picked up the instrument. 'Yes. Lieutenant Commander Frazer here.' He always hesitated, caught out by his new rank.

It was a female voice. 'Could you come to the Operations Room, sir?'

Frazer blinked. 'Surely I'm not the senior bod in the whole place?

He tried again, 'Isn't Second Officer Balfour available?' It would give him an opportunity to see her.

She replied, 'Well, no, sir.' She sounded desperate. 'And the other Two-Oh is on leave until tomorrow.'

Frazer said, 'Something's wrong.' It dawned on him. He should have known. 'Is that Leading Wren Hazel?'

'Yes, sir. Staff Officer, Operations, and Commander Prothero will be here tomorrow.' She hesitated. 'Early.'

Frazer nodded. There was a flap on. But why – ?

She said, 'She needs your help, sir. She doesn't know I'm calling you. I didn't know what else to – ' She sounded close to tears.

Frazer had seen her once, but she had not even noticed him. So it was true about her and Dick.

He said, 'I'll be right there. Three minutes.' He added softly, 'And thanks.'

It was a holiday cottage which Lynn Balfour shared with another Wren officer, the one on a night's leave.

The dark-haired Wren had to walk quickly to keep up with Frazer's strides.

She said as they hurried through the gates, 'She's not well.'

Frazer glanced at her pale profile. 'You care, don't you?'

She replied, 'She's a real poppet. She never lets anyone down.' She hesitated as they reached the cottage. 'Look, sir, there's something you should know.'

He touched her arm. 'Later. Let's go inside.'

They closed the door and switched on the lights. It was like a stage, set for a play, but still awaiting the actors. A typical Cornish cottage, he supposed, still furnished by the people who had once come here to get away from it all.

A Wren officer's jacket lay carelessly across a sofa and a tricorn hat perched jauntily on an empty flower vase.

The girl called Joanna said, 'I – I'll go and see – '

Frazer said quietly, 'We'll go together.'

He pushed open the bedroom door and saw that a light was still burning. His eyes took it in with one glance. A photograph on the dressing table of a serious-looking man with a dog. That must be her father who was a vet in Edinburgh. Leading Wren Hazel stepped aside and he saw Lynn sprawled on her side, half covered by the bedclothes, one bare arm dangling towards the floor. There was another photograph in a frame beside the lamp. The young lieutenant who must have been her lover. His eyes fastened on an empty pill bottle which lay directly below her outthrust hand.

Frazer said, 'Help me.' He cradled his arm under the girl's body and raised her to a half-sitting position. Joanna leaned over to pull her nightdress back onto her bare shoulder to cover her breast.

Frazer thought suddenly of the German girl, and Ives's anguish for her.

'Is she – ' Joanna touched her face and pushed the hair from her eyes.

Frazer hesitated and then thrust his hand below her breast. He was conscious of her nearness, unable to believe what had happened. Her head rolled against his chest as if her neck was broken. She was out cold.

He looked up and saw the girl watching him, her brown eyes very steady, prepared.

Frazer said, 'There is a heartbeat.' He lifted Lynn's face with his hand and supported her chin as she lolled against him.

'Could you make some coffee?' He saw Joanna's relief, her eagerness to help, the need to do something.

She hurried out and left the door wide open.

Frazer held Lynn carefully, aware of her body in his grip, and how lovely she was, so different too without her uniform.

What had she done? He lowered his face and touched her mouth with his. As he did so he smelt and tasted the gin. He had already noticed it but had assumed it was because she had been drinking while reading Prothero's orders.

It hit him like a club. If Prothero arrived with SO(O) in the morning it would ruin her. But why?

He heard the clatter of a cup, and prayed that she would be all right.

Aloud he murmured, 'Lynn, my love, what am I to do with you?'

He studied her face, and then very carefully lifted her to the edge of the bed and lowered her feet to the carpet.

Again, her body lolled against him and he said, 'Whatever it is, my darling, we shall sort it out. This is no way to act.'

Joanna had come into the room with a mug of black coffee but paused to watch as Frazer stroked her hair and kept talking to her in a low soothing voice. He saw her and said, 'Here, I'll take it.'

Together they forced some of the coffee between her lips.

But she showed no sign of life, and even when Frazer spread a towel across her to protect her from the coffee, she did not react. How many pills had she taken? He did not even know what they were.

He said, 'See if you can run a bath.' Their eyes met over the short, tousled hair. 'It might help. Pills and gin don't mix. Did you know?'

She met his gaze calmly. 'Some of us did.'

He put down the mug and held Lynn's face against his shoulder. 'But why?'

The other girl paused by the door. 'It's the war, isn't it, sir?'

Frazer stared with sudden anxiety and waited for some sign that she was still breathing.

He saw her lips part slightly, the faint movement of her breast.

'Come on, you can do it.' He got her to her feet and carried her around the room, their shadows leaping across the walls like two wild dancers.

He could hear Joanna running a bath and wondered what they could say if the duty officer or almost anyone else walked in. It did not seem to matter that he had broken a man's wrist during the raid on the Italian general's house. This would be seen in a very different light.

He lowered her to the bed and reached for the coffee again. He had to keep trying, no matter what. Or should he call the MO? With a sudden start he realized that her eyes were wide open, unmoving as if she had indeed died.

There was no recognition, no understanding. She just watched him, their faces almost touching. How blue her eyes were, so close they filled her face.

'It's you.' She lifted one arm very slowly and tried to put it to his shoulder but it fell to the bed again, and she moved her gaze for the first time to stare at it.

'It's you,' she tried again. 'You came.' She sounded different, far away.

Frazer hardly dared to move. She thought it was the lieutenant in the photo. Somehow he had come back. It was all she ever wanted. He was sad for her, hurt for himself, as if a stranger stood between them.

He said, 'You must try to get up, Lynn. You have to walk.'

But she was looking at him again, her features relaxed.

'I shall try.' He helped her to stand but she rested against him, unable to move further. Her shoulder had fallen bare again and as he lifted the shoulder strap to cover her breast she said, 'I knew you would be like this.' Her head lolled against him. 'Gentle. So gentle.'

The door opened and the Wren said, 'She's looking better.' But her eyes were anxious.

Lynn stared at her. 'Hello.' Then she smiled. 'Jo.'

She allowed herself to be guided to the bathroom and Frazer said, 'Can you manage?'

Joanna nodded.

Lynn Balfour turned her head. 'Don't go yet.'

Frazer shook his head. 'I'll wait in there. Don't worry about anything but getting better.'

As he made to leave she said, 'I'm glad it was you, Keith.'

Frazer shut the door, stunned.

She had not thought him to be someone else.

He looked at the framed photo. So perhaps at long last he was dead in her eyes as well.

15

No Secrets

It was a bright clear morning with a hint of overnight frost still in the air. Commander Prothero stood before a fire and rubbed his hands. He felt tired after a fast drive from Plymouth, but wide awake with excitement. His companion, the admiral's Staff Officer, Operations, Commander Whitley, perked up as a Wren entered the office with a tray of coffee.

Prothero said, 'They pulled it off, dammit. The reports are coming in now.' His small eyes looked through the window as if he could see it. The explosions, the midget submarine, the victors.

Whitley allowed the coffee to sear his throat, then said, 'You sound as if you thought it would end otherwise, Aubrey?'

Prothero nodded. 'I did. It was asking the impossible. That's commonplace these days.'

'What about this two-ringer of yours, Allenby? Is he the hero everyone thinks?'

Prothero would not be drawn. He smiled. 'You'll meet him soon. They entered Falmouth last night.' Hero? What a question. Of all the brave men Prothero had met and used Allenby was probably the most remarkable. He seemed unable to stop himself, even though he must be half crazy with fear.

The other commander persisted. 'Captain Heywood says – '

Prothero held up his hand and grinned. He had just remembered what Goudie had said to the captain. He toned it down and said cheerfully, 'I don't give a damn what he says!'

Leading Wren Hazel entered with a sheaf of signals.

Prothero eyed her gravely. She looked clapped out and her eyes were red.

He said, 'You can stop worrying.'

She stared at him, unable to speak.

Prothero added gruffly, 'He's back, safe and sound.'

She left the office and Whitley said, 'You have an odd way of dealing with your people, Aubrey. Just like a family, eh?'

'Yes. They are to me!' He pressed his buzzer and frowned. He had heard something about Second Officer Balfour. He could not keep ignoring it. Things were getting keyed up for the invasion. It had to be sooner rather than later. Everyone was screaming for it. Those, that is, who would not have to take part in it.

Lynn Balfour entered and smiled to Commander Whitley. 'Sir?'

Prothero studied her curiously. Bright as a button, her skin glowing, a sight on any morning.

He said awkwardly, 'Lieutenant Allenby will be here shortly, Lynn. He is being debriefed.'

She said, 'Won't you send him on leave, sir?'

Prothero toyed with her words, her voice. She had changed in some way. For the better? He could not tell.

He replied, 'I expect so. We'll see.'

'That means you might be thinking of transferring him back to general service, is that it, sir?'

'Can I ask you something?' Whitley leaned forward in his chair. 'Is it your place here to question a superior's orders?'

Prothero moved as if to defend her but she said, 'I think it is, sir.' Her eyes flashed and she went very pale. 'May I ask *you* something, sir?'

'Of course.'

'When did you last go to sea?'

Whitley flushed. 'I wanted to.'

He had been on staff work since being recalled to the navy from an unwanted retirement.

She said, 'I'm sorry, sir. That was cruel.'

Prothero looked from one to the other. 'You'd both better know that I make all the decisions round – ' He snatched up the telephone as it broke the tension. '*Yes!*' He had not meant to shout. It was just in time, he thought. Lynn Balfour looked as if she was about to throw up.

'He's here.'

Outside the building Lieutenant Richard Allenby paused with his raincoat slung over one arm as he stared down at the river. It was bitterly cold, but it helped to clear his head, to think. He had seen several people watching him both here and at Falmouth when he had said his goodbyes to Quinlan and his crew. What had those glances said? Surprise that he was back? Or were they merely curious to see what it had done to him?

He tried to examine his feelings as he had taught himself to do. In the past he had laid them out seemingly alongside his tools as he had prepared to defuse a mine.

This time it was different. He felt nervous, afraid that he had lost control in some way.

A shadow fell across the wall and he turned to see a tall petty officer saluting him.

He returned the salute and would have continued towards the door had not the man blocked his way. It was Ives.

Ives looked at him anxiously. 'It's me, sir!' He saw Allenby's uncertainty and added, 'I've been made up to PO.' He grinned. 'Lieutenant Commander Goudie says it's to make more room on the messdeck for the others.' He leaned forward. 'You all right, sir?'

Allenby held out his hand. 'I – I'm sorry. Congratulations. You earned it ten times over. I'm glad.' He stood staring at him helplessly, unable to go on.

Ives said, 'Look, sir. I know what you must have gone through. Why not let me see the Boss and tell him you're going to get your head down for a bit, eh?'

Allenby stared at him, his nerves screaming. *Stop it. I can't take any more. Not even your kindness. Especially that.*

He said, 'No. But thanks all the same.' He walked to the door and knew Ives was watching him as he entered.

The entrance hall was deserted although he heard a man's voice coming from the communications switchboard. He braced himself, remembering the Chief Yeoman and his bicycle. In turn that reminded him of the Jersey engineer on his cycle. The bravest, most courageous act he had ever seen.

A door opened and he saw her standing there, hands at her sides, her eyes fixed on him as he walked across the hall.

Just a few paces yet it took an eternity. In that time he saw her concern, the pain in her eyes as she looked at him.

He had it all ready. What he had intended to say. If he ever got back.

He threw his arms round her and pressed his face into her hair.

She held him tightly, her voice muffled against his chest. 'It's all right, Dick. It's all right now.'

Allenby tried to hold back but it was useless. He could hear himself sobbing uncontrollably, and hated what she must think of him.

And all the while she spoke to him, small, lost phrases as she held him. If she felt anything at that moment it was a combination of pride and surprise.

Pride that he could show his innermost feelings to her and nobody else. Surprise that she knew she loved him, and had since his letter.

Captain Jocelyn Heywood, Royal Navy, surveyed the seated officers and gave a small smile.

'You have had a full week to grow accustomed to your
boats and to each other's idiosyncrasies.'

There were several grins as he had expected. He had used
this introduction many times.

'There won't be much spare time from now on. You will
be working with the other special units and alongside the
assault groups which will eventually spearhead the invasion
into Normandy.'

Frazer sat near a window and saw the bare trees bending
to a stiff southwesterly. It had been good to get back to sea
again, in his own boat. Goudie had driven them through
every possible manoeuvre, in the Channel, and into unfamiliar waters as far as the Welsh coast. They had watched
commando units and infantry sweating ashore from their
strange, boxlike landing craft, and clambering up seemingly
vertical cliffs in full kit.

It was doubtful if anyone round here knew or guessed
much about Prothero's new flotilla. A navy within a navy.
The three boats had been painted in accepted patterns that
you would see in any Coastal Forces base along the southern
coast and the eastern coast as well. Frazer was glad that he
had the same boat for his own. Once known as Able One,
it now sported new pendant numbers, as did the others.

He glanced across the big rectangular room which had
once been the hotel's billiard hall. Now, austere and lined
with maps and warship silhouettes, it had cut all links with
the past. *Like us.*

The others were outwardly attentive to Heywood's words.
Archer, now a lieutenant and in command of MGB 194,
looked older and had lost some of his bite. As if he had not
recovered from the Med. His second in command was a
subbie named Lockyer from Coastal Forces, who had served
a year in MTBs.

The skipper of the third boat was a Lieutenant Kellett who
had also been in MTBs but had come to Prothero's Navy
via another mysterious section called the Levant Schooner

Force. It was quite common for them to work amongst the
Greek islands and even to make their bases on those occupied
by the Germans. His first lieutenant, another subbie, had
only just been commissioned. 'Biff' Tanner had apparently
been too good as a boxer for his squadron to be allowed
promotion to the wardroom. His admiral had rated sport
and athletics far higher than the business of waging war.

Frazer considered his own small command. Allenby, his
acting first lieutenant, was listed first as the section's explosives expert. Just as his young sub, Alex Balfour, would
be used mainly for intelligence and radio work where his
knowledge of languages would be of paramount importance.

Goudie commanded all of them. Despite his wound and
the pain it obviously gave him, he showed no sign of slowing
down.

He had just said this morning, 'Well, Keith, if I buy one
in the next fiasco, you'll be in my shoes. How does it feel?'

Frazer could not recall his reply. He knew Goudie better
now and did not rise so easily to his brutal wit.

He ran his eye quickly over the newcomers. To the public
at large they would look like typical wartime officers. Young,
keen, and somehow vulnerable.

Did we look like that too, he wondered. Then he thought
of Allenby. He would be back from his short leave today.
He had heard that Prothero was worried about him, but too
protective to show it. Heywood would expect results. If
anyone died in the process, too bad.

There were a few staff officers at the back of the room
and two Wren petty officers taking shorthand. Prothero and
Commander Whitley sat side by side but were a hundred
miles apart, Frazer decided.

He turned his head slightly to look at Lynn Balfour. He
had barely seen her since that night when he had lifted her
out of bed. They had all been too busy, and he knew she had
the additional anxiety of her young brother joining Special
Operations in spite of all her arguments. He was to have

joined Archer's boat, but she must have pleaded with Prothero to arrange the change to his own command. He was not sure that was a wise thing even now.

When they began training in earnest it would be even harder to see her. Perhaps impossible.

He looked up startled as Heywood said dryly, 'You have been given a few new pieces of equipment and will have to squeeze in some extra hands. But radar,' his tongue lingered on the word even though his eyes were on Frazer, 'will play an important, perhaps a conclusive, part in the months ahead. I assume, Commander Frazer, that you are well versed in such matters, however dull, eh?'

'Sorry, sir.' He had not heard a word and saw the others grinning at him, glad it was him and not them.

He saw Lynn raise her lashes from her pad and look directly at him. Her mouth moved slightly, although it was hardly a smile.

Heywood tossed his folder to the paymaster lieutenant who was his secretary, a man nobody envied, and said, 'Until tomorrow then.'

Lieutenant Kellett stood up as the others rose from their chairs. 'Off to sea again, I'd say. It's worse than the real thing.'

Frazer watched as Heywood murmured something to Prothero, and saw Lynn take up her pad as if to leave with the Boss.

He hurried across the room and confronted her.

'I wanted to see you, Lynn.' He dropped his voice as one of the Wrens watched them curiously.

'Yes. I'm sorry. I really can't – ' She looked at his face and said, 'It'll get busier from now on. It's like a flood. Ships, men, vehicles, there's hardly a square yard left in the southern counties.' She smiled sadly. 'That's not what you want, is it?'

'No. I need to see you. Talk with you.'

She dropped her gaze and said, 'I've never really thanked you for what you did.'

'That was nothing.'

'It was *everything*.' She put her hand on his cuff and stared at it as if she could not believe what she had done. 'I was ashamed.' Her eyes lifted again and fixed on his. 'I still am, deeply. Maybe it was what I needed – ' She turned as Prothero called her name. Then she shrugged. 'You can see how it is.'

She nodded to her two Wrens and said, 'Anyway, I'll see you at the admiral's party tonight. You *are* coming?'

He raised an eyebrow. It sounded like a royal command. 'Yes, I'll be there.'

She smiled. 'You're off to sea again tomorrow.'

'You know everything about us, don't you? Where we go, what we do.'

'Does that bother you?'

'I care about you and what you think. You must know that.'

Prothero called testily, 'Lynn, when you have a moment!'

'Blast him!' Frazer said quickly. 'Tonight then. I must talk.'

She studied him gravely, her eyes very steady. 'Yes. If we get the chance.'

Later that evening, as the stewards finished the ritual of fixing the blackout screens and curtains, Frazer understood what she had meant.

The place was crowded with noisy, jostling figures, most of whom were in uniform. All the services were represented including the Wrens and some VAD nurses from the local military hospital. There were even some Royal Marines officers, attached to another hush-hush unit along the Cornish coast, who were said to be doing 'things' with canoes.

In the midst of it all Rear Admiral Percival Oldenshaw, the head of Special Operations (Navy), stood and beamed like a small monkey. He had been retired years ago, but had been recalled to the service he loved and offered a post that most people thought would soon cease to exist.

Dunkirk, Singapore, names written in blood, had made most doubters see the war as purely defensive. Oldenshaw, with his ruthless and eccentric enthusiasm, had changed all that. Small raids on enemy-occupied coastline, pinpricks at first, had been the start. Then more daring attacks with carefully picked volunteers, most of whom were misfits in their more conventional roles.

Now the talk was of a final invasion of Europe. It presented problems undreamed of by any previous military planners, and would involve an armada so vast that it was a wonder the enemy had not already discovered the plan and the objectives.

A small orchestra made up of part-time musicians – Frazer recognized the violinist as one of the base cooks – did its best to compete with the buzz of voices and laughter.

Goudie was standing by a long table converted to a bar and looked as if he had been at it for some time. Frazer nodded to him and received a glassy stare in return. It no longer worried him. Whatever it was that held Goudie together seemed to carry him through each crisis, no matter how much it demanded of him.

He saw most of the flotilla's officers dotted about amongst the crowd. Archer, unusually animated, his ginger hair standing out like wings as he made some point or other to a wide-eyed WAAF from the local fighter station. Prothero, red and sweating badly, was discussing something with the admiral, and Heywood, somehow aloof despite the press of people around him, watched in silence, his pale eyes everywhere.

It was lucky they were not putting to sea until noon, Frazer thought. There would be hangovers in plenty in the morning.

Then he saw her auburn hair between two army subalterns and plunged towards her.

She was laughing, pretending to be shocked by some joke which one of them had told. But she saw Frazer, and again their eyes seemed to lock, to exclude all others.

He exclaimed, 'You're hard to find, Lynn!' He was shouting.

One of the soldiers said, 'I'm the one who's hard, chum.'

Frazer ignored him. 'Come and have a drink with me.'

The officer who had told the unfortunate joke muttered, 'Bloody colonials!'

Frazer found a corner and turned his back on the rest like a rugby forward.

'You look lovely.'

'Not you as well!' She held up her glass and studied him over the rim. 'Here's to you.'

He clinked his glass. 'To us.'

She said, 'Thank you for taking Alex with you.' She moved nearer so that he could hear above the din. 'He's really just a kid.'

Frazer smiled, 'Not like you, eh?' He could smell her perfume. The same as she had used on that night when he had carried her. When her breast and shoulder had been quite bare. He hoped she did not remember it.

'Can I see you for a few moments after this?'

She looked up at him in the same searching way, as if she was doubtful about something. 'Don't you care for *this*? I'd have thought it would be just your cup of tea.'

Frazer did not know if she was goading or testing him.

'I can live without it.'

'I've been asked to join the Boss and the admiral afterwards.' She saw the disappointment on his face and added, 'You once told me that you were a fan of Nelson's.'

Frazer started, off guard. He barely remembered it. On one of those fleeting visits to the pub she must have brought it out of him.

He grinned. 'So what?'

'What would *he* have done, d'you think?'

Her eyes were very bright, very steady, as if she was trying to conceal her thoughts from him.

He held her hand and replied, 'Nel would have said that orders are no substitute for initiative.'

She pulled her hand away and tugged her jacket into place. 'I must mingle.' She reached up impetuously and touched his mouth with her fingers. 'No wonder Emma fell for him.'

Then she turned and was swallowed up in the crowd.

Another admiral entered with his aide, and Frazer recognized him as a flag officer from Plymouth. But he did not care who he was. He turned away and touched his lips as she had done. What did she mean? Who was she behind her careful defences?

He saw Lieutenant Quinlan and his first lieutenant by the bar and made his way towards them. Nobody in this strange navy within a navy had been left out. Except those who would never be able to come, ever.

By the entrance doors Allenby stared at the swaying figures and grimaced.

'God, what a riot!'

The girl slipped her hand into his and looked at him steadily.

'We needn't stay. But the Boss would be hurt if we dodged it.'

He looked at her and squeezed her hand. She would never, could never, know what she had done for him, how close it had really been.

It had been an enchanted week, and even her home in Devon had lost its threatening atmosphere. Probably because her father had been away in London.

They had walked together for hours, no matter what the weather had been like. Her mother had been at the house, and several visitors had called, some to take lunch or dinner with her. But to Allenby it had been on a different plane. Magic. He had found that he had been able to sleep at night, and only once had a nightmare jerked him upright in bed.

He had heard not the thunder of the X–Craft's charges demolishing the German supply ship, but the pathetic clatter of the bicycle on that unknown Jersey road.

She had come to his room. He must have been making a hell of a noise although she had denied it. For several precious minutes they had clung together, she with her face against his hair, while he clutched her body to his and, despite all he had told himself, had stroked her, feeling her respond through her nightdress. He mother had come to the room eventually. He still wondered if her delay had been deliberate.

The next day, the last one, he had explained, had tried to apologize. She had not been able to face him as she was now.

'I did not know I could feel like that, Dick. I have never been with a man. Not that way. And yet I felt – '

He had held her, desperately, protectively. 'I have never been with any girl.'

It was so easy that he was still amazed. No lies, no boasts to impress others more worldly.

He said, 'I love you, Jo.'

She kissed his cheek. 'I love you.'

They did not see the expressions of the chief steward and his assistant.

The steward gave a silent whistle and said, 'All right for some, innit, Fred?'

Inside the big room Allenby said quickly, 'There's your father.' He found he could say it without discomfort. In one week she had done that for him.

She stared across the room and saw the familiar straight-backed figure with the red tabs on his collar. For some reason she felt a sudden anxiety. Her father was speaking to the admiral from Plymouth.

She replied, 'They went to school together.' She squeezed his hand tightly. Nothing must spoil things for him. Nor would it if she had anything to do with it.

*

The room was just as Frazer remembered it when, out of desperation, Dick Allenby's girl had called him here.

There was no fire in the grate but Lynn switched on an electric heater and busied herself with the curtains.

Frazer said, 'Your friend's not here yet?' He glanced towards the adjoining room. 'She'll probably come in smashed in a minute.'

Lynn kicked off her shoes and sat on the sofa. 'Help yourself to a drink.' She watched him as he opened the sideboard. 'I'd have been smashed, as you so delicately put it, but for you. You know that, surely?'

He slipped out of his jacket and sat beside her. He was very aware of her nearness and the fact she was watching him. One stupid move and he would destroy everything. If there was anything to destroy. Maybe his need for her outweighed both caution and common sense.

'You must be tired,' she said. 'And you've another long day tomorrow.'

It would soon be over. Either she would ask him to leave or her housemate would arrive. Drunk or sober, it would make no difference.

He twisted round and looked at her. 'You really are marvellous.'

She held up her hand. 'Easy, Keith. I'm not marvellous at all. I'm just an ex-secretary who wanted some excitement. I never thought I could get involved as I did and so badly hurt. I'm very ordinary really.'

He took her hand and held it firmly. 'I know better, Lynn. It's why people like you.' He felt his will weakening under her blue gaze. 'And why I love you.' She made to pull her hand away but he persisted. 'I guess I felt like that the first day I saw you at Portsmouth. It was there, but you were so wretched about Paul you couldn't see it. I loved you then. It's never stopped even though I thought it was hopeless, a non-starter.'

'You remember his name.' She watched him, his uncertainty. 'And I can hear it without pain. It's so strange.'

She stood up so suddenly that he thought she was already regretting her words.

But she said, 'I think I will have that drink now.' She waved him down. 'No. Let me. I need to think.'

She walked past the fire, her stockinged feet soundless on the old floor.

She said. 'If you're not ready to leave, I'm going to change, all right?' She made to smile but it only half came. 'Change into something more comfortable, as Bette Davis would say.'

Alone by the unblinking fire Frazer wondered what he would say to her. He knew it was important, vital that he should get it right. A car halted outside the cottage and he heard a door slam. He groaned; he had missed the moment.

The other door opened and she came in again, her glass in her hand.

From throat to toes she was covered by a peacock-blue robe; in the fire's glow it seemed to shimmer like her hair. Only her face was still as she watched him. Like a lovely mask.

She said, 'Nice, isn't it? Real silk. The Boss got it for me on one of his North African jaunts.'

She put her glass on a small table and held out her hands to him.

Frazer held them tightly and drew her towards him. 'I think we're about to have company.' He barely recognized his own voice.

The car started up and drove past the cottage, the sound dying and leaving the room silent again.

She said quietly, 'We're not. Jane's not coming back tonight.'

He stared at her, seeing the look in her eyes, like a plea, like defiance.

'I told her not to come, you see.'

She slipped down beside him and raised her face to his, her lips slightly parted like that night when she had known nothing about his concern, his desire for her.

They kissed gently at first and then with an eagerness that left them dazed, startled even. She nestled her head against his shoulder as with great care he slowly unbuttoned her robe. She watched, her heart pounding as he lifted her breast in his fingers, caressed it and squeezed it until he could barely contain his longing.

Then they stood up and she waited motionless as he let the gown slip from her shoulders and fall to the floor.

She watched his eyes as he picked her up and said, 'I carried you before, Lynn.'

As they entered the bedroom she put her arms round his neck and kissed him again, and again until they were breathless. He laid her on the bed but when he went to switch off the light she said, 'No. I want to see you. No secrets. Promise, no secrets.'

He threw his clothes anywhere and then knelt on the bed beside her.

'I love you,' he said. '*So much.*'

She reached up and held his shoulders, her fingers hot on his bare skin.

'I never dreamed.' She studied his face feature by feature. Only the quick movement of her uplifted breasts told him that her need matched his own. She added, 'Oh Keith, was it meant to be?'

He stroked her breasts, and felt the nipples harden under his fingers, saw the way her lips moistened as if she was losing control. Very gently he knelt over her, her legs parting as she continued to watch his eyes.

She said, 'I knew you would be gentle. I just knew.' Then she seized his arms, her nails digging into them as she murmured, 'Come into me, now!'

Even as he came down on her she gasped, 'It's been a long time. It may hurt. But don't stop.'

Frazer heard her sob, saw her eyes close as he pressed into her. But her body arched to receive him, to hold him and carry him down until they were one together.

16

Sunset

Lieutenant Commander John Goudie stood by a small fence above the river, one scuffed boot on the lower rail as he watched the activity below.

Prothero ambled over to join him. He looked and felt tired. His flotilla had worked and trained for weeks and months, so that some of the crews as well as the operational staff had begun to believe this was their only purpose.

Prothero looked down and followed the other man's gaze. The river was packed with craft, and yet when they came to this new HQ they had imagined the place already full.

Some landing craft were disgorging soldiers onto a pontoon, harried and controlled by the harsh tones of their NCOs. Even at this distance Prothero thought the men looked dispirited, resentful. You could take only so much training. Then tempers frayed and you got careless. It could be a fatal disease.

Goudie said, 'They'll be refuelled right away, sir.' He watched the three MGBs swaying together beneath a faint haze of petrol vapour. Their crews, in a mixture of sweaters, woolly hats and seaboots, looked like pirates. Lines snaked ashore, and he picked out the people as individuals. If he had been that kind of man Goudie might have admitted he was proud of them. Pride was not something you tossed about.

The boats had lost their newly painted image too. The hulls were stained and bore a few scrapes, marks of unexpected encounters in pitch darkness. But he knew there was nothing wrong with the machinery of war, the new guns, the big Packard motors which in spite of some extra gear could still offer forty knots.

Prothero pictured the maps in his Operations Room, the bright arrows and stars, a gathering of armies never seen in a lifetime. But there was still the Channel. It had stopped plenty of England's enemies. It could just as well stop Overlord as the secret files had labelled it.

Goudie glanced at his profile. 'Weeks not months is my guess, sir.'

Prothero grunted. 'Maybe.' It was as near as he could give to agreement.

He saw the first of the sailors clambering ashore, grubby, outwardly weary. But he knew his jolly jacks by now. In an hour or so they would be thronging the local pubs, smart as paint in their tiddly suits and gold badges and facing the taunts of the military or a few unwise civilians. 'Home again, Jack?' But it could not go on.

Prothero thought of Second Officer Balfour. How she had changed. She seemed to work longer hours, but nothing ever riled her. He had noticed that when Frazer had visited HQ ostensibly to study the plot or obtain intelligence reports they had kept apart, and yet it did not take a genius to see their oneness, their ability to touch even at a distance. He felt the old envy rising, and said, 'There's a job on. One boat. I suggest Frazer. But no heroics, d'you hear?' He glanced at Goudie's uncompromising features. 'I can't afford to lose a boat. Not now of all times.'

Goudie frowned. 'What's wrong with Coastal Forces? Surely they can handle it.'

'They'll be involved, of course.' Prothero sifted through his thoughts. He knew so much that he was always afraid he would let something slip.

'We've had word from the admiral's Intelligence Section. About a Dutch agent. We've got to bring him out.' He saw the argument on Goudie's face. 'No other way. The Germans have got the whole coastline buttoned up.'

Goudie nodded, his eyes distant. 'My old stamping ground. The Hook of Holland. Ah, well –'

'He's important because of the invasion.'

Goudie shrugged. 'Aren't they all?'

'Don't be such a bloody cynic. Do you imagine I like it?'

Goudie eyed him flatly. 'It *looks* good for your SBS, sir.'

Prothero glared. 'Not this time, damn you!' They both grinned at each other. It was like an old rehearsed act.

Then Prothero said, 'Frazer has the right temperament. It's not the time for Archer's death-or-glory attitude.'

'What about me, sir?'

Prothero smiled. 'Too valuable.' He saw Frazer and Allenby climbing the steep track from the river past a sand-bagged Bofors gun.

Prothero said abruptly, 'Say nothing, John.'

Goudie groped for his pipe. He did not need to be told.

Prothero strolled away. 'See you at the briefing then.'

Frazer and Allenby paused on the track and turned to look at the boats.

'D'you think we'll get a break for a few days?' Allenby knew Goudie was watching them but did not care. 'Surely we've worked up enough now?'

Frazer nodded. 'Likely.' He could not get over Allenby's recovery. During the many and sometimes complicated exercises at full speed Allenby had usually been the first to encourage the hands when things went wrong. He was like somebody rebuilt, so different from the broken man who had returned from the Channel Islands raid.

He thought of his own new life with Lynn. People thrown together by war and danger, but it had worked. They met as often as possible. When Lynn's obliging housemate Jane was absent, they made love, they talked for hours, or merely lay in each other's arms, strangely content although their longing was never far away.

Allenby said hesitantly, 'We're getting engaged, Keith.'
He flushed as Frazer looked at him. 'That's between us, see?'

Frazer wrung his hand. 'You sly old son-of-a-gun! Why
the hell didn't you tell me sooner?'

Allenby smiled. 'It always takes me an age to do anything.'

Frazer thumped him on the shoulder. 'Not this time,
dammit!'

Goudie greeted them with, 'Something to celebrate, have
we?'

Frazer nodded. 'Getting back in one piece. Give me a *real*
battle any time.'

Goudie gave a lazy grin. 'Liar.' Then he said, 'There's a
flap on. We'll need just your boat, it seems.' He thought of
Prothero's words. 'No heroics. So stay around the base.
Local liberty only for the hands.' He looked from one to the
other. 'What, not smiling any more?'

He sauntered away, pipe smoke trailing over one shoulder.

'What does that mean, I wonder.' Frazer glanced at his
friend. It was bad luck.

Allenby said, 'I'll change and go over to HQ.'

Frazer watched him hurry away. 'Give her my love, Dick.'

That seemed to help in some way. Allenby turned and
grinned. 'Not bloody likely!'

Sub-Lieutenant Balfour and Ives tramped through the gate
and Frazer told them the news. They both took it in their
different ways. Ives expected it. Balfour was keen just to
show what he could do, no matter what it was. His sister
would not be pleased.

Later, as Allenby, shaved and changed into his best reefer,
entered the HQ building, he saw Second Officer Balfour
looking at a notice board.

She turned instantly and Allenby thought of Frazer when
he had told him his secret. He had beaten her and Keith to
it. He could barely stop himself from chuckling despite the
news of another mission. It sounded a straightforward one
this time. And the team would be together again.

She said, 'Good to see you.' But she looked suddenly uncertain.

Allenby had the strange feeling she had been waiting just for him.

She said, 'Joanna has got a draft chit.' She watched his dismay. 'Only to Plymouth, but I know how she feels. I wanted to tell you myself. She's upset. She told me about your news. It will stay a secret as long as you want it to. I'm so happy for you.'

Allenby barely heard her. Plymouth. They would be separated just when he had hopes of seeing her more often. Thoughts raced through his mind like wildfire. She might meet someone else; Plymouth was a big naval base, not like this place. Then it hit him, and in his mind's eye he saw the Plymouth admiral speaking with Jo's father at the party. He should have seen her change of mood then. *They went to school together.* So he must have fixed it to keep his daughter away from him.

He asked wretchedly, 'Couldn't you do something to stop it?

She touched his arm. 'I tried. It was useless. Joanna is very experienced in her job. It's her sort of skill they need at Plymouth.' She did not sound as if she believed it herself.

She said, 'Be gentle with her. She loves you very much.'

Allenby nodded. 'Thanks.' He hurried towards the office but she called after him, 'She's in the signals room.'

For a moment their eyes met. It was a spare room for storing boxfiles of signals and only rarely used.

They stood pressed together for a long moment without a word being said. Allenby stroked her hair and made every second count.

She said in a small voice, 'You've heard.'

'Yes. Just now.' He pushed the door shut with his foot. 'Try not to worry about it. We'll be together again soon.' He spoke with a brightness he could not find in his heart. 'I don't want you to be unhappy.'

She looked up, her eyes red as if she had been crying. 'It's not fair. I need to be here. In case you – '

Allenby touched her face. 'In case I need you, is that it? I shall always do that.'

They walked together to the window and stared out towards the river. It was harder to see now that the trees were covered with leaves.

It all flashed through Allenby's thoughts. Their walks in the rain and the driving wind. The first sunny days when they had looked for a quiet place to talk, to touch, to thrill at each new discovery.

Now it was to end. It could be months before they met again. And when the Second Front was mounted he might be killed.

Allenby held her more tightly. 'I don't want to lose you.'

She leaned back in his arms, her eyes suddenly very bright.

'You never will. If you're thinking what I believe you are, then stop it. There's been no one else. I *want* nobody else. I love you.' She put her arms round his neck and spoke in a fierce whisper. 'I know about the next mission. It should not take long, my dear. Then – ' She lowered her face and he could feel her tremble. 'And then I want to go away with you. I want you to love me, do you understand?' Her voice was muffled and he could only guess what it had cost her to say it. 'Anyway, every way you want. Then nobody can ever take it away from us, or separate us again.

Then she did look up at him, her face flushed, but her gaze quite steady.

He said, 'We will, my darling Jo. We will.'

She stood back and straightened her tie. 'And then, if you like, we can announce our engagement.'

Outside by the same notice board Lynn Balfour heard their voices, merged in laughter and tears. She was deeply moved. Because of the happiness she too had discovered, and which she could still so easily lose.

*

They stood round a table and stared down at the chart. It was in the centre of the room with a light directed straight down onto it. Outside the shuttered windows it was light. The days were drawing out, the nights warmer.

Goudie said, 'As you may know, there are rescue floats moored along the Dutch and Belgian coasts.' He gestured to a glossy photograph which showed something that looked like a conning tower. Goudie explained, 'When pilots ditch in the sea they can make for these rafts. There's shelter inside but not much else. They're visited after any big air raid by rescue launches, just to see if they've got one in the net, theirs or ours. A touch of unusual humanity, although the cost of training new air crews plays a large part, I suspect.'

Frazer leaned on the table. Trust Goudie to spoil it. He seemed unable to stop himself.

'Our man will be dumped near one of these floats.' His eyes settled on the sub-lieutenant. 'Your German may come in handy.'

Frazer glanced at Allenby. He was not even listening. Miles away.

Frazer asked, 'Why not send someone else?'

'Orders from on high. Just pick him up and leave. Don't touch any other airmen, if there are any. It might wreck the whole rescue agreement.'

Frazer looked at his pad. They would leave at dawn. Refuel at Felixstowe and pick up an escort from the base there. By then they would know if it was on or not.

Goudie said, 'If you tangle with the enemy, E-Boats and the like, get the hell out, right?'

Frazer smiled. 'No heroics, you said.'

Goudie eyed him coldly. 'You have to be back within the week. *Have* to.'

Allenby had joined Balfour to look at the chart; they did not even notice. But Frazer felt a sudden chill up his spine like ice. When he met Goudie's eyes again he knew he had not been mistaken. The invasion was on. *Within the week.*

'Christ Almighty,' he said softly.

Goudie's face softened. 'Oh, He'll know all right.'

Frazer looked at the others. 'Get your gear and return to the boat. If any of the libertymen are adrift tell me first before you blow the whistle.

He walked with Allenby to the door. 'You OK, Dick?'

Allenby sighed. 'She'll be gone when we get back.'

'I know. I'm damned sorry, for both of you.'

Balfour said, 'I'd better drop in on my sister.'

Goudie said, 'Obey the last order. Get aboard.' He ignored the young sub's crestfallen look and waited for the door to shut. Then he said, 'She'll be browned off enough without both of you dropping in.' He glanced at the clock. 'Off you go. I'll bring your sealed orders myself before you cast off.'

Frazer crossed to the Operations Room where the usual clatter of teleprinters and typewriters greeted him with noisy abandon. The Leading Wren's desk was empty, the typewriter covered.

Frazer grimaced. No wonder Lynn had been terrified of another attachment, a new love.

She was in her office, a telephone jammed under her chin as she searched through some papers. She saw him and made a kiss with her lips.

Then she said, 'Here it is, sir. Number thirty-one. All right, sir?' She slammed down the phone and said, 'Silly old sod. Too lazy to look it up.' Then she got quickly to her feet and almost ran to him.

'I'm not going to be silly, Keith.' She searched his face. 'But do take care. For me, this time. For us.'

Frazer held her very gently. Feeling her supple body through her shirt, remembering each discovery, the way they gave freely to each other as if they had been meant always.

He said, 'I'll be back, my darling, never fear.'

She looked deep into his eyes. 'You've guessed, haven't you?'

'Well, it had to come soon.' He held her more tightly

against him. 'The Boss would never forgive me if we missed the big one.'

She touched his mouth with her fingers like that first time. 'I do love you, you know.' Somewhere a bell rang and she said urgently, 'Kiss me!'

When they forced themselves apart she said, 'Go now. I'll be thinking of you. Always.'

It was over and Frazer found himself outside the door, his back against it as several pairs of eyes looked up from the busy machines.

One girl said, 'Good luck, sir.'

'Thanks.' He blundered out into the hallway. This feeling was something he had never known before. It was as unnerving as it was exciting. No wonder Dick had changed.

He picked up his cap and walked to his quarters to change into seagoing gear. Once he looked back, but in his heart he knew she would not follow, nor would she try to see him before he sailed.

Outwardly she would be as normal. She knew that if she gave way now she would be beaten.

A door opened and Prothero came out into the corridor folding a tiny pair of old steel-rimmed glasses.

'Look after the boat, Frazer.'

Frazer nodded. He had never seen the great man in spectacles.

Prothero added vaguely, 'You as well, of course.'

Frazer walked on, his mind returning to Lynn. She had not even asked him to take care of her young brother although it must have been on her mind. She was too professional for that, and knew that he had enough to cope with.

Frazer joined Allenby in the crowded chartroom forward of and just below the bridge. It was even more cramped now that it had been partitioned off to make room for the new radar set. On deck there was little to show of their new

strength, just a little jampot perched on top of a tripod
abaft their mast. Goudie had remarked suspiciously, 'Hope it
works better than it looks.'

As in the Med, the first part of the operation had gone
like clockwork. They had entered Felixstowe at dusk,
refuelled, and had been visited by an intelligence officer from
the admiral's staff. It was all a question of timing, he had
said. The German forces had the coast completely hemmed
in. Nothing could pass without proper authority. A Dutch
tugmaster was to drop the luckless agent at sea near the
prescribed float while on passage from Flushing to Kiel where
he was to pick up a tow of barges. All coastal traffic was vital
to the Germans, especially as the Allied air forces bombed the
roads and railways with regular persistence. If the tugmaster
was caught he would pay dearly before he was permitted to
die.

Frazer often wondered how many of these brave men and
women were scattered across the occupied countries, risking
death, trying to follow instructions on their makeshift radios
while they waited and prayed for the invasion.

It had to work. There could be no retreat, no second try.
It was all or nothing.

Frazer found it helped him in a strange way when he was
being sent on one of these missions. If he was captured he
would with luck be treated as a prisoner-of-war. If he was
killed it was a small sacrifice when compared with the war's
vast appetite.

These agents and members of the Resistance had no such
cover. Nobody would have blamed them if they had sat
passively by and done nothing, like the majority of their
countrymen. It was for them a savage, personal war. After
it was all over the vengeance and recrimination would be
equally terrible for some.

Allenby shut his ears to the squeak and whirr of the radar
and peered at the chart.

'One hour from now, I'd say.'

Frazer nodded. 'That's what I think.' He tapped the chart. 'Our escort will be about there.'

There were three big motor gunboats and an MTB for extra strength, keeping station to port.

They peered around the black curtain and stared at the blinking radar which reflected on the intent features of Crocker, their only operator. He was a failed candidate for a commission, but seemed to have settled down with his new toy.

Allenby gestured to the screen as the scanner found the four escorts. Little, shimmering blobs but easy to distinguish. Before this the majority of MGBs had been blind, with human resources which had changed little in a hundred years.

Outside on the open bridge they waited for their eyesight to recover from the piercing chartlight.

Frazer looked at his luminous watch. 'Go round the boat, will you, Dick? Check all the gun positions and make sure we're properly darkened.' He saw Allenby's teeth, very white in the darkness. He knew the boat was ready, had been since they had closed up at action stations. But you had to check. Also it helped to be kept busy.

Frazer walked to the gratings at the forepart of the bridge and tasted the spray on his lips. Like her tears.

Ives was at the wheel, a lookout nearby.

On either side of the bridge was a new machine-gun mounting. Twin Vickers .303 with drums instead of trailing belts of ammunition which could become a snare for the unwary at night.

Able Seaman Weeks was at one of them. He smiled. Jack of all trades. At the rear of the bridge Balfour's shadow detached itself from the flag locker and swayed towards him.

They were moving slowly on wing engines only, but the motion was bearable, especially for the North Sea.

Balfour said in a hushed voice, 'Pretty calm night, sir.'

As the deck rolled to starboard the two officers brushed against each other.

Balfour grinned. 'Oops, sorry, sir.'

Frazer watched the sea ahead of the bows. It was an odd feeling. Like being with part of her. An extension. He shook himself angrily. *Don't start getting morbid.*

He said, 'The RAF are supposed to be dropping some anti-radar foil over the coast tonight. It will mess ours up too, but it should help in the long run.'

New inventions on every hand, he thought. If only they had had them at the beginning. The terrible harvest in the Atlantic would have been halved if not prevented altogether.

No moon. Just a few bright stars, very pale and fragile. Frazer could see their stumpy mast spiralling gently across them, the ensign whipping out from the gaff.

He heard Ives humming gently to himself. He had meant to ask him if his relationship with Sullivan had improved or worsened since his promotion to the petty officers' mess. Once at the shore HQ Frazer had called at Ives's quarters to tell him about the new crew members. Ives had not been expecting his visit and had been shaving at the time. He had been stripped to the waist, and Frazer had understood why nobody ever picked a fight with him. Around his neck, on the same cord as his identity disc, there had been another, made of metal.

Ives had seen his glance and had said defensively, 'Well, who knows, sir? I might meet her again when this lot's over.' He must have taken the German girl's identity disc while he had been caring for her. It was becoming a strange war, Frazer thought.

Now, Ives was just another shadow, legs braced, eyes on the shaded compass as he held the boat on course.

Down below Shiner Wright and his two stokers would be crawling about their greasy world with one eye on the rev counter. The new telegraphist, 'Blondie' Page, a deceptively innocent-looking youth, would be listening in case of a recall or cancellation. Did he ever think about the one he had replaced and how he had died? And up forrard Leading

Seaman Sullivan, Bert to his pals, was at his two-pounder, a key man when the guns began to bark.

Allenby returned. 'Everything's fine, sir.' In front of the others he insisted on the 'sir' no matter what Frazer said about it.

'Stand by.' Frazer raised his night glasses and heard the caution whispered around the boat. He examined his feelings. There was nothing. Just a kind of numbness. Like cramp.

Ives leaned forward on the spokes, his eyes glinting faintly in the compass light.

As usual he was composing another of his imaginary letters. It was quite mad of course, and he would never tell anyone about it. But he often thought about the frightened girl called Christiane. It was stupid, nothing could ever come of it, but still –

He tried again. *My dear Christiane, Tonight we are steering towards the coast of Holland. I have never been there. I never went anywhere until I joined up. Perhaps after the war –*

The crash of an explosion seemed to lift the hull and a blinding flash laid bare the sea and one of the escorts far away on the port beam.

Frazer, shouted, '*Full ahead all engines!*' He leapt for the other side, his eyes seared by the flash. His ears heard the startled roar as the escorts threw themselves into full speed, but his mind was still dazed by the sudden explosion. Then he saw the other vessel. She looked like an old trawler, with a tall funnel and outdated bridge. But Goudie had warned him about these craft. The Germans had dozens of them, and had fitted them with a few heavy guns and made them almost invulnerable with layers of plastic armour which was said to be as tough as concrete. They cruised or just floated motionless up and down the coast waiting for a marauding MTB or gunboat. They were too shallow-draught for a torpedo and could take a lot of punishment.

They must have thought the MGB was alone, but as the

star shell exploded almost overhead they had seen the escorts. A gun shot out a long orange tongue and again a deafening bang seemed right alongside. But the MGB was gathering speed, cutting the tired water into great banks of white foam as she tore diagonally past the armed trawler.

Tracer lifted overhead, and Frazer saw it slash the water into curtains of spray. But the trawler was turning to bring another gun into play and had already shifted target to the escorts. Frazer saw the shells burst dangerously close to the leader, the haphazard necklace of tracer dazzling green as it ripped across the sea in reply.

'Hard a-port!'

Frazer felt the hull roll over, the sea bursting over the bows like a group of angry spectres. More, more. Shots crashed past or shrieked close astern as the escorts came in to the attack. Frazer tried to level his night glasses, but it was hopeless in the fierce motion. He pointed across the screen. 'There! Red four-five!'

Balfour, his face alive in the glow of tracer, shouted, 'I see it!'

The lookout called, 'W/T reports they're transmitting, sir!'

Frazer kept his eyes fixed on the rescue float. It was an odd-shaped raft with the tower in its centre. It was garishly painted with white and orange stripes which made it all the more unreal as the crash and rattle of cannon fire ripped the night apart.

Frazer thought rapidly. They were only ten miles from Rotterdam, the nearest E-Boat base. They could scramble in minutes.

'Get ready!' The trawler was ignoring them completely and heading purposefully to close with the escorts, a powerful froth rising beneath her fat counter.

Frazer thought they probably imagined the MGB was a rescue launch which had got caught up in the fight. There was not time to mess about.

He heard a chorus of cries and turned in time to see one of the escorting MGBs explode in a sheet of flame. The others were still coming in for the kill, tracer, cannon fire, anything that would bear. There were shell bursts all over the trawler and her mast with the radio had already vanished over the side. Not soon enough, Frazer thought wildly as he said, 'Starboard a bit, 'Swain. Slow ahead. We're going alongside.'

Balfour stared mesmerized at the blazing MGB. She was down by the head, and her shattered bows were scooping in water as her props still churned ahead. Perhaps her bridge was manned only by the dead. The light vanished, snuffed out instantly as the boat rolled over and disappeared.

'Can't we pick some of them up?' Balfour sounded stunned.

'Don't be a bloody idiot!' Frazer shook his arm. 'Get down and be ready to board that thing. If anyone tries to stop you – ' he tore open the sub's holster for him, 'then use this!'

He hated himself, his voice, everything. But it was no time or place for party manners.

Balfour leapt across the surging trough of water, followed by an armed seaman. He could not concentrate and his head cringed at the noise of battle. It was all so bright and savage, like nothing he had expected or experienced. The trawler was ablaze but still firing with barely a break. The MGBs had separated to divide the enemy's firepower while the MTB was circling like an assassin, ready to dash in and drop depth-charges right alongside the enemy.

Balfour clambered down the tower, half expecting a shot and yet with his pistol still in its holster.

A feeble battery light was switched on and he saw there was only one man in the swaying uncomfortable refuge. He was dressed in crumpled RAF flying gear and Mae West, and looked exactly like a ditched airman. Balfour found time to wonder if the Germans would have accepted his disguise as genuine and marched him off to a PoW Camp, or by interrogation would have discovered he was leaving rather than arriving.

He gasped, 'Who are you?'

The man was already hurrying to the ladder. 'Redskin,' he replied.

Balfour grinned shakily. He had almost forgotten the password.

They climbed up and over the tower and after waiting for the right moment the agent, holding on to the seaman, leapt aboard the MGB.

One of the other MGBs tore past, guns painting the sea in red and green tracer. The trawler had stopped at last, but was still hitting back. The passing MGB's wake lifted the rescue float and parted it from the boat alongside. Balfour was just groping for a handhold when the gap widened and a wave knocked him from his feet and he fell choking into the sea.

Allenby dropped his glasses to his chest. '*E-Boats! Dead astern!*'

Frazer ran to the side. 'Cast off!' Then he saw Balfour floundering in the water. If he started the engines now the screws would slash him to ribbons. If he waited –

He yelled, 'Get him aboard!'

The E-Boats – it looked as if there were six of them – were coming in at top speed. But they did not fire because of the trawler. It was only a matter of a few seconds, but it saved Balfour's life. He was dragged, streaming and retching, to the bridge and Frazer shouted, 'Emergency full ahead! Hard a-starboard!' He felt the deck lift to the sudden surge of power and tore his glance from the trawler as a depthcharge, then another, exploded right against her bilge. She began to settle down immediately, and he saw men hurling themselves into the water, some even swimming towards the empty rescue float.

'Midships! *Steady!*' He heard Ives swear as some stray bullets whimpered above the bridge.

A running fight had developed but was falling farther and farther astern. The old enemies. Goudie would be at home here.

Frazer felt his limbs unwinding and he tried to control his breathing. Their escorts had won the day, but it had cost them dearly, and for what, he wondered.

Balfour dragged himself to the forepart of the bridge. He was shaking badly. But he was very young. He'd get over it.

Balfour gasped, 'Thank you, sir. For saving my life.'

Frazer grinned and knew he must look slightly wild.

Not a man lost and no damage. It helped to even the score.

He shouted, 'My pleasure, Alex.' He faced up to the stars. 'Now for home, my lads!'

They were met off the Isle of Wight by a harbour launch and their passenger was transferred aboard. Frazer recalled afterwards that he had not said a word since he had offered the password to Balfour. The following evening they cruised slowly up Carrick Roads past the crowded moorings, the rank upon rank of landing craft. Then up-river until the green tiles of the old hotel came into view.

'Fall the hands in, Dick.' Frazer studied the moorings, the lines of expectant faces on the other two MGBs. Some were already waving, and there were some ironic cheers from a tank landing ship nearby.

Frazer felt strangely elated. He had done it. He rubbed the screen. In his own command.

They turned and headed for the mooring where seamen were waiting to take their lines.

As they came alongside and the head and stern ropes were made fast Frazer ordered, 'Stop engines.' He looked at their faces. 'Well done.'

A smart petty officer in white belt and gaiters was the first to board. Some anonymous wag called, 'Don't come too near, mate! This is a fighting ship.'

The PO found Frazer and saluted. 'Beg pardon, sir, but Commander Prothero would like to see you immediately before you dismiss your company.'

Trust Prothero to be waiting. To hear it all before anyone else. It was *his* navy after all.

He hurried up the track, past grins and salutes. He felt like a victor.

Prothero was waiting in his office, his buttocks towards an empty grate. Frazer thought he had been standing like this for some time.

Prothero shook hands and watched him without speaking. Then he said quietly, 'I thought it might come better from you, Frazer.'

Frazer felt the same chill again. 'What's happened, sir?'

'Last night there was an air raid on Plymouth. Leading Wren Hazel was killed.'

Frazer said, 'I'll tell him, sir.' He looked away, his eyes blind. 'Somehow.'

17

Countdown

Frazer lay on his back and listened to the wind as it moaned around the cottage. It was afternoon and yet the room seemed dark, as if dusk was already closing in.

The girl propped herself on one elbow, her other hand occasionally stroking his chest.

She asked quietly, 'Was it as bad as you thought?'

Frazer put his arm round her and touched her spine.

'It was worse in some ways.' He pictured Allenby's pale face. 'I thought he might snap completely. You remember how he was the last time? It would be enough to destroy anyone. I'd sent Alex off the boat, I was expecting – I don't really know what.' He clasped her tightly so that her breasts touched his skin as she looked down at him. 'Instead he said something like, "I think I knew." That really shook me.'

A shutter clattered against the wall, and he added, 'They'll have to call the invasion off. It will be a fiasco otherwise.'

Her hand moved slowly over his skin, exciting and yet soothing.

'They won't. One postponement is enough.'

Frazer looked at her steadily. He was conscious of their love and also of the great sadness that hung over them.

He said, 'You always think you're the one who's going to die. You worry about those you'll leave behind. God, he must be going through hell.'

'The Boss offered him the chance to transfer, but he refused. He insists on staying with you. I'm glad in a way.'

Frazer smiled. 'Yes. If he were thrown adrift now there's no saying what he might do.'

He thought of their orders. Operation Neptune, the naval phase of the Normandy Invasion, was already under way despite the foul weather. It was more like January than June, and there were even tossing white horses on the river. It was to be hoped that the troops, packed like sardines in their landing craft, would not be too sick to dash ashore.

Frazer could think of what lay ahead and yet remain very aware of the girl beside him. Perhaps he had been a navigator for so long he could stay detached from facts and figures and accept that a destination was less important than the means of getting there. Perhaps he was wrong to take Allenby. If he broke down there could be no turning back. He dismissed the idea instantly. Loyalty was all important, but it had to stretch both ways. Allenby's last words before he had gone to his quarters were, 'I was going to buy the ring next leave.'

Frazer said, 'If anything happens – '

She laid her hand on his mouth. 'Don't.'

'But if it does. Write to my mother, will you? Tell her how it was.'

'How it *is*.' She studied him gravely. 'How many times have we made love this afternoon?'

He smiled. Her eyes were very blue in the filtered light. 'A lot.'

'Just think of that then. Of us.' She reached out and caressed him with her fingertips. 'Of this.'

He kissed her lightly. 'You know I will. You're my whole life.'

She stretched across him to the bedside table and lifted her wristwatch to look at it.

'You must go soon.'

He held her closer as she leaned over him. Feeling her, smelling her body, her warmth.

'I know.'

She said, 'I try to understand what it must be like. What

those involved feel and think, not just a mass of stars and arrows on the Boss's maps.'

'Just be here when I come back.' He felt her hand fasten on him and then she said huskily, 'Once more, my love.' She thrust her leg over him. 'Oh, my dear love. Do take care.'

Later they walked to the track by the river and looked down at the three MGBs. Most of the other vessels seemed to have gone already. Heading at their various speeds to the great whirlpool of shipping that would gather in the Channel south of the Isle of Wight before forming up for the final assault. The assembly area was to be nicknamed Piccadilly. In pitch darkness, and with every class and size of ship involved, it was very apt. All their exercises and manoeuvres would be tested to the full.

Prothero had code-named their little force Jupiter Two. They would sail ahead of the invasion fleet and intercept some coastal transports that were reported as heading west from Rotterdam. Each transport was said to contain German Beavers, two-man submarines which the enemy had been testing in secret in the Black Sea and the Baltic. If they got among the invasion fleet with its rigid lines and close ranks it would be hard to detect them. The effect on the landings could be disastrous and any delay would allow the enemy time to move his Panzers to the beachheads, which would then be obvious even to a blind man.

Frazer suspected that the agent they had dragged from the rescue float might have had a lot to do with it.

She took his hand. 'I wish I didn't know about it.'

'I know.' He returned her grip; her skin felt like ice.

Neither of them mentioned the real snag. The little convoy of transports were able to move close inshore. They had an escort of German Vendettes, fast, fifty-foot launches which were heavily armed for their size. In addition, coastal batteries would be covering the transports every mile of the way.

It would have to be a night action. Fast and effective. It was their reason for being. The cost could not be counted this time.

He saw Goudie on the shore chatting to Archer and Kellett, the two other skippers. Each boat had been loaded with extra depthcharges and ammunition at the expense of fuel. The planners obviously thought it might be a one-way trip.

He studied his own boat and remembered his elation when they had returned here, the dismay at Prothero's news. He had to go.

He said, 'Don't wait. No goodbyes, Lynn.' He raised her chin with his fingers and kissed her very gently.

She brushed something off his jacket. 'I can still *feel* you.'

She stood back. There were no words but her mouth said, 'I love you.' Then she turned on her heel and walked towards the HQ entrance. She did not look back but once the door was closed he had the sensation that she was watching him.

He touched the peak of his cap and said softly, 'And I you.'

He stepped aboard his boat and saw that the pendant number 193 had been freshly touched up with paint to cover a scar left there by chaffing against the fenders. Even the White Ensign, stiff in the wind like metal, was a new one.

Ives, who waited with the side party to greet him, saluted and grinned. 'Must do it right, eh, sir?'

A launch cast off from the outboard side and Frazer saw it was the mail boat with its crew of Wrens. Last letters to mothers, wives and lovers. With the age of his crew it would mostly be the former, he thought grimly.

Goudie was in good form. 'I've spoken with the others. Each boat has photographs and silhouettes to study, so don't let's make a balls of it, eh?'

Frazer watched him. It would be the last time they spoke until afterwards. Maybe for ever.

He said, 'Piece of cake.' He held out his hand. 'Last one home sets up the drinks.'

Goudie returned the handshake and then, surprisingly, saluted. 'Keep your head down.' Then to the trill of calls he strode across to 195, Kellett's boat, where he would take overall command.

Frazer saw Allenby waiting for him with Balfour. 'Ready to proceed, sir.'

He looked like death and his quiet determination made him seem worse.

Allenby was glad to be moving and doing things, anything to escape from the glances and the sympathy.

He had endured something like torture when the mail boat had come alongside. The coxswain had clattered down to the wardroom and had asked, 'Any letters, sir?'

Allenby had stared at her, then at the blue anchor on her sleeve. A Leading Wren like Joanna, yet not like her at all.

He had written a confused letter to his parents. It had been hopeless. His mother would not understand. Would put her own family first. 'Never mind, Dicky.' He seemed to hear her.

He had crumpled the letter into a ball and had shaken his head. The girl had lingered on the steps. Like everyone on the base, she knew about Allenby and his girl. Secret it might be, but this was no ordinary service, it was more like a family. When Prothero had sent a squad of frogmen to be dropped along the enemy-held coast to search out and examine the anti-tank defences none of them had returned. Nothing was said, but the family had its own, private grief all the same.

She had said, 'We're all so sorry, sir. She was a lovely girl.'

Allenby stared at the seamen who were loosening the mooring lines. *Was. Was. Was.* The word crashed like a hammer in his mind.

Ives had said uneasily to his friend the ERA, 'He'll get himself chopped if he doesn't keep his mind on the job.'

Shiner Wright, the oldest man in the boat, a veteran of twenty-nine, had replied sadly, 'Inside, he's dead already, if you ask me.'

Frazer walked around the small bridge and when he looked up saw a line of faces along the protective fence of the old hotel.

Prothero and the engineer officer, some Wrens, maybe even Captain Heywood.

There was so much he had wanted to tell her. There was never any time, and the words always eluded him when he needed them most. He turned his back and saw a light flash from the leader's boat, a cloud of vapour from her outlets as she started her big Packards. Frazer tugged his cap tightly across his unruly hair.

'Here we go.' He smiled at Ives and the others near the bridge. 'One more time.'

The river quaked to the combined roar of engines as one by one the little group idled clear of their moorings to fall in line behind their leader.

Frazer waved to the HQ building. Everyone waved back in return. He smiled. But she would know it was only for her.

By nightfall the three MGBs were deep into the English Channel and steering east. The atmosphere in Frazer's boat seemed relaxed. He knew it was often the case before beginning a final run-in. It was soon pitch dark and yet he had the feeling that the Channel was full of vessels. They would be creeping to their selected rendezvous and trying not to collide with one another, or to betray their positions when they responded to challenges from wary patrols.

Once or twice they had heard dull explosions, a long way away, and when Frazer had turned to Allenby the lieutenant had said in an empty voice, 'That takes guts. They're sweeping mines in the dark.' They had passed several sweepers, some new, others converted fishing trawlers. Allenby would be thinking back, remembering how a trail of events had begun with sweeping mines.

There was a brief signal from the Admiralty. The enemy convoy was on course and keeping to time, its destination Le Havre. About the worst place for a nest of midget submarines so far as the Allied invaders were concerned.

Frazer went to the chartroom and studied his calculations and compared them with the intelligence notes. They should intercept the convoy at about three in the morning northeast of Dieppe. The name reminded him of the costly raid in which so many Canadians had died or been captured. People were still very bitter about its failure.

He returned to the bridge, glad to be in the open air again.

Ives said, 'Permission to be relieved at the wheel, sir.'

Frazer nodded. 'Granted. Don't be too long. We'll close up at action stations in fifteen minutes.'

Ives made his way to the ladder and someone called, 'Goin' to put yer brown trousers on, 'Swain?' It sounded like Sullivan, and Ives ignored him.

The rating who had taken the wheel said brightly, 'I just realized somethin', sir. The numbers of this boat add up to thirteen.'

Frazer said sharply, 'That's all I need.'

Allenby lowered his night glasses. 'From Leader, sir. Form line abreast.'

As they waited for the signal Ives brushed past and resumed his place at the wheel.

Frazer noticed that in seconds Ives had donned his best shoregoing jacket, gold badges and everything. He recalled what he had said before sailing. 'Must do it right.'

Allenby strained his eyes. 'Execute!'

With a minimum of fuss the three boats broke from their

line and formed up abreast of the senior officer. A cable
apart. Just enough.

Frazer found himself listening to the engines. Throttled
down, throaty. It always made him doubt, think that one
might stop.

'Pass the word. Action stations everyone.' Frazer heard
the soft patter of shoes and rubber boots.

Would the convoy be in the right place?

Why did he even question it? The convoys could only
move at night because of the prowling fighter-bombers, and
even then they took a risk in the narrow Channel.

Frazer answered his own question. Deep inside he was
hoping they might fail to make contact. It was the first time
he had really considered dying. Being killed. He did not have
to look far for a reason.

'Boat closed up, sir.'

Frazer tried to see his features in the dark. 'You get down
aft, Dick. You know the score.'

Allenby said. 'I expect it will be all right.' He sounded as
if he no longer cared.

The lookout said, 'Leader's stoppin', sir.'

Frazer leaned across. 'Stop engines.'

Goudie would know better than anyone. In the sudden
stillness the boat rolled uncomfortably in the current and the
sea noises intruded like strangers. A halliard cracked against
the mast, something rolled across the deck and was immediately snatched up by an invisible seaman.

Ives felt the wheel pulling at his grip as they drifted
aimlessly. He thought he could smell the land. It was, after
all, just a few miles away. No star shell, no sudden challenges. The Germans might be anticipating an invasion,
maybe they already knew and were waiting at the beachheads. They would certainly not be expecting this sort of
crazy venture.

Frazer was thinking along the same lines. He heard Balfour

shifting his feet and wondered how he would cope. He was glad he could not see his eyes. Blue, like his sister's.

Curiously enough it was Balfour who heard it first.

'Engines, sir.' He pointed vaguely over the glass screen. 'Port bow, I think!'

Frazer heard it too and almost fell as he lowered his face to the compass. Northeast. Close inshore. As near as they dared. It had to be them. He found that his hands were shaking and angrily he thrust them into his pockets.

He hoped Goudie and the others had heard it too. They could not use a light or the R/T. It would wreck everything.

He forced himself to remain still and listen.

Rum-rum-rum. The beat of big German diesels. Like the Siebel ferry. He screwed up his eyes to make himself concentrate, to remember what Goudie had ordered. The convoy would be in line ahead. They would not risk a larger formation in the confined waters even though they were safe from the minefields.

Frazer said curtly, 'Stand by.' His voice sounded like someone else's. He heard Ives clear his throat very carefully like a man will do in church between hymns.

'Watch Goudie's boat.'

Easier said than done. His boat was farthest abeam and had drifted well clear on some perverse current.

We could do with Quinlan right now, Frazer thought. He could tell the size and the number of vessels merely by listening to their engine beats. He wondered if the German midget submarines had their crews with them. Or their torpedoes. As they carried two per boat it might be one hell of an explosion.

'He's off, sir!'

Frazer yelled, 'Full ahead all engines! *Tally ho!*'

The other boats were instantly revealed by their mounting bow waves and careering wash as they swung round to regain their stations.

Frazer said, 'Port fifteen. Steer nor'-nor'-east!' If only they had a damn gyro.

But Ives had her, and the boat was already rushing across the sea as if she was planing. The other two MGBs vanished in the spray as Frazer continued to steer astern of where the convoy should be. He bit his lip as wild lines of vivid tracer tore across the water, twinned with their deadly reflections below. Then a heavier gun joined in and within seconds a star shell burst above the sea like a blinding snowflake.

Frazer gripped the rail below the screen as the boat bucked over some steep wavelets. He could see the dark hulls of the transports. There seemed to be three of them. Churned water rolled amongst them and he guessed that the lively escorts were forming up their defence. Or attack.

'*Open fire!*' The bridge quivered as the two-pounder and the twin Oerlikons aft joined in the din, and from the other boats Frazer saw every gun being brought into action. The star shell could cost the enemy dearly.

'Hard a-starboard!' Frazer held on tightly as a wreck buoy loomed out of the darkness and tore along the port side.

Ives brought the boat round on course again, his face set in grim determination as the sea was criss-crossed in tracer and bursting cannon shells.

He heard Weeks shout, 'Here come the cavalry!' And then his twin Vickers machine guns clattered into life as two low-lying launches burst between the transports, caught momentarily in the drifting flare.

The other MGBs vanished as Frazer brought his boat round the stern of the rear transport, the Oerlikons striking livid stars and hurling wreckage into the sea.

Allenby needed no signal and moments later two columns of white water shot up with the sound of a giant drum. The charges must have hit the seabed even as they exploded. The transport slewed round, steering gone. A quick change of helm and Allenby released another two charges right along-side. So close they could feel the scorching heat of the blast, see pale blobs of faces before the clattering guns cut them down.

Balfour shouted, 'She's done for!'

They turned on a sixpence and shot past the transport's listing bows in time to see one of the MGBs fighting a duel at close quarters with two of the Vendettes. But one was already on fire and the other was being raked from bow to stern, while the third MGB dropped her charges close to the leading transport.

A tall waterspout shot skywards just fifty feet abeam and Frazer imagined for a few seconds that somebody's depth-charges had misfired. Then he heard a flat whistle and another column of spray deluged across their course.

Coastal battery. Shooting wild and probably blind in all the confusion. E-Boats would be charging down from the northeast. It could not last.

The MGBs turned wildly with their engines screaming as they rallied for another attack. Men shouted to each other through the smoke and there was the clink of metal as fresh magazines were jammed home, empty shells kicked into the scuppers.

The leading transport and the one which Frazer had tackled from astern were out of control and listing over. They might sink in the shallows but they could not now be hidden from the air. The RAF would take care of any salvage hopes.

There was just one transport remaining. In the leaping glare of gunfire Frazer saw an MGB tearing across the water, cutting a white furrow as she went in to the attack. A shell exploded nearby and Frazer saw the boat's number very clearly 194: it was Archer.

Ives shouted, 'Something's wrong!'

Frazer stared and saw tiny figures splashing down from the transport's side and striking out in all directions. They were abandoning without waiting for a fight, and some of the frantic swimmers were swept under Archer's keel and into those racing screws before they knew what was happening.

Frazer heard Goudie's voice harsh and angry from the R/T speaker. No need for caution now. It was as if he were here amongst them.

Balfour gasped as Goudie yelled, 'Break off! She's got the explosives!' But the din of cannon shells exploding into and through the transport's hull must have drowned the warning.

Frazer shouted, 'Hard a-port!' The deck went over and the sea licked over the side like a millrace. No wonder they had baled out.

Then came the explosion. It crashed and echoed along the coast as if it would never stop. The transport burst apart in a single column of fire. It seemed to last for ever and yet Frazer knew it was a matter of seconds. The whole area was pockmarked by falling debris from the explosion, and a piece of steel plate the size of a door crashed onto the afterdeck where it missed Allenby by inches.

Frazer saw the stern half of Archer's boat break clear from the burning wreckage and vanish, her screws still turning as they carried her to the bottom.

The coastal battery used the fires to guide their aim, and shells began to fall thick and fast between the two surviving MGBs.

'Goudie's stopping, sir!' Balfour sounded frantic.

The other MGB was dropping in the water as the power died away. She must have been hit by shell splinters, and in the glow of the fires Frazer saw Goudie on his bridge, with Kellett the skipper clinging beside him, obviously wounded.

Frazer shouted, 'We'll take 'em off! Stand by to go alongside!'

They moved slowly together, the crash of the coastal guns intermixed with the cries of the wounded aboard the sinking boat. Through it all Frazer knew they had achieved what they had set out to do. He felt like laughing, like cheering it was all so mad, so impossible.

He heard a short, abbreviated whistle and then felt the jarring crash of an explosion. He reeeled against the side of the bridge and stared at the flickering spectacle of the shattered two-pounder with the remains of Sullivan hanging from it like meat.

Frazer tried to think it out. But for the two-pounder that last shell would have burst deep inside their frail hull. It would have ended. But he could not think clearly, and as he saw Balfour staring at him, his face horrified, he felt the pain for the first time. Two sharp, red-hot prongs probed deeper and deeper into his side and shoulder until he knew he would scream. Faintly, he heard Ives tell someone to take the wheel and felt him supporting him against the side of the bridge as Allenby dashed from aft.

The other boat was alongside and they were both shining redly in the reflected fires.

Allenby seized Balfour's arm and shook him violently.

'Get down there and help them!' He shook him again. 'It's what you joined for, remember!' He pushed him to the ladder and then ducked as another shell exploded on the opposite end of Goudie's boat. All this Frazer saw, even though the pain held him speechless, barely able to breathe.

Goudie framed against the flames and yelling, '*Made* it! We bloody well *made* it!' Then the explosion alongside and the lethal rain of splinters.

When Frazer looked again, the other boat was sinking fast. Goudie was still propped in one corner of his bridge. But he was headless.

Allenby cupped his hands. 'Bear off forrard! Half ahead all engines!' He gripped the helmsman's wrist so that he jumped as if he had been hit. He was still staring, sickened at Goudie's headless corpse right alongside.

'Hard a-starboard!' He watched, not even ducking as another shell exploded in a bank of smoke. 'Steer northwest.' He heard the pumps below. They were badly mauled but still working.

Frazer felt Ives's strong fingers rip open his jacket and

shirt, and sobbed aloud as he wedged two shell dressings into place.

Ives said, 'Nothing broken as far as I can make out.' He looked at the man on the wheel and snarled, 'Watch it, sunshine! You're all over the bloody place!'

Allenby watched as Ives lowered Frazer to the deck and rolled bundles of flags under his side to keep him steady.

There were no more shells and the only sound they heard was the continuous drone of aircraft, an endless procession overhead.

At first light the sea was no longer empty.

Ives said, 'Strewth, look at it!' He sounded unusually moved.

Frazer, teeth gritted against the pain, was lifted up to his old place again, his blood already dry on the grey paintwork.

He must not miss it after all they had done. Goudie would have been the same, bless him. With Allenby beside him and the new telegraphist supporting him from the other side, he watched the fringe of the armada moving towards France. Landing ships for men and for tanks, with some brave madman playing the bagpipes. Like Ives and his best uniform, he was showing his own defiance.

A destroyer tore out of the dawn mist, and astern of her a big cruiser, her forward turrets already trained, the guns at maximum elevation as she prepared to offer covering fire.

The destroyer headed for the battered motor gunboat, glasses trained on the dead and the living. She could have been *Levant*.

It would be something to talk about, Frazer thought wearily. To tell her. To be able to tell her.

He wanted to share it with Allenby but his face defied intrusion as he watched the purposeful lines of ships. Nothing could stop them. No matter what happened later, they had done what they had set out to do.

Frazer touched the punctured plating at his side and heard the clatter of an Aldis as Allenby answered the challenge.

Ives watched him and heard him murmur, 'Lucky thirteen.'

And they were still together.

Epilogue

Sub-Lieutenant Alex Balfour looked up at the bridge and saluted.

'All secure, sir.'

Like the other hands on deck and in the moored motor gunboats nearby, he was self-conscious under the combined stare of hundreds of Germans.

Ives stepped down from the wheel and looked at the wreck-strewn harbour. Beyond it there was an endless ridge of shattered buildings; the destruction from bombing seemed total.

It was hard to believe. For this was May 1945, the war in Europe was over and here they were in the enemy's stronghold, Kiel. Even in a small MGB it had been difficult to pick up safe moorings. Sunken or partly submerged ships lay everywhere. Some with famous names like the *Admiral Hipper*, now listing with her starboard side under water, internal fires still burning. And the huge liner *New York*, once a proud member of the Hamburg–Amerika Line, which now lay half submerged. It was said that her hull was still packed with corpses. Last-moment refugees who had been caught in an air raid.

Almost the worst part was the silent army of watching Germans. Waiting to be told what to do, where to go. Frazer had already been ashore before changing moorings. Near the bombed railway junction he had seen the women too. Holding up photographs for passing surrendered troops to study. Have you seen this man? My son? My husband? You did not need to understand the language, Frazer thought.

Ives took a pair of binoculars and studied a German destroyer. It had been blasted bodily out of a dock and now lay on one side. It was incredible.

He glanced at Frazer as he took a letter from his pocket. Some mail was already getting through. It was obvious from Frazer's expression who it was from.

Ives thought of the metal identity disc around his neck. The impossible seemed more hopeful now that he was here. There ought to be a sense of triumph, of their hard-won victory. They had come a long, long way together and yet he remembered most clearly that action on the morning of D-Day. It was a pity Lieutenant Allenby was not here, Ives thought. But he had been moved from Special Operations after that one.

He glanced at the listless German sailors. The enemy. Knowing jolly jack, it would not be long before they were handing out bars of nutty to the German kids.

When he turned to Frazer again he saw his change of expression.

'Something wrong, sir?'

Frazer looked down at his letter, her familiar handwriting which had helped to get him through even the worst of it.

He said, 'Dick Allenby's dead.' As he said it he could see him, as it must have been.

Ives exclaimed, 'But how?'

Frazer said, 'There was a parachute mine in some marshes. It was no danger to houses but it was near a river. Dick Allenby went to deal with it.' He did not mention what she had told him in the letter. That over the telephone line Allenby had told his rating to take cover. The mine had gone active. There were only seconds left before it exploded. Later that same rating had told his captain that Allenby had made no attempt to run, but had just waited there. He remembered that he had spoken just once. A girl's name.

Ives struggled with his emotions. 'He shouldn't have gone! It wasn't his job any more.' He felt lost and somehow cheated.

Frazer folded the letter again. 'I know.' He smiled at him as they both remembered. 'He volunteered.'

On the following pages are details of Arrow books that will be of interest.

A SHIP MUST DIE

Douglas Reeman

January 1944

Out in the wastes of the Indian Ocean, British ships are sinking. The cause: a German armed raider, disguised to deceive unwary merchantmen.

In Williamstown, Australia, HMS *Andromeda* awaits transfer to the Australian navy. After years together in bloody combat with the Nazis, the cruiser's crew will disperse to fight in other ships, in other seas.

But a call to *Andromeda*'s youthful captain, Richard Blake VC, changes everything. He puts to sea immediately. His mission: to seek out and destroy the raider.

And in this conflict, one ship must die.

THE GREATEST ENEMY

Douglas Reeman

Twenty-five years ago HMS *Terrapin* was part of a crack hunter/killer group in the Battle of the Atlantic. Now she is working out her last commission in the Gulf of Thailand.

To Lieutenant-Commander Standish, the frigate seems to mark the end of his hopes of a career in the Navy. Then a new captain arrives, a man driven by an old-fashioned, almost obsessive patriotism. And under his stubborn leadership Standish and the crew discover a long-forgotten unity of purpose . . .

SURFACE WITH DARING
Douglas Reeman

Hiding, lying in wait on the sea bed, is EX 16, one of the most important ships in the Royal Navy. She's not much to look at, and she's only 54 feet long, with no defensive armament. But her four-man crew know that the outcome of the war could depend on this midget submarine.

Seaton, her commander, understands what his men face. There is the boredom, the discomfort, the jealousy and bickering; and already they have confronted enormous dangers on desperate raids into Norway. Now, poised for the attack on a secret Nazi rocket installation, Seaton must hold his crew together for the hell that awaits them . . .

THE PRIDE AND THE ANGUISH

Douglas Reeman

November 1941. Lieutenant Ralph Trewin, DSC, arrives at Singapore as second-in-command of the shallow-draught gunboat, HMS *Porcupine*. To Trewin, still shocked from wounds received during the evacuation of Crete, the gunboat and her five elderly consorts seem to symbolise the ignorance and blind optimism he finds in Singapore. And the *Porcupine*'s captain is as unwilling as the rest to take heed of Trewin's alarm, for to him the gunboat represents his last chance.

The following month, the Japanese invade Malaya, and in three months Singapore, the impregnable fortress, knows the humiliation of surrender.

Through the misery and despair of this bloody campaign Trewin and his captain are forced to draw on each other's beliefs and weaknesses, and together they weld the little gunboat into a symbol of bravery and pride.